CRUISE CRIME II

BLOOD DIAMONDS

Stuart St Paul

BLOOD DIAMONDS

Version Draft 26th September 2021

DORIS CRUISE BOOKS
Northwood, England.

ISBN: 9798735493730

This is totally a work of fiction. Any references to ships, locations and characters are invented and incidents are all a product of the author's wild imagination.

**Just because it never happened,
… doesn't mean it isn't going to.**

1 – BLUE HAZE

A steely blue haze hangs over Miami; one that will only shift when the sun forces it away. The lack of light from the dead concrete city fails to make the impression on nature it would have just five years earlier. It may well be an enjoyable time to be out running, and exercise is allowed within the restrictions, but it's a long time since Dwight ran anywhere. His ear is lit by the glow of his cell-phone wedged by his shoulder.

It is so quiet, the whole derelict square of 1960's units might have heard the conversation if there was anyone to listen. He powers around the corner avoiding the potholes. His converted double-cab truck is left parked alone in the large square to leave the front parking free for customers. That's a habit he had no need to keep today.

"If you could solve it, you wouldn't be ringing a black man in a wheelchair for help," Dwight says, knowing he has the upper hand.

"It's a theft. That should be at a basic rate," says the formal female voice that he is negotiating with, coming via his speaker.

From his powered chair, he fondles with a bunch of old keys that defy technology. One will open the door recessed in the entranceway to the diner. Only a designer could waste such space, he thinks, his large machine awkward to manoeuvre in the alcove.

"The bigger problem is what you're not telling me. It always is. Which is why you're ringing our agency, and why we have our fees, and why we dictate the number of agents. Plus, there's an extra: one-thousand-dollars bullet money."

The door has not been opened for weeks, yet Wild Mary's Diner is still intact. Unlike a few shops that have been looted in the lockdown, there is nothing of value here. No stock and nothing to sell for quick cash, though cash is becoming less and less useful. Food is a commodity in this third phase of lockdown, but the stock that was in this kitchen got split and moved home weeks ago. Mary and Stan had a chunk, but their kids, who now share the apartment Mary bought them, had what remained. They are all twenty years old, and burgers won't have lasted long.

"Bullet money?"

"One thousand-dollars for every bullet fired at any of our agents, but that shouldn't worry you," Dwight fires at him.

"Why not?"

"If it's an easy job like you say, no one's gonna shoot at them."

Dwight won't get breakfast. He can't smell the grill. He can't hear the daily concert of Stan's songs; the ones he's been singing since his days of touring music theatres; from Pensacola to the pier at Cocoa Beach along Florida's Emerald Coast. Stan's journey might have ended at any of the State's twelve coasts, Dwight could have set down anywhere in the USA, but they both struck gold here.

"Them's the terms. Now we got that out of the way; why are you really ringing us?"

No one at CSCI knows much about Dwight, but during the 'Art Theft' he added two freelance agents to the workforce: ex-soldiers from his old unit. Their calm helped avoid a near full-blown shoot-out on the pier in what many still called Indian River City. After that job successfully wrapped, the new mixture of agents found much to talk about. CSCI's own agents, Kieron, and Hunter, found out a lot more about Dwight Ritter.

"The jeweller's safe has been opened; it was emptied yesterday afternoon or overnight, but before seven a.m. Diamonds worth way over a quarter-of-a-million, maybe half a million will have gone."

"Can't the ship's security deal with it?" Dwight asks.

"They don't know it's happened," the woman says.

Dwight pulls up sharply, the remark stopping him in his tracks. He remains planted, looking at the small plaque, 'Cruise Ship Crime Investigators' on the otherwise innocent black cupboard door in the side wall of the diner. It hides a steel door into their secure unit just four feet behind it.

"How do you know, back at your head office, before the crew do at sea?" Dwight asks, typing 'diamond heist' into his cell-phone to update all staff. Now he knows this is a job for the agency; he smells dangerous rats on that ship.

"A whistleblower," he hears. "So, we had the choice of calling ship's security to discuss it, or, in case they were in on it, calling you, while no one knows we know."

"See, it ain't ever easy. That's why people ring CSCI. My team'll be on that ship before it gets dark."

"Keep the cost at a team of just two."

"I'll keep you informed as the cost rises, and it will. Two won't work. We start with four. I want the purchase order here by the time I finish my coffee," Dwight insists.

The glow goes out as he ends the call.

"Finish my coffee…" Dwight laughs to himself, looking at the lifeless grill. "…Starting a mug of coffee would be nice."

Beyond, in the preparation room, the refrigeration doors hang open to air. Despite the lack of breakfast, he decides to stop at his usual table by the opening in the counter. The bag slung over his shoulder is thrown onto 'his' table. All the other tables sit between two traditional red and cream art deco bench seats, but here at the end, one bench has been removed for a mobility chair. It's been that way since Dwight became a fixture, and Dwight has been on wheels since he jumped on an IED whilst leading his men from the front. It never hurt at the time, but he knew his legs were gone. Maybe one of his team had hit him with morphine but the mind and body do strange things in trauma, even without drugs. His mind still does. His team got him back, and he owes Billy and Zack his life. They will get called when CSCI need extra agents, but this is not one of those jobs. Not yet. However, Cruise Ship Crime Investigators never get called in for the easy operations. They get high-stakes complicated crimes to unravel because they not only know the industry, they know how publicity can turn bad; social media is so fast there is often no time to refer to head office. CSCI know cruising and are trusted to make quick decisions.

Dwight's cell-phone is on the surface, ringing out. A deep female voice answers with a muffled Eastern European one-word drone; nothing recognisable.

"Bedi, get your ass in the office, girl, and read your texts on the way," Dwight instructs. He doesn't want a conversation, and he doesn't want to give her the chance to say no; she is still grieving. Work will be good for her.

He spins his chair and hits the cell to end the call. Before any of these lockdowns, Dwight was considering the world class prosthetic limb centre in up-town Miami. It had taken a lot of targeted banter for him to rise above self-imposed barriers. Fighting to walk again is not only a physical torture but an explosion of his post-traumatic stress. He may have commanded a major military special-ops unit and now be the quick thinking CSCI point man and head of their technical hub, but he conceals his own dark periods. He doesn't have time for those thoughts; he makes another call.

"Croc. Send a stage one contract. Details to you on a text. I'm gonna need a plane, stand by on that."

Dwight hears the door open, and Kieron Philips arrives in the diner. He was a commander too, in the same war zones. He is very British; originally from a tank regiment but since spent many years working deep cover behind enemy lines; exactly the type of operator Dwight's unit was sent in to get out when everything went 'tits-up', as Kieron would say. Women especially love Kieron's posh British accent that draws the listener in. However, they have all been locked down again for ages and seen no one.

"Philips reporting for duty, Commander Dwight Ritter, Sir," Kieron says formally as he drags a finger along the table for dust. He is pleased there is extraordinarily little dirt, considering the place has been closed for at least six weeks. Cars, planes, and ships have all been grounded, due to the latest D-variant of the virus entering the country, so there has been little pollution again.

"Stand down, Philips, and stick this up your nose, Kieron."

The amusing pizzicato banter is back. Dwight telling Kieron Philips to stand at ease when he is outranked here in the business and by past military rank. Kieron is his boss.

"Are we not going next door?" Kieron asks, pointing to the innocent black door that once was a utilities cupboard. Dwight ignores him, tossing COVID test packs onto two of the dining tables away from him.

Wild Mary smashed a hole in the wall between the units to mend a leaking pipe. The hole got filled by a reinforced wall and steel door as they moved in and built the hi-tech hub. Now, using the 'broom-cupboard' as the entrance to their unit has become a habit. Even though they park around the corner in the shopping centre that closed long before the pandemic, they all walk past their own street door, past the corner of the diner and around to the front of the attached unit. The restaurant has both aspects, front, and side. The 'L' shaped diner has become 'home'. Mary and the 'kids' have all become essential parts of the extended investigation team who all want to get onto the cruise ship every time CSCI have a contract. However, no one will race to volunteer this time; these ships are locked down and going nowhere. They have no guests so will feel like soulless, floating tin prison ships. Maybe that is why someone, or a small team, think the valuable gem-safes on board are easy pickings.

"Yo!" Hunter says, as he swings the door open and the tiny bell above it rings for the third time. His entrance is louder and less formal than KP's. He sees Kieron at a table by himself, reading the instructions on the sterile pack.

"Won't they do that at the airport?"

"I send them tests done in the last twelve-hours," Dwight says. He is in charge at CSCI although it's owned by the two men before him: Commander Kieron Philips and Hunter Witowski (of undisclosed military rank).

"There's a system ripe for abuse," Hunter offers, stating the obvious flaw in the structure.

"You'll be shipping out today," Dwight says.

"What's the rush?" Kieron asks, not that he is objecting. He doesn't have a wife and new baby like Hunter.

"We need to be all over that ship before it gets around there's been a robbery," Dwight explains. "No one knows."

"We'll keep it secret while we're investigating then," Kieron says, sarcastically.

The two powerful men sit and wince at the uncomfortable deep swabbing of their noses, then wait for the flow test results. Dwight is on the phone, organising transport. It is remarkably quick and easy for him. Hunter has his cell-phone to his ear, but while waiting for a reply he is watching Dwight.

"You not opening the hub? Or we not allowed in 'til we pass?" Hunter asks, when Dwight finishes his call.

"I thought this job might be easy enough for me to run from home," Dwight says.

"Home?" Kieron questions.

"This is your home?" Hunter says, still waiting for someone to pick up his call and the test result to appear.

"I got my friends."

Both men look at Dwight in surprise, then almost in harmony, though with different accents, say "You don't have any friends."

"Me and the Amazon delivery guy have got real close … and I've built a state of the art gaming console. I'm making more friends there."

They both continue to look at him in amazement, wanting answers.

"My chair moves and shakes like I'm piloting a spaceship. World moves. It all moves with me."

They study him in silence.

"I'm in a team, same people every day," Dwight says. "Made some good friends."

"Avatars," Hunter states, as he throws his test-slide at him. "They ain't real people."

"An avatar says more about a person than their name because they chose it. They're free to wear it."

"Pardon?" Kieron says. "You want to run this mission, from your avatar-infested home, of surreal guests who could be our diamond thieves in disguise."

"Or perverts, or under-age girls," Hunter suggests. "No, sorry Elaine, that was to Dwight," he says, focussing back on his cell and addressing his call. "I gotta fly out and search a ship. Might be gone overnight. I'll call you when I know more. Love you."

"What's your handle?" Kieron asks Dwight.

"They're not called handles."

"Bet it's got legs," Hunter digs.

He and Kieron have been mercilessly pushing him to walk again.

"Look, guys, mobility is under consideration. I'm looking into it." Dwight concedes.

"How many legs your avatar got?"

"Eight. My name's Spider and spiders always have eight legs."

"And how many do you need?"

"Two! Hunter, I'm going to have two legs made and you're paying."

"We'll pay every damn nickel," Hunter drills.

"This eight-legged avatar: male or female?" Kieron asks.

"It's not male or female!"

"I worry about you, Dwight. You have so many life-decisions to make," Hunter says, rising to look over the counter to see nothing. No food, no coffee. "Why we in here? We've got a coffee machine next door."

"You need to get to the airport."

"What airport?"

"Might be upcoast. I don't know yet, but you will be leaving. And I do have a female friend," Dwight states.

"Seriously. Where is our information support?" Kieron enquires, looking at the closed door.

"Look. I could run it from on the ship," Dwight says.

"It's a better idea than toy town," Hunter jumps in.

"But no!" Dwight insists. "My opportunity to cruise will be wasted on a dead ship; then I'd be bottom of the stack to cruise again."

"A woman, did you slip in? You and a woman?" Kieron poses, wanting to know more.

Dwight smiles, but there is no answer.

"What? You found yourself a dame? Does she know that you are …" Hunter starts.

"What, that I'm in a chair? Yes."

"No! That you're fat. You've put on a hundred pounds," Hunter teases.

"That's the thing about an avatar, she doesn't know that, and I'm cutting back," Dwight says.

"So, she doesn't know you? And you don't know her?" Kieron attacks.

"I see her every day."

"But you don't," Hunter drills.

"It's a trust thing, we explore worlds together. Fight side by side, like being in a unit."

"But it's not, is it? What's the name of this avatar? I wanna meet her before she dates my boy? I wanna vet her," Hunter says.

"Rocket."

"Rocket! That's all you got?"

"You don't need much more to be a friend. We clicked just like that." Dwight snaps his fingers.

"So, you want to live in your bedroom now?" Hunter teases.

"With an avatar." Kieron adds.

"Here's how it will go, they will feel bad, you'll help them with advice, become real close, then wham! They'll need money for their puppy or child or whatever…" Hunter explains.

"No," Dwight insists.

"Truth is, you just don't want to be face to face with a bunch of killers out there at sea," Kieron retorts.

"It's shoplifting. No one's getting killed," Dwight says.

"It's diamonds," Hunter insists. "They call them blood diamonds because people die for them."

"How much are these diamonds worth?" Kieron asks.

"Quarter of a million dollars," Dwight reveals.

"Just across the i95 in Overtown, people get killed for a fraction of that money," Hunter adds.

"I know, I've advised the client of the bullet-money clause."

"Bullet money?" they both pull up in harmony.

"It's that new clause for extras, based on you being shot at," Dwight informs them innocently. "It's the clever clause Izzy came up with."

"How do we know how many bullets?" Hunter says, at the lunacy of the clause.

"Count them," Dwight insists, straight faced. "Then forward me the inventory with the times, and places."

"Sure! And we need a clause for being killed! Anyone who steals that value of diamonds is a potential killer!" Kieron fires at Dwight.

"Sure, that's why head office hasn't even told the resident security."

Both men shoot a puzzled look at Dwight.

"Who's gonna ring my wife and tell her it might be longer than one night?" Hunter growls, thinking.

The exchange has made all realise that they are on another 'kill or be killed mission' just like when conscripted. These missions all add to their PTSD and none of them talk about it.

2 - CROC

Croc is short for crocodile, an animal whose thick skin is worth more than its meat. This fast maturing twenty-year-old is having to toughen up to the banter and being the brunt of jokes. He is an IT genius, who, as a teenager, was nearly jailed for hacking. Mary, the owner of 'Wild Mary's' diner, a short powerful woman of African descent that few would disagree with, saved him back then, just as she had paid for all his college fees. He loved her like a mother until he found out she was his mother and now he can't get his head around it. What he wants to get his head around is a cruise ship. He has worked with Dwight as an analyst and assistant point man in the tech hub on every mission, and whilst well paid, he has not yet been on a cruise. He could pay for one, but while everyone else, including his two sisters, have managed to cruise for free, it seems wrong to pay. Then there was lockdown, a break, then lockdown, and again. So, having been in a small apartment with his two other triplets for months, he jumped at the call to stay-cruise.

He stands with his two luggage cases, alone in the small area that says, 'departure lounge', but it's not his vision of an airport. There is not another person, nor an airplane to be seen. He even has a mask on, making it more like it's the end of the world. He could be in a zombie movie, or some post-apocalyptic disaster and he is being set-up to be in the wrong place at the wrong time. He didn't even know there was an airport on this small island off Miami's mainland. Maybe the imposed stay-at-home has had him seeing too many movies. Worried he's got it wrong; he turns and walks away quickly.

"Croc!"

He is called by both Hunter and Philips. He beams as soon as he sees them.

Much nearer than the main airport, Watson Island is just a few blocks from the CSCI office. It sits between the mainland and Miami Beach and is next to Cruise Island, also known as Dodge Island. Dodge and Watson are joined by an undersea tunnel that is nearly a mile long. The little island in the Biscayne Bay is Miami's sea-plane port. That doesn't mean it has every flight-answer to every island, because most flights to where they want to go would be from Fort Lauderdale. However, there is almost no air-traffic, and just a few passengers can make a scheduled-flight change. Dwight certainly can.

Both masked agents stop yards before they meet Croc, subtly miming shock. Croc slows down.

"I passed my test. I don't have Covid!"

"We'll need two more parachutes," Philips says.

"Small ones," Hunter says, pulling his cell out, worried.

"What?" Croc asks.

"We're being dropped into the sea, near the ship," Kieron says.

"Dropped?"

"You ticked 'can parachute' on the job application," Kieron replies, with a straight face.

"I need two luggage chutes," Hunter says, into his cell.

"Did I? I filled in loads of job applications, so many I made shit up. I can't remember which one you had, but it was…"

"What? You ain't coming now?" Hunter asks, lowering his cell. "I just got the US Coast Guard looking for two small luggage chutes."

"Sorry guys… I… I've never jumped."

Croc is deflated. The agents stand staring at him until he begins to warm. He does not yet have the tools to match their repartee.

"You guys! You had me again," he says, eventually laughing, but they are not, and he sees they have not broken stance.

Hunter holds his hands up to stop him dragging the cases.

"No luggage," he states sharply.

"For real?" Croc asks, even more worried.

Kieron shakes his head. The two huge men each, take a case from Croc. He's been double-had, but even more, he knows he is one of the team and he follows them. He would follow them anywhere.

With luggage thrown on an x-ray belt, they turn to see Bedriška, the tall, leggy, Russian member of their team, as she arrives dragging her rucksack. Croc mocks shock.

"I'm on it. I'll see what I can do," Croc plays out.

"Do what?" she spits in her direct, unforgiving hard accent.

"We're being dropped into the sea, I'll arrange a chute for your case," he tries, the best he can.

Without taking another breath, Bedriška lifts him up, one hand grabbing a chunk of the back of his pants, the other the scruff of his neck. His feet are swept, and she throws him along the rubber conveyor belt into the luggage x-ray machine. She walks through the human x-ray arch, leaving her case on the ground for Kieron to deal with.

"Ma'am, that's strictly not allowed, I'll have to ask you to go back through the arch and wait the other side until your luggage is through," a security guard says, putting his hand on his gun.

She looks at him with her death stare.

"You be dead before gun raised. Say more, you die. That my luggage. Pick it up," she demands, as it comes through the machine after Croc who is falling off the moving band.

"Stand down agent Kossoff," Hunter orders, to diffuse the situation. He and Kieron walk in to support her.

"I'll need an apology for that, sir," the officer says, trying to find some dignity faced with three massive physical units.

Kieron looks at her face. "That's the best one I've ever seen her give."

Hunter ushers Bedriška through. Croc lifts her case off the end of the belt, watched by the other smaller officer.

"Don't you look at me like that, I'm just as deadly," Croc tries.

The officer snatches at his clipped-in gun. Croc dives for the floor using the case for cover as they both roll, the lid coming open and his clothes coming out.

The others turn as Croc apologises, letting the immigration officer, now towering over him, spin the case and hold the lid up.

"You got a gun in here, kid?" The officer torments.

"No. I carry all guns," Bedriška announces, her face stern. Every word true.

3 - FISHING

Croc follows the other three outside to a small propellor plane. It is a nine-seater commercial flight out to the islands. The CSCI team are the last to board the Cessna Grand Caravan Amphibian which is rarely this full. The two other passengers are seated at the back. Croc is in front of them. Kieron and Hunter sit together in front of him so they can chat. Bedi sits alone right up-front. She is in a dark place, stoic and not in any way engaging with the others. The pilot worries as she watches him take off. He fills with relief as he levels off, and she looks down at her cell. On the screen, she has stored the deck plans of the MS Aerwyna. She knows ships well from her years as a spa manager, but not these ships; not that they are hugely different.

"Why do they leave stuff in the safe?" Hunter whispers closely into Kieron's ear, just loud enough to work over the engine noise.

"Who knew the lockdown would carry on and on?" Kieron postures.

"Thieves did, obviously," Croc states, leaning in from behind trying to be involved in the quiet exchange.

Both investigators turn to scold him for his flippant comments.

Hunter leans into the boy's ear, "No one starts a world pandemic to steal a few diamonds."

"Shop couldn't know," Croc whispers, a little embarrassed.

"Why?" Hunter asks.

"Or they'd have a better safe."

Croc spins through his cell messages to the photo Dwight sent, which is from the whistleblower.

"On second look, I guess it's got a key. But the numbers panel; any good hacker could open it."

Both agents stare at Croc.

"I guess. I've never opened a safe but there's a few underground chat sites on digital safes," Croc says, trying to restrain himself. He wants to join in, but he is also petrified of them.

"So, Croc, option 1," Kieron starts, "A team board the ship mid-lockdown just to steal the diamonds. With them they have number-crackers, and a key?"

Croc looks puzzled at his own summation when it is laid out. "Yeah. They are diamond stealers."

Both Hunter and Kieron think for a moment. Croc is like a sprung coil that needs to be flicked.

"Generator modification engineers, carpet layers, or, yes, IT specialists," Croc says, looking at his cell for the lists of workers.

"But what don't they know?" Hunter asks Croc.

Croc shakes his head thinking. "That we're coming?" He offers.

The two agents wait and wait, and Croc feels he must fill the silence. They are used to silence; it is an interrogation tool.

"I guess they should have figured out someone would be on their way," Croc begins.

"Why?" Hunter challenges.

"Because the safe was left open," Kieron says. "Big mistake."

"Yeah. That had to be a mistake," Croc agrees.

"Why couldn't they close the safe?" Hunter asks.

"I'll work that up," Croc says, keenly tapping that note into his cell. "That had to be their big mistake."

"First mistake," Kieron says.

"Yeah. Second mistake; they won't be expecting us."

"Us? You been watching super-hero movies?" Hunter asks Croc.

"Yeah. Loads." Croc admits excitedly. "We need lycra!"

"No one's expecting super-heroes," Hunter says. "Not even if we get new pants."

Croc nods slowly. He realises that he is falling into elephant traps and being shat on by banter, so he delivers a deliberate answer.

"We're gonna catch them out big time then."

Croc dares to raise a very limp fist and push it very hesitantly upwards. The ratchet movements don't get far before they're reversed. Philips and Witowski wait a moment for that to settle, before shaking their heads.

"One. They don't know the robbery's been discovered; and we keep it that way," Kieron starts.

"Two, they ain't getting off with the diamonds. No one will be expecting a complete ship lock-down," Hunter says, almost lost in the increasing power of the engine.

"How?"

"A Covid outbreak," Kieron says, right into his ear.

"But the whole ship is tested twice a week. Who's got Covid?"

"You," they say, one into each ear.

He drops back, leaving the conversation.

Croc wakes from a daydream, frightened by the sudden propellor noise-reduction of the small plane. He slides across to the window seat.

"We're falling!"

"Landing," Hunter growls without effort.

"You know why it's called a landing?" Croc asks the others, looking at the beautiful shades of green and blue waters below.

He is ignored by all as the plane loses altitude.

"Coz, you meant to land on land!" Croc shouts in a panic.

"Can't you swim?" Kieron asks.

"Me?" Croc tries to deflect.

Again, he is ignored, but everyone has gathered that he can't swim, and have no doubt stored the knowledge for future use.

"I'm landing on land," the man in the back adds smartly.

"Where?" Croc asks in a panic.

"GHC!"

"That's it. GHC. I'm getting off at GHC," Croc shouts, now believing they have been winding him up about landing in the sea.

"Our ship's nowhere near Great Harbour," Hunter says dryly.

"Then we'll get a boat."

"Croc. This plane also stops by our ship," Kieron insists.

"It ain't a bus!" Croc argues. I'm doing GHC." He turns to the man on the back seat. "Can I hire a boat?"

"Sure. Everyone has a boat on the islands. You fish?"

"Yeah."

"Fish? You've never been fishing in your life," Hunter enjoys.

"Never," Kieron adds.

"Big-game fishing here," the man in the back starts.

"That's what I do. Got my own rod," Croc throws in fast.

"The rod comes with the gig, kid," the man says.

"Even better! My names Croc," he says, reaching back to shake hands, but it is ignored. "Ah, sorry," he says, offering the elbow that doesn't connect. "I'll be fishing all the way to the ship."

"You had a flow test?" the man asks.

"This morning, before flying."

"You on holiday? Looking to relax in sun, or for sex, or a little gambling?"

"Work," Croc says, embarrassed as the offers get more dangerous.

"What do you guys do on the ship?" the man asks.

Hunter presses Croc's shoe with his, just to remind him that idle chatter is the worst kind. Hunter is recording sound on his cell-phone.

"Just here with my team," Croc says, controlling himself.

Hunter releases his belt and slips behind into Croc's row and mimes a fist bump with the man without touching, it is returned.

"Name's Hunter, I'd love to take you up on that offer to fish some other time. I'll even buy the beers. If we get a day off. Never been around these parts."

"You met the right guy. Name's Havana Rock. You in a rush?"

"They can't make us work 'til we arrive," Hunter says, testing him.

"Doug," Havana Rock shouts forward. "Take her around again."

"Yes Sir, Rock," the pilot says, and the engines gun back up as he radios the local airport to say he is going around one more time.

"We're the only bird in the sky today," Havana Rock explains.

Hunter leans into Croc and shares some private words. "Get the names of ships, all the boats, all the islands, and distances between them."

"A lot of Islands," Kieron says, picking up the baton.

"Thirty Berry islands; Sandy Cay, Whale Cay, Chub Cay, Hog Cay, we've even got a Cockroach Cay."

"What's that one nearest to the ships?" Hunter asks, watching Croc start to plot.

"That's Cistern. Development there didn't work out which is why it's up for sale. The runway would need some work before that airport could open again. Perfect for another cruise line; it'll get bought."

"Cruise line?"

"Yeah. Royal Caribbean's already got Little Stirrup, and NCL's got Great Stirrup Cay. Down there, that's Bullock's Harbour; you get a great night out there. You could buy that cay too if you've got the right money."

The plane pulls around in a full circle, low enough to view everything.

"Must be thirty ships?" Hunter provokes.

"That's a lot of money in one fishbowl," Rock says.

"How many fishing boats down there?" Hunter asks.

"Hundreds and hundreds. Must be way over a thousand boats in the Bahamas," Rock answers.

"That's a list I bet no one keeps," Kieron says.

"That would be like trying to list the millionaires here and what they do to make their money. Lists you ain't gonna find."

4 – MIX AND MATCH

Croc learned his skills through trial and error. His no-fear, touchy-feely approach is how most kids pick up their computing and hacking skills. He never made general grades at college and his IT qualification wasn't good on paper. Bored with the restraints of the course, he spent too much time learning to jive and flip burgers at Wild Mary's. There he became the only one permitted to assist Stan on the grill, and the only one ever to be allowed to cook Wild Mary's fried green tomatoes. That was the highest honour he ever achieved. At night he would use the diner's computer to hack into digital wormholes he had no right to be in.

In total contrast, Commander Kieron Philips went straight into officer school and rose through the ranks. He is studious and super bright at everything including languages. He survived authority in a long army career, eventually working deep behind enemy lines in the Middle East. He portrayed many facades, from a journalist to a baggage handler. He also executed many illegal and invisible payoffs with leaders for a government that would disown him in a heartbeat.

Croc has been sending and receiving texts with Miami since the small plane flew out and that has intensified on the short hop back into the sea. It is touching down on the water before he can object or worry; his work is full-on already. All four investigators have been sent and have learned their new cover story before they step from the floating plane to the lifeboat that will tender them the short distance to the ship. Their cover-stories and working qualifications are all written by Izzy, Croc's sister, who has been called in to assist Dwight.

The story goes that the four of them are a cyber-crimes team sent to test the ship's newly installed IT software and they answer to no one. They are to act as guests and exhaust everyone but find weaknesses. The best lies are the ones closest to the truth. The job title suits them very well, and it lets them play with the ship's security, even though the ship has been told to give them no access whatsoever. They are to be treated like guests.

Croc and Hunter are at check-in where their cell-phones have been loaded with the ship's app. They are being shown the many features from menus and maps to news and the daily programme. They will be using them around the ship to pay bills, and to open their cabin doors. They also linger at reception because they want plastic card door keys as a back-up despite being told repeatedly that they won't be necessary. The other two, claiming no smart phone and not liking the free plastic wrist 'tracelet' and medallion, go across the atrium. They have plastic door keys, but the shop has opened for them to upgrade the medallion; an up-sale the ship encourages.

Kieron and Bedriška have a special bond and have learned to look out for each other, but the death of Georgie may have tested that. Bedriška has refused to take his calls since her partner's death, so they haven't spoken. Two shop assistants are supervised as Kieron acts the posh British guest buying the expensive watch that does everything. He may understand a lot of what is being said, but he insists it is fully explained to him again, especially the medical emergency features. He is testing the shop assistant but also observing the IT engineer who is training her - a man who is unaware that Kieron's cover story is to test their software installations. Neither of them has a clue that he is looking for diamond thieves.

Bedriška is the perfect difficult non-English speaking guest with no digital skills and claiming no smart cellphone. She was given the wrist band and a necklace to hold the medallion - the alternative technical track and trace disc-shaped requirement. Neither the necklace nor tracelet in numerous colours meet her demands. Reluctantly giving in to the need to open her cabin door, Bedi goes through the process. These items were on sale before the lockdown, but the new software is far more advanced; or should be. The engineer helping Bedi receives a call on his cell, and he listens to the caller without a word until he says "OK," and ends the call. He holds eye to eye with Bedi, a dangerous thing to do. His vision widens and he focusses on Kieron. Bedriška and Kieron see that the IT team have clearly been told the purpose of the CSCI team. Everything has changed and the cover story now must be played out in public.

"Find anything you don't understand, just come and see me, first. No need to report up if I can sort it. There's always a way to sort things out," he tells the agents.

Bedriška snatches the medal. "I can work stupid tracelet out."

5 - AUTHORITY

"Dwight Ritter?" a young sounding female voice says firmly. "I think we should meet."

In the dark room, her picture pops up on a video screen with an invitation to a video call. Dwight mouths 'Oh really', shaking his head as he rejects the camera request. He has always hated authority, especially young ones. Izzy imposes herself on him while listening. He waves her away from engaging their camera.

"It's Commander Dwight Ritter, and no we don't have to meet."

"You're reporting on my company, we absolutely must meet."

"I absolutely don't have to. I don't report to you."

Izzy is thrown by Dwight's attitude to the young woman.

"Oh, I think you do, I'm JJ. JJ Easterbrook, the Executive Director of External Communications at Easterbook/William."

"Hope your family are real proud, but with respect, it means nothing to me. Now if you will excuse me, I'm busy."

Dwight hangs up and Izzy looks at him aghast, her hands splayed out to gesture.

"What the...? You could have been more friendly to her."

"Why?"

"Why were you so rude? Was it because she was a woman?"

"She shouldn't have this number."

"We're in the phone book and she was an Executive doing her job."

"We have one contractor; we answer to them and to no one else."

"But she deserved respect," Izzy insists.

Dwight thinks on it.

"Izzy. You handle the press, and you handle them well. I think you should do all public relations, so as operations chief, I hereby appoint you Executive Director of External Affairs. Overstep normal company protocols and you answer to Commanders Philips and Witowski. Congratulations."

"What?" she yells.

"First job is to get a door or desk sign made, name and title, big."

"You're winding me up, and I don't think this is funny."

"Seriously, you are our in-house copywriter and journalist, that makes you press and PR. I thought it was a good title but come up with a better one and I'll consider it. I'm entering the promotion into the daily log."

Dwight formally types away. Izzy's phone buzzes and she knows that was him informing everyone including her. There is a second buzz, and she looks. A smiley face from Kieron. Then a thumbs up from Hunter.

"He's got to learn that the thumbs up is not so cool," she mumbles.

Then there is the text message from Croc. 'Congratulations. I left a present for you in my desk drawer'.

"How did he know I was going to get promoted?"

Dwight tries to throw a look of real confusion; hands up, face in a kind of 'I don't know' grimace.

Izzy opens the drawer and screams leaping back. There is a small family of baby rats suckling off the mother, who looks up at her frightened.

"That's a strong young woman there, needs a little TLC, not WTF. Croc named the little guy Ben before he left on assignment. The other four Randy, Tito, Jermaine, and Reynaud. You better do a second count, but there are a few spare names. Then they need to be re-homed; externally."

6 - THE GRAVEYARD

Hunter kicks the large case Croc pulls, so it turns sideways from the long corridor into the cabin doorway. Croc heaves it in but is distracted, in awe of the cabin. Hunter lifts it, then the second case that he was pulling for Croc, tossing them both onto the nearest of two beds.

"Nice," Croc says.

"Sorry I forgot; you live in a derelict unit."

"Not anymore. You should come over to our apartment for dinner one night."

"Let's start with a beer on top deck. Let's go."

"I need to unpack."

"You never need to unpack; we don't stay long enough."

Croc flips the lid on his huge case. Hunter cringes at what he sees inside.

"What?" Croc asks.

"You know the people who pack the most?"

"No?" Croc asks, falling in line with the lead.

"The ones with least inside them. You got a dinner suit?"

"No."

"Nice evening clothes?"

"No."

"What's in here?"

"Pants, shirts."

"Denim pants and tee shirts?"

"Yes."

"And they fill a case that size? My case rests," Hunter asks and answers.

"You've got a dinner suit?"

"First and sometimes the only thing I pack."

"In your small sports bag?"

"Plus two pairs of shorts, casuals and two sun shirts. Bag zipped, I'm gone," Hunter confirms.

"Zipped?"

"Not close to being full. And I bet Kieron's got his military dress suit. He wouldn't be able to stop himself."

"With his medals?" Croc asks.

"And shiny boots."

"No!"

"You know what's wrong with a big case?"

"No," Croc almost whispers embarrassedly.

"Takes you ages to pack, takes you ages to unpack."

Hunter flips open the second case. It is full of technical equipment.

"This one I kinda get."

"But, no point in us bringing all this if they've left with the diamonds," Croc agrees.

"Let's go. Beer time," Hunter says in a hurry.

"But."

"OK. You're on your own. I'll see you in the Sunset Bar, above the pool deck."

"Hey wait," Croc splutters.

"Map is on the ship's app, Bedi's next door feeling sorry for herself," Hunter throws back.

Croc is not familiar with ships, unlike Hunter who spent years in cruise ship security teams after 'separation'. Croc eventually decides not to unpack and leaves, but way too late; Hunter has gone. He wanders helplessly confused into Bedriška's cabin next door.

"Sorry, the door was open. They've gone for a drink; Hunter says we should hurry."

Bedi lifts her glass and downs it in one. Croc looks around and sees the tiny spirit bottles discarded on various tops. He realises she has emptied the mini bar. Bedi can drink a lot.

"Do you have evening wear with you?" he asks.

"Of course. It is cruise ship. Do you have mini bar?"

"Of course. It is cruise ship," Croc tries mocking.

From her small rucksack, she pulls a hand sized pouch. Almost the kind that holds a large shopping bag. Inside glitters silver, but the material drops before his eyes, unrolling with a flick it turns into a sheer silver evening dress.

"Wow. Next you're gonna make the underwear appear from …" Croc slows to a stop. Her look has blocked his further speech.

"Nothing under dis dress."

Croc is embarrassed, he tries to change the subject and his mind anchors on the one thing he has never braved to ask, and he asks exactly the wrong person.

"Do you think we'll die on this mission?"

"Don't know, don't care."

Croc is shocked and finds himself uncontrollably defensive.

"But you're not in the KGB now."

"Same job. Different boss."

"No…"

"Yes. Policeman. Army. Security. KGB. I trust this team. I never trust my country. They want to kill me."

"So how do we do," he stutters, "how do you do it?"

"Never fear death, we all die. Just be smarter than other guy."

"Or shoot them fast like you did in that drug house. I couldn't shoot anyone."

"That was smart move."

"Guess so, we're both alive. And that was just over some paintings. This is diamonds."

"Take baby from mother, she become killer. Mad woman kill Georgie. No reason to kill most gentle woman in world," she says, as flatly as everything she says anything, but there is pain in each word.

"Yeah. Sorry, you must have really loved her."

"I did."

She continues to take off her clothes. Croc is spellbound and must shock himself free. He turns in embarrassment to see her cabin door still open. He darts back and slams it and by the time he blushingly turns back, she is dressed in silver. The material has melted onto her body and there is not a line to distract from her perfect curves. She brushes her hair and clips it back on one side, adds lipstick, and then rouge while he is still in a coma.

"Wow! I can't see where you've stashed your gun."

"We go. Your gun needs to relax."

Croc is embarrassed but must follow.

7 - ELECTRIC BLUE

Smelling of fresh coffee, the hub is alive as no bedroom could be. It has its own version of Miami's blue haze that started Dwight's day, but the neon electric glow of digital information ignores time. It might be evening outside but the unit where work has begun will merge into a Groundhog Day and possibly weeks if the mission drags on. The row of computer screens all the way down to the end large monitor are alive and healthy, but human life is suspended in a quasi-space-station. The hub is effectively a hard vacuum plasma containing a low density of particles of hydrogen and helium, as well as electromagnetic radiation, magnetic fields, and cosmic rays; he could be an astronaut.

"Chief Operations Officer, Casey B. de Michelle" he explains pulling a picture of her onto the large screen at the end of the desk. "I feel she has mixed feelings. I can't work out whether it's because she's a broken woman who doesn't think the cruise company can survive further lockdown, or that the jewellers are her most precious client, and she doesn't need this aggravation on top of the past year they've all had."

Many cruise ships sell tickets at cost. The profit is from upselling and the art gallery, and jewellers are main players that must be kept sweet.

Dwight turns to the other screen where he has Ms de Michelle's ID card, driving licence and passport on the smaller work screens. A CV going back to her time as a chef in France, a restauranteur, hotel manager, and a hotel manager on the group's ships. It is a progression that shows knowledge of the industry, not just a fast-tracked executive. Dwight's attention is broken by a door alarm. Different cameras show angles of a delivery driver with a box, who stands waiting at the hub's real entrance.

"I'm gonna buzz the door. Leave it on the shelf, not the floor," Dwight instructs.

Dwight hasn't eaten all day, which can affect his mood. The burgers, fried green tomatoes, and potato fries from next door have not been available. Wild Mary has always insisted her diner is there to sit down and eat in, or to learn to jive in, but she does not and never will deliver food. If life never opens up again, she might have to change her stance, but then, she could cook and supply from home.

Dwight collects the box and rips it open as he motors around to the kitchen. He must negotiate the end of the main desk, Izzy's screen and discussion area, and the temporary beds that have all become part of the space along with the kitchenette in the fast expansion. The destroyed box exposes a large white plastic tub with brown and green artwork. His diet of coffee is about to be supplemented by raw organic juiced greens in powder form needing water. Not totally inspired by the imprisonment of lockdown, Dwight is to turn his life around. It is a mental position not every bilateral above-the-knee amputee manages to arrive at. Kieron and Hunter have barraged him to get off his ass and will take full credit for it. Dwight has decided that he will master his prosthetics and will only use the chair as the other option and not let it be his warden. He knows if he wants the slightest chance of controlling prosthetics, he must drop some weight and get back to near military fitness. Above the knee amputees find it physically and mentally tiring, having to practice constantly and concentrate hard to master walking, stairs, slopes, and uneven ground.

With a shaken green suspension in the chair's usual flask holder, he speeds back towards the desk as Kieron is calling.

"Dwight, I'm more interested in the whistleblower."

"Kieron, you have it all."

"Can't you trace the guy down?"

"No," Dwight says, as he can add nothing to the conversation.

They tend to talk to each other as if an answer is not required. As if each line is a report, which it is when sending detail like Casey de Michelle.

Dwight brings up the electric code of the call Casey had with the whistleblower. He plays it.

"Hello. I am in the stock room. The safe is empty. Door open. Safe door never open, not open yesterday."

"Can I get your name?"

"Not yet."

The call is ended.

"The voice is male, he's Asian," Kieron ventures, you must have more than we can hear.

Dwight is running code.

"It is a mobile phone, pinging off the ship's system," Dwight says.

"Every call should be on their track and trace; let's find him." It is an order from Kieron. Dwight is not yet up to speed. His mind is on new legs and romance.

He starts to type on the main system. 'Rocket. Sorry. Can't make the team for a few days...' But he stops and deletes it, realising he shouldn't expose the system to an outside trace even though it has firewalls. He rolls his phone over and ensures 'share location' is off, and 'allow location' is off. He spools down, making everything safe, then types with his large thumbs while the cell is in his hefty hands holding the unit.

'Can't make the team for a few days, sorry.' He pauses then adds, 'miss you'. Then after a thought, he further adds 'all'. That ensures the message is generic, but it is not.

A reply flies back.

'No worries.' Then there are emojis showing crying, love hearts and kisses. These warm him inside and he smiles.

'Why are you not at home? Where are you?' is the next message he receives.

Dwight becomes serious. He checks his phone is location safe.

"How does she know I've moved?" He mumbles.

"What was that?" Kieron asks on the screen.

"Just thinking out loud, boss. Looking at the same old walls," he says, as he switches his cell off and takes the battery out.

8 – NAUGHTY NYMPHS

Kieron is leaning on the rail looking out to sea, a glass of rosé in one hand, his cell in the other showing Dwight in Miami. Hunter strolls over and joins him, examining the head on his newly poured beer against the dropping sun.

"Hey, Dwight, there might not be any guests, but the crew keeps the beer from going flat, and someone's delivering new stocks."

"Local barge out of Great Harbour Cay about twenty miles away. Cheers," Dwight replies. "While you two are being serious, I just want to report; this soldier has decided to turn his life around and look for love."

"Kieron, swipe left. I prefer action movies," Hunter says.

"We'll report in later. Good luck Dwight," Kieron says quietly. He has just lost Georgie and knows it can't have been easy for Dwight when his wife left him. Sipping his wine, Kieron's gaze remains fixed on the horizon. "I think the group below are carpet fitters, the team over on starboard section are the haberdashers, and just behind us are the IT crowd. I met one in the shop. He wasn't happy we were inspecting their work."

"No kidding."

"Three lockdowns and the sea has become a cruise ship graveyard," Kieron Philips says, of the tens of ships anchored before him. "But yet they decorate the mausoleums," he concludes, in his best British accent, almost Shakespearean.

The world, the past, and questions about the future would flash through Kieron's mind as he was powered fast and low in a chopper towards his drop zone. But he would shake those unwanted thoughts away, for a lack of concentration could be terminal. Under no threat in his Miami apartment, memories lingered, and the future sometimes seemed empty and pointless. He needed this mission to escape the twisted deliberations of Georgie's death.

Georgie was special but it was a disastrous romance. She was never a member of Cruise Ship Crime Investigators; she was an Entertainments Manager on a ship. She became intertwined with Kieron as they avoided a heist, before having to resolve it to save Hunter's wife, Elaine. Part way into the twisted venture they had four million dollars in cash which they sneaked off a ship and invested in Bequia. The thing about a cruise is its programme doesn't stop, not for life, rarely for death, and never for thinking time. Their decision came in a mad short affair while her first female partner was away on leave. They left the island owning two beautiful Caribbean houses together which had to be explained to Bedriška. Only Kieron with his calm and charm could get away with being the seducer, and then become Bedriška's first real male bed partner on her debut mission for CSCI. It was never simple, and they both loved Georgie to the end, and they both hurt.

"That's the Amatheia, the nurse to all fishes, or ships. I've often moored next to it. I should think it's the same as this inside," Hunter starts. "The one behind it is Ianassa. All eleven ships in this fleet are mermaids."

"Ianassa is a nymph."

"Is there a difference?" Hunter asks.

"My Greek mythology is not good enough for detail, but nymphs are female spirits of the sea who accompany or support gods. I think Ianassa is the daughter of Doris, and maybe of the Ionian Sea."

"There's a Doris in Greek mythology?"

"Wife of the sea-god Nereus."

"What's a mermaid?"

"This is a mermaid," Philips says, turning to toast glasses with Bedi. She has a large bowl glass full of ice and he knows the liquid will be neat vodka.

"Skol."

"Quite a disturbance you've left in your wake," Hunter growls.

"Naughty mermaids lure sailors to their death," Kieron offers. She gives him a long hard look as if he owes her money.

Oblivious of any atmosphere, Croc steps in and clinks his beer bottle.

"All good in the hood?" Croc says jokingly.

"What you drinking?" Hunter asks the young lad.

"Small beer. I paid by my cruise cell phone through my cruise app."

"You're not old enough to be served!"

"I can confirm the guest cruise-app works. I've already hacked into their system and changed my age by just a year, and I'm now officially old enough to drink."

"Already?"

"A real simple buffer overflow. Because they're using too many different code writers. It's a predictable site."

"Croc, let's not get carried away with the 'cover job'," Kieron suggests. He turns back to the sea and looks at the Amatheia, the nearest anchored ship. "Diamonds. How long would it take you to swim to that ship?"

Croc falls silent, Hunter is in play.

"About a mile?"

"I guess," Kieron confirms.

"Night?" Hunter asks again.

"Sharks hunt at night," Bedi stabs in.

"No, trick question. You wouldn't swim with diamonds," Croc answers worried.

"I'd let you have a sea-scooter," Kieron suggests to Croc.

"Still no," Croc says. "Whatever that is."

"It pull you. Shark like moving food," Bedriška explains flatly. She is killing the conversation rather than joining in.

"I'd want a powered inflatable kayak," Hunter suggests.

"Me too," Kieron agrees.

"I'd use a drone," Croc says.

A moments silence reveals that is an inventive idea.

"Drone? Not carry half-a-million-dollars a mile over sea," Bedi states. She never questions.

"Break the load; do more than one flight," Croc suggests.

"Then double risk. Each flight, risk," she says.

"I agree. Plus, one diamond alone was worth a hundred-and-fifty-thousand-dollars," Kieron adds. "Could you land a drone on that ship, from here?"

"You'd need someone there, talking it down, unseen," Hunter considers.

"It has a camera. It can see what it's doing," Croc argues.

"Sure, but we're not talking military-tech," Kieron says, now worried.

"Drone technology will be way beyond what you had in the military," Croc argues.

Kieron turns, holds his empty glass up towards a waiter and finds immediate attention. But he is looking at the IT crowd.

"Tech guy doing 'staff track and trace' instruction today, he could be ex-military," Bedi says, looking at their team.

The IT guy has his eye on her. He stands and raises a glass. Kieron's new full glass arrives in time, and he returns a high confident toast, then reaches with his arm so his watch can touch the waiter's machine to pay.

"Stay out of our way, clankies," is the order shouted from the IT guy

"Clankies?" Croc asks.

"Army term for engineers. Can a drone remote on that ship steal control of a drone from this ship mid-flight, take it in and land it?" Hunter asks.

"Like two remotes?" Croc asks.

"Exactly. Two operators, one on each ship. That ship's having a refit; it's got the same teams," Hunter joins in.

"No. Each drone is encrypted to a specific remote. They are bound together by code as well as frequency; that way you can have any number of drones flying on the same frequency," Croc explains.

"Could techie break code?" Bedi asks.

"In theory."

"Like they break safe code?" she states.

"Sure. But why fly diamonds between ships? None of the ships are locked down," Croc offers. "They simply take them off on a boat or supply barge. The diamonds could be long gone without drones."

"Forget drone. They break gem-safe code on both ships, all ships," Bedi adds.

Bedi points to the Ianassa.

"We need to close all the ships down now, right now," Kieron states with a determined urgency.

Hunter finishes his beer. Croc copies him.

"I'm ready. You need me to have Covid, right?" Croc fears.

"No," Hunter drawls. He and Kieron both stare at the IT crowd.

"They have Covid," Bedi spits as she swaggers off ahead, towards the IT crowd.

"And it's gonna happen now," Hunter says, walking after her. "And we need boots on the other ships," is fired back at Croc.

"Report back," Kieron tells Croc. "We're about to get into the medical centre."

Croc hesitates.

"You sure you don't need my help?"

9 – CODE RED

Unusual for a ship with no guests, at just past midnight, the noisy medical centre is full of patients but has only two nurses covering the shift. A crazy end to the first day. A security guard either side of the wide entrance parts for a third to push the last man in. At the opposite end by the reception counter, Hunter pulls Croc towards him. To make the smart young man look less clean, he twists his mask a little, and smears some blood across it. He and Philips had hit each other to ensure blood when messing up the IT guys. If there was a real military man amongst them, neither of them found him. Before Croc can complain, he is given orders.

"Work the other end. Every time the nurse comes back this way, faint or be ill. Keep her away from us."

Croc is pushed off.

"Two metres distance guys, some respect," Kieron barks loudly in his very British army voice. He wants an excuse to use the space behind reception.

Trying to keep socially distanced is impossible. They all wear new disposable blue medical masks, issued by the clinic, which means there is no chance to see any wounds.

"Everyone, listen! New rules! Anyone who fights, causes a blood injury to another, or who steps into this medical centre must take another Covid test. That includes security," the senior nurse shouts. She is reading from a sheet of paper then she holds it up as proof. The security guards ease themselves outside the door and wait there. The crew inside are the two sides of a drunken brawl that calmed down as soon as it was broken up.

Croc walks past Bedi and takes a position nearer the door, then collapses.

"Get up," Bedriška demands.

Confused Croc stands up but seeing Hunter disapprove he continues to act unwell. A medical assistant walks around with a hand scanner taking their personal identification details from the smart device they must all carry; Kieron's watch, everyone else's smart cellphone, and finally Bedi's disc worn on a chain around her neck. After each personal device is scanned, a test-kit is scanned and handed to them, the two become digitally linked.

"You all know what to do. Deep long swab, dip, then just two drops on the slide and put them on my desk. It's not a race," the senior nurse shouts. "No rush to leave; you're here because you love seeing my pretty face, right?"

"Wrong," Bedi shouts back without any sense of humour. "I here because animal hit me on back of head."

The nurse holds her finger in front of Bedi's eyes and moves it left then right watching her eye movement. She moves away to another job.

As the completed slides begin to get slid on the counter, Kieron palms one away and starts work. Hunter keeps busy in front of him as a visual block, but Bedi is the best distraction at the other end.

"Don't look at my body. Perverts!" Bedriška shouts, scouring the room. She is eye candy standing central in her slinky sparkling silver long dress, she commands attention, making everyone bow their heads as they swab.

Kieron uses his thumb nail to loosen and remove the top from the plastic base of the two-piece slide. The important top that has the easy-to-scan QR code and number relating to a crew member in the room is quickly clipped to a test failure bottom from his pocket and put back on the table. The new slide that read 'no Covid' will never be seen, that is dropped in Kieron's other pocket.

"Don't touch the slides," the nurse shouts at him.

Croc collapses screaming pain and Bedi spins around. "Who touch me?"

Chaos brakes out, during which Kieron manages to change four slides, which will be enough. He moves away out of sight and finds a supply of previous tests in the medical waste bin. He easily changes seven from there and mixes six back in the waste. He drops the last one on the floor by the reception desk. Finishing, he takes a large amount of sanitising gel in his hands and rubs hard. It is his turn to shout,

"Someone has got Covid, look, I don't want to be kept in here."

The senior nurse goes to the counter and separates the pass slides from the failures. She fires the hand scanner at the QR codes on the positive tests.

"Chad Roberts, please go into treatment room one. William Stevens, treatment room one. Franklin Spender and Mike Summers, all in treatment room one."

The nurse looks at the medic who has just arrived.

"We need to follow the drill," he tells her.

She leans into a panel, lifts a rigid plastic safety cover off a set of buttons and presses 'speak'. She leans into the microphone.

"Code Red, Code Red. Alpha Team to the medical centre. This is not a drill. I repeat, Code Red, Alpha Team to the medical centre."

The two security guards at the exit stand far more formally and call for back up.

"Can we go? We're all negative," one of the IT team group asks.

"No," is the short abrupt answer from the medical assistant.

The leader of the IT crowd, Chad Roberts glowers at Kieron as he turns into the treatment room.

"Get well," Kieron offers in return.

Croc and Bedi slip back to Hunter as Kieron eases from behind the desk. Hunter is on his cell.

"Good evening, Dwight. Time to get head office to lock this ship down. The Covid outbreak is formal. It must be enough to lock us and the nearest ships down, if crew have been moving between them. We need a past log of all movement; manpower, equipment or supplies that have gone between ships. Also boots on at least the MS Amatheia and check the safe. Who do we have that could open it?" Kieron asks to end his list.

"I'll ask Billy."

"Great. Nice being on a mission where no-one gets killed," is said, full of British sarcasm.

"OK. What's up?" Dwight asks, knowing his man by now.

"Run the names of the IT team for military connections."

"Roger-that."

Hunter leans in and borrows Kieron's cell. "Sorry if we're keeping you away from your new female avatar friend," he mocks.

"No. A rest from my gaming nuance will be a good cooling period for her. She was coming on a bit strong."

"Essential. I need a face-to-face with the whistleblower."

"That was never an option."

"You should have his cell number by now. If we have his cell number; Croc can get into the track and trace. He's broken in the system already."

Kieron takes his cell back.

"Dwight. Gotta go. We need to switch the second tests."

The call ends and Hunter is still amused. He almost announces to the others, "sounds like Dwight's romance with his new female avatar has hit the rocks."

"That's avatars for you," Croc says, sheepishly.

Whilst the three enjoy the banter, Kieron is focussed on work. The nurse has the clear tests on one side, and the four fails on the other side. She counts them again.

"One short?" Kieron asks, looking around and on the floor, to be helpful. Croc joins in and sees the one deliberately placed under the desk.

"No, that's right," the nurse smiles at Kieron.

"One here, on the floor," Croc shouts.

The nurse may have her quota, but her smile drops to an inquisitive look; the one on the floor cannot be ignored. Croc hands it to her and she is confused by another positive test. The room has started to clear quickly with increased security taking non-Covid guest crew to their cabins for isolation.

"It's positive," she whispers to herself.

Kieron is waiting for his moment; he needs the new tests being done by the doctor in the treatment room next to him.

"Call the doctor," Kieron suggests to her.

She puts the failed test on the counter, alone, and rounds the desk, to the door of the treatment room.

"Doctor, I've another positive test."

The doctor follows her out holding the four new tests.

Hunter watches Kieron, he knows what must happen. He has no fear of Kieron failing but wonders what his plan might be.

The doctor is looking at the computer screen as the new failure is scanned. It puzzles them, both, and they can only talk in whispers.

"Don't you get cross contamination holding them like that?" Kieron asks the doctor of the tests in his hand.

"No," the Doctor defends, but he puts them down.

Kieron leans over the counter and the tests to steal a look at the screen, he sees it shows the ID of an officer, pictured in a white shirt with his hat on. His hand is on the four tests, and they are swapped for four known fails out of his pocket. Four people not even on the ship. If any of the slides' identities are scanned the game is up.

"OK. One thing at a time," the doctor says, with a quick look at the four tests. "They're all Covid-positive again."

The nurse leans over with the scanner, Kieron makes the start of a lightening move from his end of the counter. He must stop her. Hunter is faster; he raises a hand to cease his attack. He is nearer. To end what could have only been a clumsy burst, Hunter puts his hand on the scanner plug and eases it out of the socket just enough for it not to work. The nurse tries scanning the test, but each attempt fails.

The clock is ticking fast, and Kieron must work on the plastic cases of the real new tests but will need more time. The nurse collects the scanner lead and follows it back finding it has been unplugged. Bedi pushes Croc over.

"Be ill."

Croc hits the deck with groans that would have the audience of an amateur theatre walking out. Hunter kicks the power socket and the whole computer dies.

In confusion, the doctor barks new orders.

"Call that officer. Have him come here or go straight to his cabin, whichever is nearest." The doctor rounds the counter and goes back into the treatment room. "Gentlemen, it's bad news. A second bad result for each of you."

"What officer?" The nurse says, arms skywards. She has no screen.

"It said Petty Officer Tommy Mooney," Kieron says, standing and leaning over the desk to swap the tests back. Hunter bends down and re-powers her machine.

Two security officers enter.

"Right, two more," they shout at the CSCI team.

Bedi heaves Croc up.

"You feel better now? We go."

10 – WHISTLEBLOWER

A whistleblower can remain anonymous. A call such as this could be a spoof other than for the picture that followed the brief conversation. The picture of the safe they all have on their cell phones.

"Same as picture Dwight sent," Bedi says, comparing the open safe to the one she has on her unregistered cell that she can carry. The goddess in beach shorts and white tennis shoes, squats in front of it in the messy overcrowded stockroom. A tall woman whose leg muscles shuffle slightly but remain perfect, has blocked the other's vision of the waist height, grey safe. She pulls on rubber gloves and lifts the rejected, black velvet empty ring-trays, from the car crash of a discarded pile hastily tossed back inside. She passes them back, one by one.

Kieron is double checking the corridor, back and forth. There is no sign of life. On the door is a sign saying, 'Never Lock.' He closes it behind him and holds it closed. He holds the handle tightly in the up mode, taking pictures of the room with his unregistered cell, as far as he can, planted by his heel hard against the door.

"The cabin door is never locked," Keiron states.

"So, it junk room; how thief know dis safe not junk?" Bedi demands of the twisted logic.

"Let Croc get in there to dust, Bedi, I wanna get out of here," Hunter says, spinning a static chair around, then sitting on it back-to-front as if auditioning for West Side Story.

The room would look bigger if it were not for the rubbish massed in it, and four people filling the remaining space. It is a normal smaller cabin on a lower crew deck.

"This much crap in the room, everyone's using it," Croc says.

The last tray scratches as it slides out less easily. A ring drops to the floor. Bedi passes the tray behind her as before, but she retains and studies the ring. The centre princess diamond is surrounded by a halo of smaller diamonds on a gallery, with accent stones down the shoulder of the platinum shank. The detail implies expense rather than bling. She twists the tiny white tag that traditionally hangs from every ring, but the five-digit number gives nothing away. It is a shop code; jewellers often make up prices and invent discounts depending on the client seeking to purchase.

"Why leave one ring?" she asks.

"Why call the whistleblower line? Why not tell your head of department, your captain, or your security team?" Hunter adds.

Kieron looks from her to him, wondering if he is trying to put her down with the bigger question. Maybe he is seeing something that is not there, but in the art theft job, Hunter took a bit of a dislike to Bedi and wanted her off the team. Maybe this job is so unengaging he is looking for trouble in the wrong place.

Croc wriggles further into the open safe which sits against the side wall, but away from the back wall.

"It's bolted down, so it's meant to be here," Croc fires back.

"Maybe. But maybe the snitch wasn't. He was in the wrong place, somewhere he shouldn't have been when he saw the safe open this morning," Hunter suggests.

"That's yesterday morning now. When it gets light, the clock's on 24hrs," Kieron adds.

"To notice a safe was closed, then open, that's a daily visit," Hunter says.

"And if he is supposed to be in here, he's due back between now and then."

"But the thieves planned this on shore," Croc states, laying on the floor.

"Why?" Bedi asks.

"Who carries a code breaker? Apart from me." Croc enjoys the chance to be top-sleuth and he man-handles the circular key-pad unit that hangs on its wires from its recess in the thick steel door. He flicks the four batteries out from their holder and tosses them at Hunter. "These cells are out."

"Why?"

"To find the entry code, they would twist the keypad out from the door front," he demonstrates, by twisting the number pad from the door, where the batteries go so they can always be changed from the outside. "Attach a number-runner and wait until it finds the right code, but that rinses the batteries fast. If they take too long, they have just enough power to open the door. It's a heavy lock." Croc indicates the four protruding steel stumps. "If they use the door-lock-lever to manoeuvre the door while stealing the diamonds, and accidentally move the handle lock to closed, even if they remembered the number, the batteries are dead. The door is locked open. They would have to come back with new batteries."

"Amateur," Bedriška says.

Croc goes back to pulling small plastic stickies from the door handle. They have fingerprints dusted into them. He passes them to Bedi, who drops them in an evidence envelope.

"We might have to leave you here to finish up," Hunter suggests, standing.

"Hang on. What if the thieves come back to close the door?"

"Yeah, it's a worry," Hunter jokes.

"Thanks. Enjoy supper," Croc digs. "I'll finish this, and if the regular whistle-snitch comes back I'll take his name and address, and if the thief comes back to close the door, I'll do the same."

"They might even want to touch up the paint where they scratched the safe. Look, no thief comes back to tidy the crime scene. This doesn't take four of us and I need to think, looking at a big wall I can write on," Hunter explains standing.

"I can do that better with my software," Croc panics.

Hunter ignores him and holds his hand out, wanting Bedi's ring. He has the look of a supervisor disapproving of impropriety.

"You know what KGB officer do if another officer dislike them stealing piece of evidence? Kill them," she says firmly.

"Here," she says handing the ring to Croc, still wearing gloves and treating it with care. "Dust. Fast."

Croc is speedy; he dusts then examines it with the eye glass.

"It is perfectly polished. No one touched it," he says handing it back. He is not going to join in any conflict Bedi has; he has watched her shoot around a dozen men dead in less seconds, stopping only to change guns rather than breathe. He knows she is some form of superwoman.

She waves the ring in front of Hunter's face.

"I think, two whistle-person. One has many rings, one wants reward. That why they call Miami, and not want to be searched. Idiots."

She takes her gloves off and slips the ring on while Kieron checks outside to see if their escape is clear. It is the only piece of jewellery in an array of scars.

"I keep. We engaged as well as we own house together in Bequia. Good to have cover story near truth."

The ice has been broken, but not the iceberg which was Georgie finding that they slept together on Bedi's first CSCI mission.

"Can you two cease romancing on company time," Hunter says, moving past her in the confined space.

"If I want to fuck Kieron. Get used to it. He must." Bedi boldly leaves.

11 – DUCK

Neither Kieron nor Hunter need money, and that worries Croc. He and his sisters have set a future on the two men's toy, and they need a plan in place before the two bosses decide to close CSCI.

Hunter wants to be a stay-at-home dad and Kieron wants to see New York and travel America. That will happen when they recover their trunk full of gold at the end of the rainbow. Maybe, just maybe they might hand CSCI over to him and the others. But although Billy and Zack could join the team, K&H are the attraction.

First, he has the room stock all documented on his note pad, to form a layer of possible room-users on his software; a programme he thinks might sell. He is convinced it is smarter than Holmes 2, the system used by New Scotland Yard. Croc has yet to see any other commercial investigative software on the market that is as sharp as his, but he needs a good portfolio of jobs that would allow him to sell it worldwide. Though nervous of being left alone in many respects, he needs to focus. He counts off his jobs to test he has everything; there is no coming back.

Two: finger printing of the safe done though he expects that has yielded few results.

Three is the tough one. What Croc needs in this junk emporium is not there. He needs screens or monitors to set his software up properly if they are staying on ship. He takes a moment to look around again, not to go over the jumble, but to think. There must be other rooms like this one.

'Crash!'

He stayed a moment too long. The door is hit hard. Two people in wild Asian conversation burst in and their exuberance fills the small space where there is no longer any sign of Croc. In that split second, he had a decision to make; either stand and be brave with clever exchanges or hide. As a black kid brought up in America, his instinct is to run or hide. He knows the room well; he knows the placement of boxes and what is in them; he has mapped each one. He knows the thin space behind the boxes, to the left of the open safe. He became hidden in there before the door swung fully open, but it is a huge risk; if he is found next to the open safe, the ship will consider him the thief. Worse still, if the real thieves find him, he can expect a beating. His breathing gets far shallower as even more scenarios go through his head. He hears the movement of boxes near him. It reminds him to record their voices as he has no idea what they are saying, and it will need to be interpreted.

He squeezes even lower, fumbling for his cell, pushing himself into the ground, small as a mouse. He never knew Georgie, but pressed against the floor he wonders if she felt this panic in that moment before she died in a lower deck crew cabin like this. No, surely, he is not going to die. A huge thump and he instinctively shelters his head with his arm, laying flatter. Boxes rain down from the fight he can hear above him. He feels the two people struggle so hard the boxes might part, and the men will fall on him. He is being buried as the boxes are pushed back. It is hard to make-out what is going on, but one last struggle sends a box of flags all over him. He can't reach his cell, then remembers he doesn't have it. He and Hunter left their cell phones in their cabins due to track and trace. Above him someone is being strangled and he should help. But then he might be murdered too. He is going to have to listen to a killing just feet away from him because he is not physically capable like K&H. He can't fight.

Then the boxes start to move in rhythm, the thrust is one he recognises. The distress is from one of two people having sex, fast sex, not loving in-a-bed sex. He needs to know who they are. He will have to be the recorder that relays everything that happens. He needs to get his head up and see because this couple could be the whistle-duo. He needs to see if she has a ring on her finger like Bedi, he needs to see them. No, that is stupid. He can only lay down and see shoes and socks. They will have to ID them with shoes and socks.

As he contemplates, a hand thunders down seeking purchase, the tips of the fingers just grabbing the edge of his hair. He dares not react, not move. Croc squeezes close into the box feeling the fingers above his head. His eyes try to look up. Now captured into their grubby act, should the man grab harder and further, he will have Croc's head. There is no option other than to get free as fast as he can. He tries to pull his head away, but his hair is trapped until the rhythmic impetus relaxes, then he is gone. He slides down before the hand heaves hard on the cardboard again. Looking at it, inches from his face, he pulls a finger printing strip and holds it ready. In the momentary release of the man's strong hand, he slips the strip under the finger and then away in the next circle. Now he needs to put a face and some detail to his captured evidence.

Worm-like he tries to wriggle around the boxes, without the ones on top of him moving too much. He has not lost more than a minute. Wow, they started the sex quickly and now, before he can see them the man is leaving. Black brogues, black socks, beige pants; that is not enough detail. Then a white apron drops below knee high as he goes, and the door wipes out vision. His partner is buried deeper, and she takes effort to recover. Storage boxes get pushed out of the way as they are used for leverage and Croc is hit by the fall out and he misses the second person leave. He has no idea who either of them is so he should follow as fast as he can, but he hesitates at the door. He has the door open; he must escape; he must be brave, but he can hear voices. He bursts out, walking purposefully, not that he knows where he is going. At the end of the corridor is a general relaxation room and it is busy with male and female kitchen staff. Which ones are they? They all have black brogues and the same kitchen uniform. He can't stand and stare. He passes and travels the long corridor looking for the white painted steel stairs that will take him up. New thoughts run through his head. Is this the way he came down with his team? It looks different. What will he do when he gets to the door that leads back into the guest areas? Will he be entering the right section? Will he get caught leaving the crew zone? He has no map, no cell phone, no idea.

12 – LOVE TRIANGLE

"Am I going to get any sleep in here?" Croc asks, as he enters his cabin and sees that Bedi has emptied his mini bar, Hunter has stretched a white sheet to the wall and drawn three circles, and Kieron is being very British and has four cups of tea on the tray.

"I took a cup from each room, take them back with you."

"I hope you're not walking about with your fancy watch on," Hunter says, as he draws lines between the three circles to make a triangle. "I'm seeing three people; the thief, the snitch and the COO."

He fills the three circles with the names.

"It's not quite a good title for a book," Kieron says, offering him his tea.

"Why stupid thief leave ring?" Bedi puzzles, admiring her new jewel until stopping at the tray where she sees Kieron has brought her vodka from other cabins as well as tea. She takes two bottles, unscrews one and tips it in to strengthen her brew. She offers to do the same for Kieron.

"No sugar for me, thank you."

She drinks the second bottle offered to him and takes her tea.

"The job was incomplete; the thief was disturbed," Hunter offers.

"Disturbed? Trapped inside! Trust me, there's no way out when someone enters," Croc says, now a detective.

"You were trapped inside by who?"

"Kitchen staff, on a break."

"What were they doing in there?" Kieron asks.

"Having sex! They go there to have sex," Croc explains.

"I hope you collect cum for test," Bedi says flatly.

Croc didn't and he can't work out whether she might be serious, or it's an eastern European joke. She did throw him in the airport x-ray machine. He wonders if he is about to be verbally attacked or physically embarrassed by her.

"Lunch-time brothel," she states.

"A diamond heist, using a code breaker that can take an hour or more, would have been planned between breaks," Kieron offers.

"He took too long," Croc offers. "Just got the safe open, and crash! The doors burst open. That's exactly what happened to me. I was there maybe 5 minutes too long."

"Any good working girl see diamond in safe if door open," Bedi says, still bothered by her diamonds being left there.

Hunter takes a pen to the stretched sheet and writes under the 'snitch circle'.

'Kitchen breaks; midnight to 1am, then 5am to 6am?'

Then he writes a mobile number.

"Dwight traced the caller, so Croc, get yourself into the ship's track and trace and find our snitch," Hunter concludes.

"Yeah. I'll get that done while you three run up to breakfast," Croc says very sarcastically.

"You can eat while we interview him. You find our snitch; we find the diamonds." Kieron says slowly.

"We've got one," Hunter says, leaning towards Bedi's ring. "We're paid to get them back, right?"

She gives him a killer-stare in a slow turn. "You look for others".

Before cruising, both Kieron and Hunter had great lives in the military. Both survived a colourful list of troubled countries and enjoyed a rich palette of food and culture, but with no time for romantic partners. Towards the end of their national careers, they worked behind lines and seldom settled, rarely unpacked, and hardly ever owned much. Anything they owned or loved was at risk.

Hunter Witowski was the first to take separation from the armed forces, and he went straight into the cruise industry, being fast tracked to security. He fell in love with Elaine who worked on the ship. She fell pregnant and went to live in their house in Madeira. However, she was kidnapped and held to ransom in order to force him to get a drug baroness to Europe, with her trunk full of one-hundred-dollar bills. Without Kieron and a female officer Ronnie, when the heist got out of control, guests would have been at risk. As it was, the money got bigger and bigger, and conveniently went missing. CSCI know where it is, but the only route through customs for just under twenty million in cash might be through India where CSCI part own a refrigeration business. They just need to get their original ship with the trunk full of money there and have a fault on a freezer so they can fill it with the money and get it through customs.

The public address system in the cabin bursts in to explain the new situation for entering the buffet for breakfast. It does not break Croc's speedy, deliberate unpacking of his equipment. He is spreading it around the remainder of the room, reminding the team that it is his cabin. Each of them must move when he finds a reason to place something where they are, it is quite a dance.

"Croc. We should leave you to do what you do best; set up your digital Sherlock Holmes. We'll get in the testing queue at the buffet," Kieron says.

"I might try and plan the technical hub around a bed I could potentially sleep in," Croc offers. He is tired and naturally grumpy. "And another thing," Croc calls out to stop them as they leave. "My idea of simplifying the name to Cruise Crime Investigators, CCI; can we chat about that at one of the meetings?"

They all leave puzzled. Croc is chuffed at showing his potential and that he cares for the agency. When they've had enough of CSCI he definitely wants CCI.

13 – TEAM OF THREE

Macey sits, swinging her legs, on a desk in Miami's hidden technical hub where Dwight Ritter has spent the night. As always, she is super-casual, but is now sporting new stylish baggy denim floral dungarees. Her hair is up in a bun and paint brushes poke in and out of it like a sputnik, which implies she is still working even though she has become a minor art-world sensation. The same huge innocent smile that she had when serving burgers next door for Wild Mary, long before any of her paintings sold, shows some aspects of life have not changed since then.

"Billy is on his way in," Dwight starts.

"I love Billy."

"We all do, Macey, and I'm hoping you'll go with him as a two-man team."

"Onto a ship? To join Croc?"

"No. He's on the MS Aerwyna, a mermaid known as the 'Friend of the Ocean'. I want you on the ship near to them, the MS Amatheia. She is known as 'the Nurse to all Fishes' and I'm told is a nymph."

"You started writing children's stories?"

Dwight ignores her remark and continues. "You might have to take a boat to the MS Ianassa, 'a nymph of the Ionian Sea'. I think they are all daughters of Doris, the sea Goddess. But check that. I thought the mythology stuff might be a line to inspire new paintings."

"No. It sounds crap. Real pink pony fairy shit."

"That sells, right?"

"Oh yeah. I'm sure it sells bundles on ships, but it's not me."

"Not even a limited edition?"

Macey shakes her head, totally disinterested.

"Not even the angry naughty daughters of the Goddess," he tries, changing tact.

"Who put you up to this?"

"I'm the first person to ever buy one of your commercial pieces."

"Are you pre-ordering a set?"

"No."

"Then stop. No to painting fairies. But if you want me to assist Billy, I'll go if Ricky can come."

It shows in his face that was not the plan. Dwight has the authority to say who does what. As the point man in the hub, he can see the operation. He still wonders whether things might have been handled better if he had stayed in Miami on the last job. No one suspected it would become such an interwoven web of intrigue and that Kieron would find himself in the middle of what became a disastrous romance.

"OK, there's three ships in a triangle. Billy's got to check the gem safes are intact."

"Diamonds? Maybe Ricky can propose," she whispers while she has time.

"It's an in and out job."

Izzy and Ricky return from the kitchen area each carrying two cups of coffee. Ricky has one for Macey, not knowing why she is looking at him so coyly. Izzy has a mug for Dwight."

"No food anywhere," Izzy says.

Ricky pulls his cell up and starts to type.

"I'll get us stocked," he offers, opening the shopping app on his cell.

"Keep it healthy, Ricky. Salad. Celery and stuff," Dwight offers.

Ricky hesitates and studies him before he continues; it might have been a joke.

"Why can't Izzy go?" Macey asks.

"I need her here, covering for me."

"You on the mission?" Macey asks.

"He's going for a fitting. New legs. He's got a lady," Izzy chirps out.

Macey nearly chokes on her coffee.

"What? No, hey and go, go. But…" she pulls up. "You can't be taller than me." Macey jumps down and stands tall next to him in his chair. Even seated he is a big man.

"Good point, you've never been taller than us," Izzy says, standing next to her sister.

"I think I was, once."

"Never," Macey continues.

"She's right. Not here," Izzy agrees.

"Behave, both of you."

"OK. Serious. Ricky's coming."

"Look, Macey. Ricky's a journalist. First rule of being an investigator?"

"Don't get your legs blown off?" Macey asks.

"Bit harsh!" Izzy says

"Yes, sorry Dwight."

"No, you're right, that's the other first rule. But, get in, do your job, get out, quietly."

"But I want Ricky there," she demands.

"You can trust me, Dwight. You know that." Ricky says.

"A journalist always wants a story," Dwight argues.

"Macey's my story," he replies.

"She's old news."

"Hey!" Macey declares.

"Sorry, Macey, you are. Ricky's gonna need to move on and write something new. This gig's not it."

"Dwight, I'm here. I'll always be here, so let's agree, I leave the investigation alone: unless instructed."

Dwight pauses. He knows he will be giving in, but he needs to figure how Ricky will fit.

"Here's a story: ship's laying idle for a year yet full of technicians and fitters adding 80 km of data cable to enable 950 WiFi access points and even more spots below decks that ensure the 'track and trace' is capable of finding anyone anywhere in the near 50,000 tonnes of steel. New systems, complying with new regulations as well as future-proofing the ship and adding customer service. Carpet layers, painters and haberdashers following them around as they put the channelling and trunking back in the ceilings and floors. Over 6,500 square metres of carpets, tens of thousands of litres of paint, and bathroom fitters using miles of trimming."

"They are the images I paint. Ignored men working on the expected." Macey lifts Dwight's chin, and looks him straight in the eyes. "You want me to go? Ricky comes. And you, no taller than 5ft 7inches when they fit those legs."

"You can write that's why she is there. I'll talk to the Operations Officer."

Leaving no time to settle into coffee the door alarm goes.

"Screens show door cameras."

All screens jump awake. Billy is pulling crazy zany faces into the security cameras outside the unit's main door. Dwight buzzes him. It's such a quicker, simpler way to enter the hub it's hard to understand why it's not the first choice of entry for the staff.

"You've got a safe you need cracking?" he exclaims, filling the room with his character even though he is not very big.

"How tall are you, Billy?" Izzy asks.

"Five seven."

She turns back to Dwight and her smile expresses her desire for conformity.

"I was six four, an impressive six four. I've never felt impressive down here, and I want to stand out again. I wanna stand tall again."

Billy pulls a snub nose automatic weapon from under the desk by an unused screen.

"This is how you look impressive," he grins.

"That's just bullying with violence," Macey says.

"Works for me. I was bullied all the time at school," he answers.

"This is getting too deep," Izzy suggests.

"Bully with power, bully with money; them kids'll still be bullying somewhere," Billy insists. "They'll always be bullying, and it'll always be too deep."

Izzy turns to Dwight.

"Have you felt bullied since you've been in the chair?"

Dwight points down to a muzzle under the seat of his chair. It is only just visible when pointed out.

"I always have my hand right on the trigger down here in the trenches."

"Are we gonna need guns?" Macey asks.

"No. I just saw it under there," Billy says. "You see dead people: someone has to supply them," Billy says to Macey.

14 – TURNED UPSIDE DOWN

Hunter and Kieron burst into a small inside cabin on deck three which is in total darkness despite it being mid-morning. It is hard to imagine such blackness. Bedriška closes the door behind them. There are screams from a woman but in two steps they are at the bed. Bedriška silences the Malaysian woman she captures from under the covers. Hunter has the man on the other side of the bed.

"Cruise line security, sorry to disturb you but this is a matter of urgency."

"Here, here," the woman says, offering a ring to Bedi. Part of her face is occasionally lit by the tiny green light emitting diode from her cell charger. But even in no light she notices Bedi's ring.

"Name?" Bedi asks. She appears abrupt even when she has no intention to frighten.

"Banjo. Everyone call me Banjo."

Bedi examines the ring close to the green light, then passes it to Hunter. He fires a small powerful beam at it and holds it in front of the man.

"Where's the rest?" he asks him.

"We only have one," she answers for him. "We want reward."

It is obvious to both Hunter and Bedi that if allowed, he may have different answers.

"You rang head office?" he asks him.

"I make him ring. Someone stole everything. Not us. We want reward, then he leave his wife and I have children."

"To get reward you must leave your name! Stupid!" Bedi says.

"Did you see the safe?" Hunter asks.

"No. I never been in there. We have bedroom. "
Banjo says.

Hunter points the strong beam of light straight into
the man's face and drills him with a hard look, he edges
between them. Bedi does the same as Hunter pushes the
very frightened man into the wall, hand around his neck.

"There's a camera in that room. We saw you. I can
show her," Hunter threatens.

The man changes from defence to being seriously
worried.

"Camera?"

He is allowed enough freedom to flip open a small
bedside cupboard. Diamond rings bounce down from a
shelf. The man collects them from below. Banjo
overpowers Bedi, climbs over Hunter, beating her man.
Her native Malaysian is so fast few would understand,
but he does. In both shock and anger, she collects all the
rings, inspecting them before she is forced to hand them
over to Hunter. He drops them into a small soft cloth
bag, fifty-two diamond rings. Kieron grabs his legs and
pulls him from the melee. As soon as he has his head, he
pins it to the bed and gets in close.

"Where's the rest?"

Banjo rushes down the bed and attacks him again, all
her emotions have joined together in violence against her
betrayal,

"Arif! You cheat me. You cheat. Arif!"

Kieron is hit as much as her husband and pulls him
away as Bedriška pulls her back, now restraining her.
Hunter is checking the side area for dropped pieces that
could be worth thousands.

"We need more Arif, or this gets much worse for
you."

"We go outside," the man insists to Kieron. He is standing in his cotton knee length pants and his vest and keeping Kieron between him and Banjo.

A shaft of light scans the room as the door is opened and darkness falls as it closes.

Kieron has the man pinned against the wall in the empty corridor where he has no jurisdiction.

"I never steal…"

"Looks like you did," Kieron offers, in close quarters. He knows the risk of waking the neighbour is too great and will restrict him, so he hauls him, arm locked, fingers pushed into the back of his neck, down the long white tunnel of cabin doors. There is little resistance. Beyond the watertight doors, which push open easily, a drone of noise hits them. Kieron jams him against the white metal stair rail and below is the most unwelcome twirl of steel stairs and cacophony of engineering. They can no longer whisper.

"How did you open the safe?"

The Asian man who is part of the kitchen team is shocked.

"I never open safe. Never. It open," Arif panics.

"Who went in there before you?"

"No! I just start break."

"And you have sex?"

"Who with?"

"Ramesh."

Kieron knows that is the name of another man.

"Was he waiting in there for you?"

"No. We both on break."

"Did he take any diamonds?"

"No. He leave fast. He leave me in there."

"And you saw the safe was open?"

Arif nods.

Hunter is standing behind Kieron. Impatient, he rips the man's arm and walks him up the steel stairs. With every floor they rise the powerful drone of engines reduces. As he is pushed into a passenger area it is almost silent. He is manhandled quickly along to Croc's cabin.

15 - ARIF

"What's up now?" Croc asks, as Arif is thrown into his cabin. "Is this a prison as well?"

"New training level. Interrogation," Kieron says, and he and Hunter stand just inside the cabin.

"Training. I want to talk to you about that, and the new name."

"What new name?" Hunter asks.

"C.C.I."

"What training?" Kieron asks.

"Izzy and I have been doing some research. She is writing a paper to show the C.C.I. background, and the formal training we have and can give others."

"A paper?" Hunter asks.

"You are already cruise ship crime management trained and you are both trained in every area from crime detection through to evidence preservation."

"We are?" Kieron asks.

"So, she can submit our standards to MARAD and request to be certified as security trainers and operatives in the cruise industry."

"Why?" Hunter asks.

"Then C.C.I. will be fully compliant with the CVSSA model of training standards."

Kieron looks at Hunter. He has no idea what Croc is on about as his background is not in cruise ships.

"The Cruise Vessel Security and Safety Act," Hunter tells him.

They both turn back to Croc.

"Figure out what he knows, within the model standards," Hunter says to Croc, leaving the frightened man with him.

Croc stands aghast. A confused Arif before him has not understood a word of what has been said. Croc points at him, then a picture on the screen.

"You were in the room?"

The man nods.

"Having sex?"

The man nods.

"Two nights ago."

The man nods.

"And last night."

The man nods.

"I was in there with you."

The man looks confused.

"Hiding behind the boxes."

Arif looks at him in horror, he was sure no one was in the room. Croc turns around and stands next to him. He mimes a mental picture of the boxes for the man in his empty-looking cabin.

"Me. I am here. Your sex was very fast? Very quick?"

The man, further embarrassed, agrees with the smallest nod.

"Then you leave first? Fast?"

The man's answer takes some time. Croc's look is genuinely questioning pushing the man to answer.

"No. Ramesh leave first."

Croc is realising it might have been two men: this guy and Ramesh. That he was underneath and therefore last to leave.

"Who looked in the safe? Who took the diamonds?" Croc asks.

The man looks around. He knows he is not in a security office. He is fearful for his life.

"You? You steal the diamonds? You are thief." The man turns and bursts out. Croc is left amazed.

"No, no, no, no. Not me."

His first interrogation session turned upside down. He accelerates to the door but only to see the man has gone. He wanders next door to Hunter's room and knocks. The door is opened by a dreary eyed Hunter who must have just fallen asleep.

"What?"

Croc is even more guilty, seeing he has woken Hunter.

"What did you get that was so worth breaking my power nap?" Hunter asks Croc.

"He ran. He thinks we're the diamond thieves. He ran scarred. I ran after him, but he was gone."

16 – ANCHORED ADJACENT

The seaplane drops below the horizon and glides effortlessly on a flat sea. The only passengers are Macey, Billy, and Ricky. Unbeknown to the crew of the MS Amatheia they will be the last to join before it is hit by lockdown. Nobody and no diamonds will be able to move on or off the ship until COVID tests have been run throughout the ship. The CSCI team may have about 24 hours unless head office in Miami can extend the embargo.

Unlike the team of investigators boarding the MS Aerwyna yesterday, who had no greeting team, Macey gets special guest privileges. She is met by Captain Spinazzola and his entourage. A bearded man, he is far too like the cliché one expects: relaxed in a short-sleeved, perfectly pressed white shirt with the neck button open.

"Would you join me for dinner tonight?" he asks. "It might be my last night of peace for a while."

Macey is there to do a painting of the ship. Ricky has not yet escaped being the appendage that has to build press releases on her. Neither read much from his seemingly flippant remark.

Billy has noticed the ship's photographer as the lifeboat tender berths alongside the ship, and he has been clever enough to stay clear of any picture. For him, Macey's special talent is to take all the attention. Billy is undercover as her manager. There is no plan. He has been given a bundle of lateral flow fail-results, but he is on his own; Ricky and Macey have no skills as agents.

With no guests to fill any potential painting, Billy and Ricky argue they need ideas to bring life to the ship. With no member of the art gallery team on a dormant ship, an entertainment host is taking them on a pre-dinner guide of stock rooms that might reveal props for Macey to include in prospective paintings.

"How about this? A feather boa?"

"Tacky. How about gems? Glamour?" Billy leads, leaving the room full of junk. He knows he is after a cabin further along.

"Diamond shop is closed. The stock must be locked away somewhere," the host says.

Billy leaves and marches along, host in tow, until he reaches 219.

"How about this one?" Billy asks. He tries the door before any reply. The door is locked.

"Careful, that might be someone's cabin."

Billy knows it's not, he knows it is the stockroom where the gem-safe is kept. He points to the label on the door. 'Keep Locked HoD MJB'.

"Doesn't look like someone's cabin," Billy adds looking for a reply.

"Must be something special," the host offers.

Billy stands still, no eye movement in any direction, not a word. It is the technique of silence used during an interview that demands an answer. The Host feels the embarrassment.

"No idea," he adds weakly.

Billy remains hauntingly stoic, even Ricky feels the embarrassment.

"Never heard of MJB," the host reads. "HoD means head of department. Our rooms are HoD Ents. Short for entertainment."

Billy has his cell up and captures an image of the name tag before moving on. He is going to need some IT assistance and his mobile signal is challenged in the low decks of the ship.

"You'll need special privileges for your cell to use the relay points down this low," the host adds.

"I will."

Ricky sees a side to Billy that is dangerous and threatening without the need for him to do very much at all. Billy might argue that he is doing a lot.

"Should we not head up and prepare for dinner?" the host asks, wishing to escape.

"So early?" Billy punishes. "Loads of time to brush my teeth. Do you clean your teeth for dinner?"

The host has no idea how to take Billy.

"We're eating at the captain's table."

"I'll brush my teeth then."

"You'll need a jacket. I can lend you one... if you need."

"We're good, thanks," Ricky says, letting him off the hook.

As the host leads them up the white painted steel crew stairs, Ricky engages him in chat as Billy trails behind trying to get a signal on his cell. The new technical points have been put all over the ship, but they are under the control of head office. Below decks it is still a track and trace only whereas above decks it is also internet and cell phone hotspots. Tests are still ongoing to see what happens if three thousand guests all decide to use a software provider to engage in face-to-face calls back home, and what the system should be restricted to. All Billy wants is support. The communication an agent might expect with his handler, but as this rather mundane job forces demands, the staff at CSCI are stretched. Croc is away on the other ship with his own duties and Billy is getting a little impatient with Izzy back in the Florida hub.

"Where's commander Ritter? Can't you put him on the line?" he says, as they break into daylight and Billy walks to the rail on deck seven, the promenade deck.

"He's not available," is the line from Izzy that only he can hear. He turns and sees Ricky and the host waiting.

He hears her but it is not something he can accept.

"Look. Izzy. Just put Dwight on the phone. Damien says I need special privileges."

Damien is now worried; he wants to know who Billy is talking to.

"No. I'm your point of contact, and your request has been taken," he hears.

"Izzy."

"No, Billy," she insists back through his cell. "The longer you keep me busy, the longer you keep me from dealing with a solution."

Billy is struck dumb. The phone goes dead, and he looks at Ricky standing next to Damien.

"I know. Have you met her twin sister?"

"Where do they get it from?" Billy asks.

"You don't know their mother, Wild Mary?"

"Not really," Billy says slowly. A smile glides across his face, equally as worrying as his still look. Ricky ignores it but Damien, the host, shows his new fear.

"What?"

Billy's smile gets bigger, showing his teeth. Damien couldn't be more worried. Ricky is enjoying the game but needs to understand the answer. Billy has worked out the play.

"Do you remember the label that was on cabin 221?" Billy asks.

"No, we walked straight passed it," Damien says, but Billy's annoying fixed grin has not faltered.

"I can go back," Damien says, looking for any reason to escape.

Billy's eyes widen to suggest it is a promising idea and Damien is off. He must run down three decks

"Are you teasing him?" Ricky asks.

"No. I just need the answer."

"You think he knows the answer?"

"Lots of people might have an answer; they just don't know the answer. I need 219 opened."

"I agree," Ricky says. "And as important, we need to know who locked it?"

Billy nods while looking young Ricky straight in the eyes. There is something about this strange group and their combined talents which surprises him, and Ricky has something which he feels could have the makings of a young agent in training.

"I agree," Billy smiles.

"And did you see the label on the door next door?" Ricky asks him.

"I wasn't giving it my full attention, because it was locked by a different head of department."

"Keep locked. HoD W something H?"

"WBH," Damien says, reappearing in time.

Billy nods with pleasure.

"Game on!"

17 - OLD TYMES

"Where've you been?" Izzy demands of Dwight, as he powers in through their own entrance, not the access via Wild Mary's Diner.

"Why? You got somewhere to be?"

"I've been calling you," Izzy angers.

"I left you in charge."

Dwight is as cool as ever. If anything, he is way too relaxed for her liking.

"It got complicated."

"It always gets complicated," Dwight says, arriving behind the long desk of screens. They all appear dormant, which causes him to look at her in wonder.

"Billy was demanding to speak with you," she adds.

"He always wants to speak with me. What did you tell him?"

"Why was your cell off?"

"I never expected to be out all day; the power went out."

"You went to an induction."

Dwight is now attaching his cell to the power supply as she stands over him, nodding. It is the nod that demands a better answer.

"You fell for the sales talk. What else have they sold you?" she continues.

"Izzy, I went in for two legs. They ain't gonna sell me three."

"I hear your girlfriend Rocket has eight."

"I still haven't used my real name; not till I'm 100% convinced."

"You're gonna walk again."

"And you ain't gonna be looking down at me like that for much longer."

"My, you've got very confident."

"I met other vets there. Guys I knew. Guys that are now walking."

"Anyone wanna job? We seem to have a vacancy."

"You mean you can't cope?"

"I coped very well. Very, very well. But as I'm new to this, I just wanted a little guidance."

"So, Izzy. How can I guide you?"

"Too late. I read all the guidelines. I've done it now."

"Done what? That worries me."

"Nothing. Billy was being weird."

"Has he killed anyone?" Dwight asks. Billy getting weird has his full attention.

"Not yet. But he's seriously worrying."

Dwight's cell starts to bleep with stacked unanswered messages flooding in.

"You coped?" he says, collecting his tethered cell. He scrolls to the bottom and reads the last first, then looks up at her.

"What?" she asks.

"Game on?"

"I don't know. It's all one big game to all of you," she says defensively.

18 – MAN CAVE

On the MS Aerwyna, Croc's cabin curtain has been closed and the last of the day's sun has been left outside. Croc's room has been turned into a mini hub. Next to his own cabin television he has coupled the screens from Kieron's and Bedriška's cabins giving him a trio of monitors working from his laptop computer. The coat rail on the wall next to him is now the organised home of many hanging leads. The tablet he brought with him is the wandering device that can also give input into the mini system.

Hunter walks in without knocking.

"Did we lose a night's sleep somewhere? Oh no, you didn't. You were asleep when I got back and I guess you just woke up," Croc fires at him with edge.

"I've had a baby keeping me up every night for months," Hunter replies softly, not taking the bait.

"And what do you call Billy?" Croc asks.

Hunter slips a small laugh through a grin.

"How are Elaine and the baby? I've been awake so long the kid must nearly be at school," Croc says.

"Not walking but very demanding. That makes two people giving me orders back home, but only one keeping me up at night."

"Had the first one not kept you up all night, you wouldn't have the second. I'm glad work's such a welcome break for you."

Hunter is looking at his sheet on the wall. There is a list of departments from Entertainment to Main Dining running down the side.

"What are these?"

"All the departments with stock in the gem safe room. You like the answers up on the wall."

Hunter turns back to a screen and takes Croc's pad.

"Help yourself," Croc says, trying to become the focus of attention.

"Thanks," Hunter murmurs without giving him a look. He scrolls up and back down, finding Billy's texts on both locked doors. He lifts Croc's cabin phone.

"Feel free," Croc says, watching Hunter just use his room and feeling very used himself.

Hunter holds back on dealing with Croc and then the call is answered.

"You awake?"

"I obviously am now," Kieron is heard to say via the telephone.

"Meeting in five, give Bedi a nudge and tell her."

"That's very presumptuous."

"Yeah." Hunter ends the call.

Though they own Cruise Ship Crime Investigators together, the two men know little about each other. Kieron is a single guy discovering women, and Hunter has a new baby, albeit both late to their respective games. Both worked behind-the-lines in special-operations for their countries, which gives them a military bond of brotherhood without needing to know any history. Both are alpha males who have sparse conversation other than quips. They have only worked together on two CSCI missions, Serial Killer and Art Theft. Getting to know Dwight, their point man, Wild Mary and her triplets, Macey, Izzy, and Croc has clouded the social focus.

"You forgot to tell him the meeting's in my cabin," Croc adds.

"Well, it wouldn't be in mine; I'd never get any sleep," Hunter says.

19 – LEFT OUT

Hunter is pondering the two lines of Billy's text on the screen.

'Keep locked. HoD WBH. Keep locked. HoD MJB. Game on!'

"Billy's so annoying. He obviously worked this out and is revelling in his moment of glory. Kieron will get it. He loves this cryptic stuff."

"We're taking a run at the safe after his dinner with the captain, but we both reckon the safe will be empty." Says Croc.

"Yeah," Hunter agrees, but not giving it enough weight to ask Croc why.

Croc is tired and easily annoyed, but not least because Hunter felt him unworthy of the conundrum team. The look is enough. What might have been banter or playful digs obviously have no place with Croc as an on-site point man. Seeing this, Hunter wonders if Croc feels insulted when they report to him back in Miami, and he is often the brunt of bullish jibes. Before Hunter can figure out a way to deal with any possible insult, Kieron enters dressed in his suit, and the moment is gone.

"I thought you were asleep," Hunter mocks him cheekily.

"Why? I was dressing for dinner. I booked us a table in the main restaurant. We have to swab test outside over a drink; very civilised," Kieron informs him.

"Why didn't I know?" Hunter asks.

"I did a memo along with my thoughts on the Amatheia and how it changes everything."

"Amatheia?"

"She's moving out tomorrow."

"Why the rush?" Hunter asks.

Bedriška enters in her slinky silver dress.

"Ready?" She asks, then she specifically aims a remark at Kieron. "Good memo. I think you almost right."

"What?" Hunter asks.

"You needed the holiday," Croc says.

Hunter bites back on his anger which would be an unnecessary reaction. Let the kid have his moment; it is more important he knows what is going on. He stares at Kieron.

"I feel like Rip Van Winkle," Hunter announces.

"I think Kieron add numbers up wrong. They need two ships." Bedi says.

Hunter is no wiser and snaps from her to Kieron then to Croc with a look that questions why he does not know what is going on.

"Maybe I should have been woken up."

"You've not reported in all day, so I assumed you were asleep, sir. I can't use the ship's system to update reports, so unless you come in, your cell doesn't have the information," Croc explains, pointing to the sign on a pad on a stand he has assembled at the end of the equipment.

Bedi enjoys touching her cell to the pad hitting the sign. 'Update here.' Her cell bleeps and she grins. Kieron does the same.

"But my cell's registered next door and can be track and traced. I don't walk in here with it."

"Exactly. Kieron's and Bedi's cells are not registered. She has a medallion."

"In my cabin," she adds. "I get it on the way to dinner."

"And he has a watch," Croc says, holding the smile.

Kieron shows his bare wrists.

Hunter is not impressed. "My cell needs to be updated, even when sleeping, that's how it needs to work. Now explain the maths," he demands.

"Covid regulations state ships are currently sailing domestic routes only and at 66% guest capacity. Regulation just cut that to 55% from Monday so all the fleet's current holidays are over-sold," Kieron explains.

"Overflow from ten ships in service doing domestic staycations, too many guests for just one more ship," Bedi says.

"She's right," Croc adds, having re-done the sums.

"No, she's wrong," Hunter says, rushing into the idea.

"She's not," Croc argues. "Ten times 150 booked guests lost off each ship. They'll need two of these ships."

"That's not the way cruising works. They're only 10% over capacity and at least 10% will want to cancel," Hunter explains.

"Whatever the numbers, if the diamonds have been moved here, they're all on the wrong ship. Tomorrow, the Amatheia could take them home, if they get them across there before she sails," Kieron says.

"I'll be a few minutes," Hunter says, leaving the cabin. He then pops his head back. "I need one of those update pads in my room."

"Oh, No worries. Enjoy your food," Croc says, but Hunter has gone.

"Croc. Get ready for dinner, we can talk at the table," Kieron suggests.

"I need to get a few doors open for Billy. His gem-stock room is locked."

"After dinner. The real question now is, who locked the cabin there? And who unlocked the cabin here?"

"Billy's following up on his idea."

"Billy should share his mad ideas. Hunter is right, all information should be shared immediately."

"In case we don't make it?" Croc asks.

"Billy knows. Now, you need to eat. Join us for dinner." Kieron orders him and leaves.

Bedriška hangs back, she is the only one in the team who has previously done anything outside the Miami hub with Croc. He guided her into the projects back in Miami to discover his sister's paintings that were taken by Macey's adoptive mother's drug dealer.

"Finish. Come to dinner," she barks.

"I don't have a jacket."

"I will have one sent."

Bedriška turns and leaves.

"Hey, Bedi."

She turns back into the room.

"Thanks."

20 - WHAT A CALAMITY

Billy is very respectful of the dress code for dinner. His suit is a wonderful fit on his sharp jib, and he has no need to be in uniform for anyone to guess he served in the military. Ricky is there in his varsity suit and Macey perfectly shows off one of the many evening dresses bought for her on the last cruise, when she was paid to be on the ship as the star. She looks a million dollars.

"Susie. Is Damien avoiding me?" Billy whispers in the ear of a very pretty hostess, her name and title evident from her gold lapel badge.

"It looks that way," she says, waving to Damien to join them, but he ducks away.

"It must be because I asked him for a brief backstage tour, just the two of us."

"I'd have thought he'd have jumped at the chance. I can do that tour for you."

"Ricky," Billy calls his new partner over. "We've got our tour."

"Great," Ricky says, going along with it, not having a clue what is in store.

"We have an hour before dinner," Billy insists.

Ricky worked with Hunter in England on the agency's last mission and is familiar with the urgency agents force upon people. Even when Susie tries to use Captain Spinoza as an excuse, Billy practically drags her to him and Macey.

"Sir, Macey. Would you mind if Ricky and I avail ourselves of a short 30-minute tour by this wonderful young lady?"

Macey plays her part in encouraging it, having no idea why it is needed. It is a faith and unquestionable support the team give each other. Damien ducks back within the captain's ensemble knowing he has dodged a bullet as he watches Susie lead them off.

Both Billy and Ricky have seen theatres before but mock being super impressed as Billy almost sprints to the stage and climbs the stairs. It is as if he is leading the tour. He finds the backstage area and inspects the large flat-packed scenery tied back against the rear wall for safety in rough seas. Billy, has it untied before Susie can react, and he is asking her which shows they perform. The problem is he is moving her on with such speed she is fighting to know the answers; she is not a member of the stage cast.

"Buddy Holly, I know that one. That was on when I was a dancer, a long time ago," she says, taking a breather.

"That's where you get that marvellous figure from," Billy compliments her.

Before she has thanked him, he is turning the flat scenery pieces over until he gets to the one he wants.

"The Wild West," he exclaims. "Will Smith!"

That makes her stumble for a moment trying to recall the show. Ricky takes up the gauntlet as Billy continues to investigate.

"No," she whispers.

"Not one of your shows?"

"No," she answers him again, puzzled by the questions. "I think it's…"

Very dramatically, Billy stops her.

"Calamity Jane! Do you have the graveyard scene?"

"Again, I don't know. But what I do know is that where possible these old stage scenery sections are being replaced."

Billy finds the graveyard scene and heaves to try and set it free. Ricky helps and she feels as if the tour has gone way too far.

"Can we stop?" she asks.

"Look, Ricky," Billy encourages. "Picture. Susie, take the weight."

Ricky is captivated and is a little slower than expected for the penny to drop. She is puzzled.

"What do you see there, Ricky?"

"Can we put these back now?" Susie asks. "My arm is aching."

"Sorry, Susie. I didn't realise Ricky was letting you take all the weight," Billy says, waiting for an answer.

"The bowl on the tombstone, It says Mary Jane Burke, alias Calamity Jane. Born May 1ˢᵗ, 1852. Princetown, Missouri. Died August 1ˢᵗ, 1903. Terry, South Dakota. Her dying wish, 'bury me next to Wild Bill'."

Billy points to the head of Wild Bill Hickok, portrayed as a sculpture on the tombstone next to hers. Billy folds the large panel back.

"Wow," Susie says, relieved. "You can see why they are all being replaced."

"By what?" Ricky asks.

"An LED back curtain. It's like a huge TV screen and the location is shown on the screen behind the dancers," she explains.

"So, someone in IT will be busy getting MJB a room next to WBH?" Billy grins.

"They will. And it means they can tell more of the story. Whatever the story is," she says, trying to end the tour by checking her watch.

Billy drops to a squat turning fast and pointing. He has found a stagehand, almost invisible in the dark shadows at the side of the stage. If Billy's finger were a gun, he would have been shot dead.

"Is that what he operates?"

Billy is a gunslinger. A killer legalised and trained by his country and now working on the outside as a gun-for-hire.

"Sandip. Do you operate the new curtain?" Susie asks.

"I just switch on and off," Sandip says, frightened.

"Turn it on, turn it on. We're on the Captain's special tour by Susie here," Billy says, scampering over leaving her and Ricky holding the remaining wooden sections.

Sandip switches the curtain on, and the stage fills with light. Billy stares at Sandip with his frightening mad eyes, making him step back.

"Sandip. Help Susie with the old wooden staging."

Billy is left with the computer controls.

"Wow!" Billy says, forwarding through the still frames until there is one of a saloon bar. He rushes to the middle of the stage.

"Does that send a cold rush down your spine, Susie?"

"Why?" Susie asks, joining him. Ricky is enjoying the very methodical show which is all information gathering.

"Sandip could have shot me in the back of the head?"

"Why would he do that?"

"We're in Deadwood, where men die over gold-fever," Billy says. "Have we overstayed our welcome?"

Susie nods and leads him and Ricky down into the theatre stalls, leaving Sandip tying the stage sections back to the wall. Billy enjoys sharing the history of one of his heroes, Wild Bill Hickok.

"Gold fever! Bill was shot in the back of the head in Nuttal & Mann's casino number 10 in Deadwood. He normally sat back to the wall, but on this occasion arrived at the gambling table late and took the only seat left. He asked to swap with Charlie Rich who occupied his traditional seat, but Rich said no. Jack McCall was tried twice for his murder, eventually hung in Laramie."

"Maybe you should help these story tellers out, eh Billy?" Ricky suggests.

"Ricky. Maybe you're right. I could," Billy offers, while on the cell texting Dwight, as they stand in the theatre stalls looking back at the lit curtain.

"Where do they do they input the show to the curtain?"

"I don't know," Susie says. "Sandip?"

He doesn't answer; he must have gone.

21 - BORED AND CARELESS

Croc weaves through the sparsely populated, but no less opulent or formal, main dining room. He is sporting a huge smile all the way to the table-for-four where, he takes the last chair.

"Sorry if I was abrupt earlier," Hunter gets in first. "So, are we still looking at the IT boys?"

"We might be looking at the wrong IT crowd," Croc shares, sitting.

"Nice jacket," Kieron compliments him.

Croc rises again to model it, thanking Bedriška. Dressing for dinner is still important, even though the ship has been without guests for a year. The officers are in whites as expected, and the contractors are keen to show they understand and fit into ship life. Contracts to service ships are worth a lot of money.

"Surely IT is IT?" Hunter asks Croc, as he settles down again.

"No; there is technical shit, and then there is shit that is technical," Croc says, taking the menu.

But Bedriška takes it away from him. "I already order."

"But I might want something different!" he exclaims.

"Don't look at menu. I hate to see you disappointed."

"So, what's IT that's not IT?" Hunter asks.

"Washing machine," Bedriška volunteers.

"Excursion booking," Kieron adds.

Hunter looks at each of them disapprovingly, which encourages her to continue.

"Stock levels in bar," she offers.

"OK. Before it becomes a Monty Python re-run. What did the Romans give us?" Hunter asks.

"I've given Dwight control of the stockroom doors on the *Amatheia*; meaning any smart IT group on the ship could do the same. Him and Billy are kicking some ideas around and I'll join them after dinner to run a code-buster on the safe. We're betting the gem-safe's empty."

"If the diamonds have been rinsed from the other two safes, but then they fail here…" Kieron starts.

"This was last ship?" Bedi offers. "Job meant to finish here. Go home."

"But we're in lockdown, and the *Amatheia* is heading for the coast," Croc says.

"They failed to get the third haul, but the one thing they can't do is fail to get away," Hunter adds.

"Clock ticking," Bedriška concludes, nodding. "Then boom!" Her arms form a small explosive mushroom shape over her plate.

"Boom?" Hunter asks her.

"Lockdown?" Croc concludes.

"No. Boom is us fuck up their plan," she says.

Hunter takes a moment. As bold as her remark is, she is not wrong, and having someone in the team focus the rest of them is always good.

"OK, back to the start. Who is the right IT crowd?" Hunter asks Croc. "Is it Dwight's new gaming friends?"

Croc's brain has been walking through these patterns as he dressed for dinner. Answers haunted him though his journey up to the dining room and through his wait for his rapid COVID test clearance. However, boom was not a scenario he or Dwight discussed. His energy is sapped as he begins to understand Bedi's explosive term.

"Who locked the other stockroom doors?" Hunter coaxes.

"When engineers get bored, or think they are doing stuff below their ability, they get bored," Croc starts.

"You say cocky," Bedi interprets.

"They make mistakes," Kieron slides in. "We don't. We share everything, every little thing."

Croc is no longer full of smiles.

"Most criminals are caught because of their mistakes," Hunter adds. "We help each other out. It's a team."

Weaknesses in Croc are often exploited for team banter, but this is not one of those moments. He and Dwight have kicked around some incomplete concepts and the full team have not been involved. The moment of power Croc had felt has gone and has left the others inspecting him.

"Croc?" Bedi asks.

"I need to fess-up here, best to get it out there early. I got bored. Messed about. It got out of control," Croc says.

The others put their eating utensils down and wait for the cocky young hacker Wild Mary had to lawyer-up to keep out of jail years ago. Croc is having an internal debate and the silence feels like forever.

"I'm Rocket," he blurts out.

"Rocket?" Kieron asks.

"Rocket who?" Hunter adds.

"Dwight's eight-legged avatar," Croc explains.

The team are caught by the curved ball he has thrown.

"You make big man get out of chair and walk?" Bedi asks.

"Yes," he adds tentatively. "But that was…"

Bedi stands up, signals to the wine waiter. "One bottle champagne, one bottle vodka." She takes the glass she carried through from the bar and toasts Croc. "Skol!"

"Well done kid, nice move," Hunter says.

"So, team. How do I get out of this?"

"No idea," Kieron states.

"No, you're on your own," Hunter agrees.

22 – SHIP SECURITY

Five optimum areas are often listed as essential in large-scale kitchens, but there are six. Food preparation, cooking and service are the three that are obvious, with service getting all the guest tips. It is why they are not normally allowed to keep them, but the pot is controlled by the maître d'hôtel, or head waiter, who ensures that those who work in kitchen storage and washing are also included with the other three. The sixth area is the staff recreation and toilets.

When the midnight break is called, a cacophony of sound swells into the recreation area, but almost as soon as it builds it is orchestrated to silence. With time running out, and three times as many diamonds to find, the CSCI team can no longer hide under the cover of information technology testers.

"Where Arif?" Bedriška barks at the shocked team. She and Kieron read each of their faces as they wait for a reply, but none is forthcoming.

There are several quick fixes to interviewing a crowd. Kieron slips off the desk and walks towards the man he has chosen from initial reactions to be most likely to speak. His eyes never leave him, but they are joined by an accusing point of his finger before he meets him face to face.

"You. Yang," he says, reading a name badge. "Where is Arif?"

"He not come to work. Nor Banjo. Both, not at work."

Kieron searches through the crowd, checking name badges until he finds Ramesh who is heaved out. Bedriška is off the table behind him without the need for a cue. She and Kieron frog march Ramesh down the corridor. Bedi takes control of him as Kieron pushes the stock room door open.

"Hunter. They didn't make it to work," Kieron explains.

Hunter is straight out. "No movement here."

The three agents are all big enough to make crew corridors look narrow, but together with Ramesh, they bounce off the edges until they reach Banjo and Arif's room.

The cabin door swings open easily with a push to reveal it has been wrecked. As Ramesh looks on in horror, the three quickly inspect every cupboard, drawer and opening that has been turned out.

"They don't seem to want to leave without every last piece," Kieron says, careful not to introduce Ramesh into more detail than he has just discovered.

"Why not just keep your head down and get out of Dodge with the smaller prize?" Hunter asks of himself as he shakes his head in wonder.

"Greed," Kieron announces. "Our evolution is based on greed."

"You sound like Gordon Gekko."

"Who?" Bedi asks.

"Movie. Wall Street," Hunter says.

"Everything is movie for American," she starts. "Greed is simple. It start with greed for life."

"Don't you become a philosopher on me too."

"Russian very deep thinkers."

Hunter ignores her and turns sharply to their prisoner.

"OK Ramesh. You've got five," he shows him a hand of splayed digits. "Five seconds to show me where you would hide something."

"What do they want?" Ramesh asks.

Bedi shows him her ring. "This. He stole diamond ring."

Ramesh looks to the ceiling, but every panel has been pulled down. He looks in the shower, but the panels have all been removed. He opens his hands.

"No. Nowhere."

"OK. Where your boyfriend hide?" Bedriška demands, getting right into his face.

Once more, Ramesh looks lost. She stamps on his foot and as he bends in pain she slaps up under his chin.

"Where?" She demands.

Ramesh leads them into the corridor.

"This is Banjo's best friend," he reveals, looking at cabin A619 across the way.

Kieron goes back into Arif's cabin and lifts the telephone.

"Croc. Open up A619."

By the time Kieron is back in the corridor, Bedriška is in the cabin. Banjo is quivering with fear on the bed, pressed into the wall as if she were trying to implode.

"Where is he?" Hunter starts.

"Look! Here," Ramesh says, leaning in to snatch the ring she tries to hide on her finger. Banjo snatches her hand back and fires Ramesh a deathly look. Hunter pulls him clear of her.

"Arif taken," she sobs, her heart racing.

"Who take him?" Bedriška says, trying to make her feel easier, but she missed that semester at spy school.

"American want diamonds. Arif tell him he has none."

Hunter sees the hatred she manages to aim at Ramesh even though she is distressed.

"How did you escape?" Kieron asks her, from the back. He takes over questioning while Hunter thinks.

"I was in here. I hold door just open."

Kieron turns and holds the cabin door ajar, and he can see into Arif's cabin.

"American took him away," she sobs.

"How many?" Bedriška asks.

"One."

"Man, woman, big?"

"One man, not big like you."

"One man only explain why no look-out during robbery," Bedriška says to Kieron.

"Skin colour, hair colour, bald?"

"White man, dark hair, I think. He not always in view. Sometimes I closed door. I did not see him."

"Why take him?" Kieron asks.

"He wants the diamonds. Arif told him ship security take diamonds, so he drags Arif away, kicking him. He wants Arif to pick out your picture from crew list. He will kill Arif," she says.

"He won't kill him," Hunter growls.

The three are thinking hard and fast.

"Why didn't he come for Arif yesterday?" Kieron asks. "What's different today?"

"Ship sailing."

"Maybe."

"We put report in," Bedi then offers. "He not know Arif yesterday."

"Please get Arif back," Ramesh begs.

As the agents look between Ramesh, Banjo, and the door, a lot seems wrong.

"Croc is by himself," Kieron worries.

As they all turn to move off, Banjo stops them.

"Don't leave me here."

Ramesh is fearful of being alone too.

Bedi sees an American Baseball bat, glove, and ball on the wall. She takes the bat.

"You go. I make trap. If he come back, I kill him."

"If he lets Arif go, we need him. Arif's seen the man. If the man comes back to search for the diamonds again, we need him alive."

23 – COMPROMISED

Croc's door is closed. K&H are left in the corridor waiting for an answer, looking at each other.

"He needed sleep?" Hunter questions.

"We need him to wake up."

"But not wake the neighbours."

Kieron darts off, entering his cabin with the reserve magnetic card. He stops and looks around. His room might look untouched to many, but Kieron knows someone has been in.

He goes to the cabin house phone and dials. Then turns and sniffs gently. Stretching the handset cable, he moves to a drawer that is not closed as tightly as he left it; and he is precise. He straightens the wristwatch which has been dislodged from the USB charger; the red light shows it starts to charge again. His travel bag of few clothes that he lives out of, sits on the bed where he left it, but it does not sit the same. Looking inside he can see that nothing is folded quite as he left it.

He still has the handset to his ear.

"Come on, Croc. Pick up."

With his other hand he speed-dials Dwight on his cell but stops. Ceasing both calls he leaves his room, reuniting with Hunter at Croc's door.

"They took my cell," Hunter says.

"Did they get the diamonds?" Kieron asks.

"No," he answers, patting his front waist pocket. "But all contacts in my cell must be considered compromised."

"Time to wake up the neighbours?" Kieron says, preparing his shoulder to take the door out.

"Doors this low are meant to withstand sea water," Hunter tells him.

"Together?"

As a coordinated shunt, they take out Croc's door with such force it bounces on its hinges. Kieron pushes the door closed behind them and they look around. It is hard to know whether the room has been ransacked or it is how Croc had it, but one thing is certain: Croc is missing.

Hunter circles the room looking for clues.

"You smell that musky aftershave, that was in my room. It's old, been on all evening," Kieron suggests.

"For someone who had a major smash on the head a few months back, there's not much wrong with your smell."

"It used to be a lot sharper." Kieron lifts his cell. "We need to break silence."

Hunter nods in agreement as he backs into the cabin phone on the desk and dials. "Be brief," he says to Kieron, then into the room phone. "Bedi. Croc is AWOL, my cell-phone's been taken. They could be all over us."

"He," she says. "It one man."

Hunter puts the telephone handset back down and looks at Kieron.

"Dwight always answers," Kieron worries.

Hunter drops to the desk chair and fires up a screen. He sends a message to Miami.

'Man down.'

He spins around and they both continue to inspect the room.

"With Croc down, we need Dwight to share the thoughts on the IT crowd, or we're working blind," Kieron says, frustrated.

"Yeah. Call me old school, but I like everything shared."

The screen fires up behind Hunter. A large close-up of Dwight's face with a headset and microphone like a 1980's Top Gun pilot.

"Roll call," Dwight demands.

"Hunter Witowski."

"Kieron Philips."

They both rattle off as a response to Dwight's two-word command to take register.

"Dwight. We have an information leak. I'll be brief," Hunter starts. "Agent Bedriška Kossoff has a trap set, she is in a safe house with two potential witnesses. Third witness taken, we think to identify us by picture. Croc is missing, have you heard from him?"

"Negative," Dwight snaps back.

24 - AWOL

"Run that by us again," Kieron says, relaxing.

"I was taking five," Dwight admits, explaining why he was not on duty.

"Taking five, and we have a communications leak; it could be anywhere, top to bottom?" Hunter probes, sitting on Croc's bed.

"I left Izzy in charge. You had Croc as local point man. I'm entitled to sleep."

"But to be clear, you weren't sleeping?" Kieron asks.

"You needed to be brief, not tear me off about how I use my downtime," Dwight says, beginning to get angry, though mindful of the missing agent.

"Yeah. Yeah."

"Commander Philips, we have a man down," Dwight says, now getting angrier than them. Frustrated at their inactivity.

Kieron Philips stands up and addresses the screen as if Dwight were in the room.

"And you have no idea where he is?"

"No, sir."

"And no idea where the leak is."

"No, sir."

"But you were playing a video game with your girlfriend?" Hunter asks, sitting up, equally as casual as Kieron.

"Sir, I can vouch for Rocket. She's not the source of this leak," Dwight insists.

"You're 100% certain about this Rocket?" Kieron asks.

Hunter looks across the cabin to his partner, they are both on dangerous ground.

"Sirs, both of you. I apologise for not being here when we lost a man. And I will trace all the gamers, each last one, but I'm sure they're not our leak."

"Listen. Dwight. We're losing water. The thief only knew about Arif and Banjo after our report. So, every theory you and your team have on which IT crowd are doing what, needs to be shared," Hunter demands.

"He's not working by himself," Kieron adds.

"His puppet master might be on land, but there's a leak. We're being played," Hunter adds.

"I agree. I'll work all night. Now, should we look for Croc?" Dwight demands.

"We'll find Croc. You need to get your office sharing information and not writing papers about 'sharing information'," Kieron demands.

"That needs explaining, sir."

"Cut the sir, Dwight. Izzy and Croc are planning a take-over and not doing their jobs."

"Take-over?"

"The youngsters wanna change the name to Cruise Crime Investigators, get industry approval and then train other security staff," Hunter informs him.

"I know nothing about that, sir."

Kieron and Hunter both leap from their beds.

"Seems a few things you don't know about. Let's get each other up to speed on everything," Hunter says, hitting a key to end the call, Kieron delaying the door from opening.

"That was getting embarrassing."

Confused, Croc enters the room with his Top Gun head set and microphone still on, and his digital pad in hand.

25 – THERAPY

Within minutes of Croc's return, Kieron and Hunter had dashed back to their rooms and packed. They stand just inside Croc's cabin, both carrying their simple travel bags. They watch Croc panic to grab all his clothes from the closet and fill his giant case.

"Ready to move out?" Hunter asks, seeing he is not.

"Has Rocket broken it to Dwight?" Kieron demands.

"No and no. I'm working as fast as I can, but I should be sleeping. I gave you your cell-phone back, I explained why I was looking for Kieron's cell. Updates require communication."

"Updates? It was more important for you to share your CCI document than job information?" Kieron demands, closing the cabin door so as not to disturb neighbouring cabins. It is still incredibly early hours of the morning.

"I Bluetooth all documents to your cells when I can find them. I do not use the ship's system."

"But going into our cabins without permission?" Hunter persists.

"The three of you are never out of my cabin."

"That's different," Kieron argues.

"All our cabins are operational centres." In temper, Croc slams the lid to his case. "Actually, I'm not moving. Now you know it was me in your cabins, you know these rooms are under no threat."

"We have a leak, they found Arif and Banjo from our report."

"Maybe."

"Everything's a threat," Hunter says.

"It's the middle of the night and I need to sleep."

Kieron and Hunter look at each other amazed at the dissension on the ranks.

"If the leak is one of the gamers, I can run checks easier than Dwight," Croc says. "In the morning; our gamers do programme and firmware updates."

"So, you think you're that clever?"

"Thirty-seven-minutes," Croc announces, turning back to them sharply. He is tired and grumpy. He may have done all-nighters in Miami when his agents were away out in-the-field, but he has the pressure of being in action with them. "That's how long it took me to open the safe on another ship. Thirty-seven minutes. Except, which one of us has not slept? That's right. Me."

"Less time gaming and a lot more military discipline," Hunter states.

"Hunter, this is the outside world. Workers have rights. And gaming is an important part of the future. Not only are we the guys who fly your military drones, but surgeons-who-game are more accurate and faster. I'm faster than the idiots robbing these diamonds, and I'm your point-man here."

"I'll read your document," he replies.

"Izzy wrote it."

"Personally, I got no interest in training security staff for ships. However, I can see all your arguments. It does keep Zack and Billy working, it means you have a lengthy list of potential investigators to hand, and Wild Mary will sell more burgers. But no, I'm out. I'll take the money from the trunk we have on our old ship, and then retire to being a father. So, Kieron," he says turning to his partner. "…unless you've a better idea than Mr Rocket Crocket, I'm off to bed."

Hunter leaves the room. Kieron is nodding slowly.

"He's a new dad," Kieron says softly. "He'll calm down."

"That's just it. Izzy's been looking into postpartum mood disorders in new fathers, it's similar to PTSD. We need a company policy on mental health," Croc says.

"What about Dwight's?" Kieron asks. "Tell him you've been found. Tell him you're Rocket, but careful, Dwight is already one fucked-up man. He deserves more from you. You need me to write that in a paper."

Kieron leaves.

Scolded, Croc sits on the bed and lifts his pad. He starts to type.

'Dear Dwight. I must tell you'. There is a huge pause as Croc thinks, then he twists and angrily screams into a pillow then draws his legs back and kicks his luggage case off the bed. He lies flat and looks at his pad.

'I'm really a man, well, almost. Some still think me a boy. Rocket'.

He presses send.

26 – TIME TO STOP

In Miami, Lizzie jumps to life a moment after Croc's picture fires up on the huge monitor throwing light into the Miami headquarters.

"Do you know what time it is?" Izzy scolds, having been woken.

"You been there all night?" Croc asks.

"Does it end?"

"No," Croc says.

"You can get your ass back here and keep this job."

"Where's Dwight?"

"Mr Angry? That man's a ghost. He got up, worked out, showered in the wet room, and was angry down the phone, then threw me a sheet of notes. He left without saying goodbye. Looked real strange."

"Notes?"

"I haven't typed them up yet."

"Why didn't he type them?"

"Say's he's not using his computer, doesn't want to use any computer."

"Read them to us," Kieron asks.

"He got a movement order that fits your theory of a one-man thief, and Billy's safe being empty. A works team left Ianassa 14 days ago for Amatheia and left there four days ago for Aerwyna. Ten-day schedule on each ship. Fifty-two names, mainly fabric and carpet fitters, no IT. He said the thief must be working with a remote IT person, and that could be anywhere. Could be Billy's idea to follow the LED curtain. Last thing, lock down ends later so goods can transfer from you to the Amatheia before she sails."

"No, no, no," Hunter says.

"Yeah. I think that's what Dwight might've been angry about. Either that or me calling him Spider. He seemed fine with that yesterday."

In the hub on the ship, Croc, who is dressed in a green all-in-one engineer's coveralls, turns away from the monitor and waits for Izzy to answer.

Hunter stands by Bedriška and Ramesh who sit on his bed.

"Yeah. Roger that. Let's get that list of fitters. I'll look at the tech suggestion and try and keep the ship locked down." The call ends. Hunter gets up and pats Croc's shoulder. "Operational duties."

"Why me?"

"You look like crew," Bedi says.

Ramesh nods.

"Bedi will walk you down there, get inside if you can, as close as you can, but we want to know if Arif is in the cells. Right?"

Ramesh nods, reluctantly.

Bedi waits for them to rise and eases them to Hunter who opens the door. The force of him and Bedi walking out carries Croc and Ramesh with them. They have no option.

27 – THE STAGE IS SET

Hunter stands at the back of the theatre by the control box. It is a two-tier structure, and he has worked out that the lower desk is for sound, the upper desk is lighting. There is no obvious control for the LED wall or recent obvious reconstruction of the desk.

Bedi walks up behind him, with Croc - still in greens - and Ramesh looking like crew.

"There's something going on in the cells, but no way to get in without being arrested," Croc offers.

"You want I cause trouble?" Bedi offers.

"No. Leave that to me. I need to keep the ship locked down, so I'll start at the top. The worst result is I'll end up in the cells," Hunter says, looking at his watch. "Thirty-minutes breakfast break, then track my cell."

"I can do that here, on my tablet," Croc says, lifting his pad.

"Fifty-two names, we need more time. We need their faces, and we need Arif to ID the guy."

"One of them's gonna want to get off on that transfer back," Croc suggests. He has his green coveralls off and is dumping them under a seat.

"Too late. It's a risk. Leave Billy on that ship just in case." Hunter says.

"Breakfast," Bedi says, pointing up. "Big day."

"How about me?" Ramesh asks.

"No one's after you. They need to get off this ship, and their clock is ticking."

Hunter walks away from them, thinking.

Hunter walks down the gangway on the right, between the rows of dark red theatre stalls. He weaves around the midway divider and down steps to the lower stalls on deck five. Checking his cell-phone has service, which it does because he is in a public area, he climbs up onto the stage and looks at the LED curtain. No one is around; not engineering, not stagehands.

He moves to the side of the stage and finds a box with about twenty switches, most labelled. He flicks the one labelled 'rafters' and looks up as lights come on in the high ceiling. There is nobody hanging there.

"Hello."

Backstage he pauses to look at props and scenery additions that are stacked away. He sees only one trunk that could hold a body. He flips the lid up and disturbs the material on top, but it does not reveal Arif.

He walks down the backstage steps, through the dressing room and sends a text to all.

'Stage area clear. Going up.'

A thumbs up comes back from Kieron, then Izzy and finally one from Dwight. He knows his cell is working and he will have done enough to wake the trace system if he is being watched.

He hits Dwight's name to send a message just to him. 'Nice work. Get some sleep.'

A thumbs up comes back, but he knows Dwight won't be sleeping.

28 – THE BRIDGE

The ship is driven by a team in the bridge. The bridge, so called because it spans or bridges and then overhangs the two sides of the ship, is most obvious from the exterior. When docking, officers come to the 'overhang' which looks back, front, and down through a glass floor section in order to park the ship. It sits on the pool deck, below the equally well glazed lounge bar, on this class of ship. Some ships do not have the lounge at the front but devote this exceptional area to the few who afford the spa or visit the gym. A rear lounge can be such a disappointment on visual cruises like the Fjords or the Northern Lights. If having such views from the rear was as good, they would move the bridge there, but it is at the front.

As obvious as the control area is from the outside, it is not so easy to find when inside the ship. The power centre is behind a set of offices, the captain's suite on one side and the chief engineer's residence on the other side. Like an airplane's cockpit, the door is normally locked with no access for guests. There is an internal crew staircase which avails staff to go up or down to deck seven, the promenade deck, and Hunter uses this approach. As he expected, the door to the MS Aerwyna bridge has no need to be closed; he just needed to know how to get there.

The low early morning sun blisters through the glass as he enters and stops, allowing the crew to react. He can see a small and very strange looking hairless white cat, walk across the control desk to Captain Veronica Walker, as if needing protection from its owner. Even the animal knows Hunter is not supposed to be in there. A senior officer approaches him in the open entrance to the bridge.

"Can I help you, sir?"

"Hunter Witowski, Cruise Crime Investigators," he says, announcing himself then realising the parapraxis he made using Croc's new and preferred company name. It flew off the tongue.

"Is Captain Walker expecting you?"

"No, I'm working here undercover."

That was guaranteed to gain attention. What Hunter expects to happen now is that the officer will be asked to show him to a small meeting room, where he will be made to wait until she is joined by at least the head of security and possibly the hotel manager. Hunter would prefer this to happen much quicker and without the full senior crew.

"Would you follow me sir," the officer says, wishing to lead him off, after speaking with the captain.

"Point me to the chart room and tell her I work directly for the company's Chief Operations Officer, Ms Casey B. de Michelle. I would rather the circle in-the-know was kept small, and that time is of-an-essence. We have a communication breach and a man down. I need her help."

Hunter turns to follow the officer, wondering how the captain will react to the new knowledge. Whatever happens, his team's cover is broken, and time is running out.

He hears the door to the bridge close and lock behind them.

29 – LIFE AT SEA

The breakfast buffet is under no social distancing pressure this early in the morning. Bedriška sits with her back to the outside glass, the sun highlighting her short hair from behind as she watches the crew being temperature tested on entrance. She has finished her small breakfast. Croc is still eating, although finding time to brief Bedi.

"Explain Billy's mad idea," Bedi says, looking at the picture of the door on the screen of her cell-phone which had previously not interested her. "Keep Locked HoD WBH?"

"Typical playful techie boredom. Wild Bill Hickok," Croc explains.

"Why Americans think they are wild? Wild Mary? Wild Bill?"

"Wild Hunter," Croc adds.

Bedi twists her head, thinking.

"Yes. New name of agency; 'Wild'. I be Wild Bedi, you be Wild Croc. We all be wild."

Croc ignores it as another moment of her madness.

"It appears a wild techie joke, possibly by the guys digitising the stage show Calamity Jane for the LED show."

"Why not Wild Jane?"

"Whatever, IT don't know or use door names. Computers just deal in numbers for cabins. They would never know or put names on the door. Pointless."

"Were Bill and Jane married?" Bedi asks.

"I haven't seen the show. Actually, they were real, but it was a long time ago and they weren't married, but that don't matter, right? Just like ships."

"Ships?"

"Arif had a wife back home and a woman here?"

"Yes," she begins to agree. "Many crew have ship wife, and wife back home."

"Two wives. And Arif's relationship with Ramesh? Is that normal too?"

"Don't know," she answers, as if to question why Croc might think she is the expert on relationships.

"But you slept with Georgie, entertainment manager and also Kieron," Croc says, before realising he has gone too far. "I meant, how does the at-sea family work?" he tries, digging a bigger hole.

"You and Dwight two men? Or are you transgender avatar?" she bites. "Is Spider still your friend, Rocket?"

Croc stops eating.

"I haven't told him. Is Kieron still your friend?"

"Kieron my only friend."

"Hey. How about me?"

"Not friend. You not include me in your company take-over."

"What?"

"I hear, you take over company. Call it CCI. Employ Billy and Zack."

"What? No."

"You make CCI?"

"It's a better name," he argues.

"Izzy write long paper?

"Yes, but.

"Is there Russian version?"

"What?"

"Did you translate for me?"

"You speak English," he says in panic.

"But you never consult me."

"Sure. I do."

"Why not CCII?"

"What?"

"International! Cruise Crime Investigators International! Why you not want me, Russian? Why you not want Prisha, Indian?"

"I do."

"Breakfast break over."

Bedi marches off. Croc turns to his food in shock and as he stares down at his plate. It comes up into his face. Red ketchup sauce is everywhere.

"Ha," Bedi laughs unemotionally, leaving again.

Croc is puzzled.

"That was a joke, right?"

"No," she shouts back. "I go find Bill and Jane."

30 - THE VILLAGE

Ship life is confusing.

Kieron met Bedi's partner Georgie on his first cruise where Hunter was surreptitiously saving the life of his kidnapped wife Elaine. Hunter, then head of security, had one selfish goal in mind: to free his wife, even if he did support a south American drug gang who used the ship in an unseen heist. Kieron got involved, and to this day has never analysed how or why. The trunk with millions of dollars seems one of the many byproducts, like Kieron falling hopelessly in love with Georgie.

Georgie, the entertainment manager, however, was in her first female relationship with Bedriška, who worked in the spa but was on leave.

Since Georgie's death, despite catching her killer, whom Bedi cleverly snared into a fatal end, neither Kieron nor Bedi can have her. It was a disastrous romance. Now they have an awkward relationship that is only just beginning to thaw out. Kieron and Hunter were never glued at the hip, and Hunter has never been a huge fan of Bedi; he thinks she's a drunk. Croc doesn't understand any of it. Working on a cruise ship appears to be a dangerously small village, and although this one is populated with outside crew, there is no telling which of them is Bill or Jane.

31 – BROKEN COVER

Tea is about to be served to Hunter in the Captain's meeting room, but Hunter refuses.

"I'll wait for the captain."

"Sir, Captain Walker insisted that you are comfortable, in case she is delayed.

"She won't be," Hunter says to the waiter who steps back against the panelled polished dark wood wall and waits. Models of great ships stand on plinths and plaques from cruise ports adorn the walls with flags. It is so traditional that Hunter does not bother to look, whereas Croc might find it fascinating.

Captain Walker enters with her head of security, Selma Gomez. Hunter stands and then is put at ease. As they sit, tea is served, and he thinks that Commander Kieron Philips would have preferred this task. Two senior women in uniform would have had him in a spin. The captain encourages him to start but Hunter looks towards the waiter. Veronica Walker understands the request for security, and with a nod, the waiter is asked to wait outside.

"You said we have a man down?" the captain starts.

"Arif, kitchen staff in cabin A620."

"He works for you? I wasn't expecting that."

"No. He was a witness to a diamond robbery from the locked safe in the general store cabin near their recreation room. He called the whistleblower's hotline."

"Your purpose on my ship?"

"To catch the diamond thieves and recover the diamonds," Hunter explains. "So, I need your ship to stay locked down."

"That would help you, would it?"

"Yes, ma'am."

"Because the thieves could be any crew member on board?" the captain asks.

"Anyone. But, we think the 52 fitters who have moved from ship to ship in the last few weeks, might just have a white American among them with dark hair who could be called William, or Bill," Hunter says.

"He's all alone?"

"We had to stop the diamonds leaving. We caused the lockdown."

"Do you carry a weapon?" Selma asks.

"No, ma'am."

"Would you submit to a search."

Hunter stands, his arms out.

"Would you prefer a man?"

"No ma'am, I would like this circle to remain small."

Selma, the head of security, pats and rubs him down, always asking permission first when in sensitive areas.

"I spoke with our company COO," Captain Walker says.

"Ms de Michelle."

"Yes. She said he'd never heard of you."

"I'm under cover, ma'am."

"Or," Captain Walker starts. "You are the thief, and you want me to help you get the gems off ship. Ms de Michelle suggested you are put under arrest."

"May I?" Officer Gomez asks. She pulls the small felt bag from the front pocket of Hunter's denim pants. The diamond rings are tipped out on the shiny dark wood table.

Hunter slides his mobile next to them and it is obvious from the screen that it is live.

"Have you been recording our conversation?" the captain asks.

"Not here. In Miami at our headquarters, so let's both of us do this by the book."

32 – THE LADDER

Ramesh has never been in the massive, steam-filled laundry. Neither has Croc, but they are told the green coverall is their pass to go anywhere. Kieron could only watch and learn during the extensive briefing they were given from Hunter and Bedriška because he is not as ship-worldly.

"If you see a stool, or a ladder, or anything, carry it in. People look at the absurd tool, not you," was the only addition he could make.

That is what they both remember now, staring at a six-foot stepladder left in busy wide i95, the working centre vein of the ship. Croc reaches forward and takes it.

"Come on," he says, leading Ramesh in. They look more like a TV sketch show waiting to go wrong than agents working behind enemy lines.

They walk between rows of workstations and machines. Croc looks from his pad and then all around him. He doesn't even need to do the challenging work; the supervisor in charge nods and points to a pillar with a newly fitted yellow digital transmission relay disc.

"Why did she think we came for this?" Ramesh panics.

"Because it is a new installation, and it's a mystery," Croc explains as he expands the ladder. "I can make this work as an information feed in Hunter's room."

"But he's been arrested."

"They don't know that," Croc says, now being the experienced one.

"Go on then, take it," Ramesh argues.

"I can't. I don't have any tools."

Croc climbs the ladder and makes a drama out of checking the newly installed communication and track and trace point. The audience he gains allows Bedriška the ability to slip in for one of her familiar tricks.

Unnoticed, she sorts through the rows of clean and pressed uniforms. She takes one that will fit her, and one for Kieron, and lifts a few shirts before she wafts out.

33 - ONE DOWN

Standing on the promenade deck, twenty miles off the coast of Great Harbour Cay and 100 miles from Freeport, Bahamas, Kieron and Bedriška might look like two fine officers, but neither are relaxed.

"Piece of that uniform missing, soldier," Dwight barks at them on a video call.

"We know," Kieron replies, one eye on his phone showing Dwight in a gym at the rehab centre, the other focussed on the MS Amatheia, which is being made ready to sail back to Miami.

The excitement of the other ship's crew can be heard easily from a mile away over the quiet, flat ocean. It will be the first time many will have seen land in a year. Up-anchor is planned for 1900hrs, and the easy sail home is likely to be a party, berthing at Port Miami, Dodge Island early morning.

"If I can see the badge is missing, others will," Dwight adds.

"You're special, Dwight. Not everyone has your talent," Kieron says. "Izzy might have rung Miss Casey to challenge her disowning Hunter, she might have got a second payment, but it's not adding up."

Bedi digs him to look at a lifeboat leaving the other ship. He acknowledges that he has seen it.

"I need some time out, but I'm across what's going on," Dwight insists.

"Are you? We need to know a lot more about our employer. Never assume you know who you are talking to, or who you are working for. Is Izzy out of her depth?"

"Izzy? Look Kieron, the kids are the future. They just think it's nearer than it is. We have to give them some rope."

"And let them hang themselves?" Kieron asks.

"Not a helpful approach," Croc adds. "Some of those old school tactics might be too outdated."

"Croc. The cruise line is a corporation. Unlike you, the staff do exactly what they are told. And they don't step out of line."

Croc is silenced for a moment. His actions have reverberated around some senior agents, and some have not yet played out.

"In war, a soldier never knows whether he's fighting for the right side, or the wrong side, or who he is up against," Dwight adds.

"They never ask," Bedi fires in. "We need to ask."

"Something's niggling my legs, the two I don't have and the eight I do. I don't know whether it's this gym, but I have an itch. Give me an hour or so here, I'm looking for my own clarity; then I'll go and see where she's at."

The call goes dead.

"That boats heading for us," Kieron says, watching their lifeboat speed towards them.

"We need lapel badges."

Croc, who has been listening and deliberately staying out of any picture sent to Dwight, opens the 'crew only door'. "He'll come back."

Kieron looks back out at the approaching lifeboat.

"We should go," Bedi says. "Forget badge."

As they begin to walk away, Ramesh rushes up through the crew door followed by a worried Banjo. He hands over two gold lapel badges. One says Ramesh, Kitchen Washer, and the other Banjo, Kitchen Utility.

"I did not want to be alone," Banjo says.

Bedi slides the name and job title out, turns them over. Banjo copies with the second badge. Bedi writes on the blank side as neatly as she can.

Kieron is watching a craft approaching fast.

"We need to go," he says. "You two. In your overalls, stay behind us, we might need back up."

"Don't leave me," Banjo worries.

"You come too. When we give you a wave, rush to get on the tender."

"We leave the ship?" Banjo asks.

"No, we arrest you. You'll be safe in a cell in the brig until this is over. Hunter might be there."

Bedi and Kieron rush off and the other two follow a few paces behind, puzzled. They go inside at midships and rush down two decks. The watertight door is closed, so they run down again to deck four where the door is open to the sea.

Engineering and safety staff wait on the pontoon, boxes of materials, bags of waste and other crew wait. The two officers try to analyse who and what is there and look for the American with dark hair who could be jumping ship with the diamonds.

"What are you thinking?" Bedi asks Kieron.

"Rather than us try and arrest our thief, we get our three to charge off when we see him go. Security will arrest all of them, including him. We should have to do nothing."

"Good plan. But how we get the diamonds?"

34 – EXPECTED PRACTICES

Selma enters the crew security office and sits in front of Hunter. She dismisses her two security officers who leave the room.

"We seem to have got off on the wrong foot," she starts.

"Is this necessary?" he asks, raising his wrists that are cable tied together.

"I just read your jacket, and I figure if you wanted them off, they'd be off."

"Cable ties?" he questions.

"If you didn't want to be in here, you wouldn't be"

"So why am I still under arrest?"

"I've not charged you with anything?"

"I'm free to go?"

"I didn't say that either."

"You want me to suggest what should happen?" he asks. "You have to hand me over; Freeport is way too far to transport me. Great Harbour Cay is still a few hours but the nearest; they have police, immigration, and an airport."

"I can hold you overnight to cool down, but why are you here?"

"To say hello to the neighbours."

"You don't have any neighbours."

"Do you have Arif in the brig?"

"Follow me," she says, getting up and leading him to four small cabins she has at the back of the area. Swinging each door open, she shows they are empty.

"If you've not had a crime reported, then you should give me back my diamonds."

"That's debatable because there's a limit on the amount of money you can travel with. Let's just say they're in here until the morning." She opens the safe with her thumb print and throws them in and closes the door. "They're going nowhere."

"So, who is reading the rule-book on what to do with me?" he asks.

"Apart from your office in Miami who seems to know the book back to front?"

"Izzy." Hunter nods, with a wry smile.

"Captain Walker has been dealing with her. We know who you are, if you are who you say you are?"

"All that established I have no reason to be in here," Hunter tells her.

"Don't set me a challenge," she says, with a huge smile.

"No. The challenge is to figure out where the thief is, and yet more difficult, where his IT support comes from. His IT guy has broken into your system."

"If they've broken in, it's a case of who, how far and how wide," she says.

"And is this petty diamond theft just a test?"

Their chat is broken up by the sounds of an approaching argument. She looks to see security with crew under arrest, rushing towards the offices.

"Is this your doing?" she asks.

"Is it an American with dark hair, carrying diamonds and trying to jump ship?"

Hunter holds his hands under the table and tries to sit as ordinarily as he can with his wrists bound. Cable ties are strong shackles.

A man fitting exactly that description is pushed against the wall. He is held by an officer standing to the side of him.

Banjo is pushed to the other wall, along with Ramesh and Croc. Two officers face them to keep them in place. The room is busy.

"Can I suggest we move a couple of these to cells in the brig until we've processed the others," Hunter suggests, awkwardly sitting at the desk like a small country dictator. He flicks his head to Croc and the lad knows that means get out of the way. He and Ramesh are led to the brig which has four cabins at the back. The first door is opened. Ramesh is pushed into the cell.

Meanwhile Selma approaches the thief. A flick of disapproval sets in on Hunter's lips, but he cannot get up or intervene or undermine her. What is she doing? This is not the Wild West, he ponders to himself.

Selma looks down to the money pouch around his waist and cuts the belt with a knife, so the sack drops into her hand. Hunter eases his chair back; he hates each of her moves.

Holding the knife awkwardly in her hand, she unzips the pouch and lifts out two self-sealing, transparent plastic bags of diamond rings. She tosses them onto the table.

"And that makes three," she says, side stepping to the safe. The door opens on her thumb print. She takes out the diamonds that were already in there.

"Is this it? Just the three ships?"

"Four," the thief says, pushing his right hip pocket forward.

Hunter can no longer watch her handling of the situation. He barks at the prisoner.

"No. You didn't even manage two properly. Step back Gomez," he says, giving her an order that he knows will save her life.

35 – TOO LATE

Selma glances back at Hunter.

"Watch your prisoner," he shouts.

But it is too late. Hunter didn't train her.

The thief grabs her knife and heaves it back into her stomach as if he is pulling a rope. The strain in his eyes shows he is lifting. He means more than just to stab her.

"Medic. Call medic, now," Hunter shouts, rising fast. "Croc, make that call."

The thief kicks the table forward, momentarily trapping Hunter's thighs and tipping him forward. Before the kick settles, the killer's whole-body twists, and with a wide scoop of the air he aims the knife straight at Hunter's neck.

Hunter's bound arms manage to palm the knife down but cannot take the power out of it. The blade digs straight into his side, between his ribs. Hunter drops in pain and gasping for air.

Far too late, the ship's guard reaches for the thief. But the slayer moves well and drops flat down on the table. The knife goes up into the guard's stomach. In the same motion the thief's leg flicks the guard over the top of him with a classic Tomoe-nage throw. The body fires straight into the advancing Croc. Croc is pulled down and slashed from the side towards his stomach; he can feel the cold steel.

Banjo makes a grab for the diamonds; her hand is stabbed right through. The knife pins her to the wood. She screams in pain but at the same time aims abuse at her attacker. She is hit hard on the jaw; silenced she hangs down.

"Call medic," Hunter tries to shout again, but with half the power. He takes the taser out of the dead guard's belt and slides under the table to grab the thief's leg.

By the time the thief has the three bags of diamonds and has pulled his knife which releases Banjo to drop, he is held. He raises his knife, but Hunter stabs his groin with the taser.

"Call it in. Call a medic, Medic." Hunter fires the taser but at that point he knows he has lost. "Is this set for, tasering rabbits?" is the last thing he tries to say with no wind.

The knife goes into his shoulder, just under his neck, and his senses stop.

36 – TRAINING

Croc drops to his knees beside Hunter, himself gasping for air, tightening every muscle in his face to help his boss. He pulls his elbow hard into his own side and stomach as he tears a strip from the bottom of his tee-shirt. The cloth is way too little to stop Hunter's bleeding. Forcing himself not to scream with pain, Croc uses both hands to rip the shirt off his back and violently tear it in half. He pushes the first length deep into the hole in Hunter's neck and the other in his ribs. It is impossible to know whether the blood is coming from him or Hunter. He slaps Hunter's face.

"Stay with me boss."

Hunter's eyes open a little. "Always…" He fights for breath. "Always search a suspect before you travel them." Fighting to talk he coughs blood. "We never trained this team, eh?" He passes out, blood coming from his mouth.

The first medic comes rushing into the brig and Banjo confronts him with her stabbed hand.

"Stop. She might be armed. Get down here," Croc insists, ordering him to work on Hunter. He moves the table to expose the three in need of serious help, Selma, the guard, and Hunter.

Croc yanks the fighting Banjo away from her priority position at the door and into the guard who took him and Ramesh to the cell. She is immobilised.

"Search her, and lock her out of the way," Croc demands, beginning to feel faint. He lifts his cell and types.

'Man down'.

He staggers to the wall for support. Below him is a blood bath.

"This one's dead," a second medic says, examining Selma.

"Guard with a stomach wound, agent with two stab wounds. We need two stretchers, blood, and plasma," Croc orders with control and authority. "His blood type is O-positive."

Blood-soaked bandages are appearing everywhere as they try and save both men.

"What about me?" Banjo cries, being pulled backwards.

Croc finds everything he has left and takes a soft pad and a roll of tape from the open green medical bag. He wraps the pad around the wound but uses the tape to bind her hands together. He tapes her mouth to stop her screaming. Finally, he squeezes her hands until she screams into the tape, and he slips her diamond ring off. She is pushed in the cell.

"You're under arrest," he says firmly.

"That's mine," she tries to say through the tape.

"That's evidence," he says to her. He pockets it as he addresses the guard. "Lock the door."

Croc lifts his cell again, but collapses. He sends no further message.

37 - WEARABLE

The fitting room at the prosthetic clinic is a cross between a surgical operating theatre and a craftsman's workshop. It is equipped with every required tool and strap for building and fitting a prosthesis. In case there is a medical emergency it has equipment on standby, and hidden from view but easily accessible there are panic buttons. The raised bed is strong, oversized and bolted to the floor. Its shiny leather sections can be raised and folded into numerous positions.

Dwight lays flat. Both of his stumps end below the thigh; he has no knee either side. When exposed it is a harsh message that serving for one's country can rob a soldier of the human body as well as dignity and confidence.

"I'd ask how your diet was going, but…." Amy pauses. She has a special rapport with Dwight which allows her to punish him with a joke.

"Fifteen pounds so far this month."

"How is it actors can lose weight, and put it on so easily? And yet none of my patients ever-"

"Get great acting jobs?" Dwight snaps in.

"Touchez," Jake, the prosthetist says.

The medical staff have played every routine many times, heard all the answers, and they always have a smile. However, they keep pressure on their patients to lose weight by the time they need to start to walk again. Walking is never easy for a bilateral above-the-knee amputee.

"Have you not told your friends and family yet?" she asks.

"Who is there to tell? Wife went with the legs. Hey, Jake, you couldn't make me a new one of those. I'd like to look at the available upgrade and modification options."

Amy takes a tissue and playfully pushes it into Dwight's mouth. He, just as playfully grabs her digit and for a second, she is held. The tissue never stays in his mouth, but her finger does, for a moment longer than it should. Life at the centre must be fun, it has to be fun; however, there is a limit to which the staff can allow themselves to get close or bond with patients. They have all been through enough pain and disappointment.

Jake nods, looking incredibly pleased with his work.

"What do you look so smug about?" Amy asks, saving herself.

"It fits pretty good."

"We'd all be pretty pissed if it didn't. You've made impressions and measured enough," Dwight says looking down his body.

"For such a simple job. Did you want two, I can't remember," Jake asks, with a cheeky retort.

"Get on with it, soldier."

Jake pulls up the second moulded transparent plastic socket. It also sits on an aluminium pole and has a basic hinged foot. He begins to fit it to Dwight's second stump. There is a mood change when Dwight sees a full body again.

"It's not my colour, Jake," he manages slowly, his voice giving away a million emotions.

"There's a long way to go before we get away from temporary models."

"Hear that, Amy? You're just temporary," Dwight says.

It is banter, but Amy is temporary and everyone that leaves is a loss for her.

"Shall we see how comfortable they are, and how tall you might be?" Amy encourages, flatly.

"If it means standing, no."

Amy gives him a disapproving look. Dwight sits up with Jake moving the new legs. He spins ninety degrees, and the artificial knees bend down over the edge of the bed. Dwight draws breath in shock, his world turning profoundly serious again. He is saved by his cell bleeping. Rescuing himself, he reads it. 'Man down'.

"I've gotta go. Now. Fast."

"We can be done with this in an hour," Jake offers.

"Just take them off. Amy, I need the chair. I need you to take me to my truck. Sorry."

"Dwight, slow down," she replies.

"Amy. I've a man down in the field. I'm needed. Not in an hour, but now."

Dwight makes a call as Amy pulls his chair over.

"Jake, leave them on. They're visiting HQ with me today."

"You can't drive with them on," Jake says.

"Get me a taxi-cab. I have to go, buddy."

Dwight's cell is at his ear and connects.

"Izzy. Who's down?"

Dwight listens. His face falls.

"Keep trying him. Text all agents. I'll be there superfast."

Amy and Jake know this is serious. They help him into the clinic's chair.

"We have an ambulance. They love using the blues-and-twos. I'm going with you," Amy starts, as she pushes Dwight out. "You said you were a computer analyst."

"I didn't say who for."

Jake collects tools and Dwight's pants and rushes out behind them.

The clinic ambulance reverses up to the glass doors, its lights already flashing. Jake momentarily pauses at the door and addresses the receptionist.

"Reschedule the rest of my day."

"You don't have anything," the receptionist replies blankly.

38 – PANIC

Kieron and Bedi watch the lifeboat's final loading at the open sea door. It is not like the rushed loading and unloading on most port days when groceries are delivered, trash taken off, pianos tuned, equipment sent ashore to be repaired. On such days, a movement order and schedule are circulated. Those directives are sacrosanct. No department can take time from another. The process is then martialled by the Loading Officer who spends time between port days with departments, listening to their cases for time and prioritisation.

As duty martials are watching for a fugitive or his escaping IT partner whom they have never seen, Kieron and Bedriška are both distracted by their unregistered bleeping cells fired by the ship's system.

'Who's down? Roll call please. Billy. Three all present and correct on the Amatheia.'

"Why is Billy calling this?" Bedi asks, knowing he has broken their radio silence.

Kieron types. 'Bedi and Kieron together, Aerwyna. Going to investigate.'

His phone beeps back.

'Dwight Ritter, leaving gym in Miami for office.'

'This is Izzy, Miami HQ. Part message was from Croc. No reply to me since message. No reply from Hunter.'

They know, whatever has happened, it is serious. But they still have a job to do and need to split.

"Stay here and ensure no one leaves this ship," Kieron says, taking off at speed.

Bedi eases towards the lifeboat, now wanting it to leave as soon as possible. However, it is going nowhere until she is certain no one has escaped. On hearing the command for local crew to step free, she walks into action.

"Wait. Final security check. Company agent Bedriška Kossoff."

She steps onto the boat. Her harsh tone and fearful accent make everyone stand back. She walks around the lifeboat, looks everywhere, then checks over the sides and in the water, finally looking up at the decks above.

"Go," she says, stepping back onto the floating pontoon. She fires an order back at the boat crew. "Stop for no one. Pick no one up from the sea. She lifts her cells and dials as she watches the boat leave. "Billy. Boat with you in twenty." Still on her cell, Bedriška turns to the engineers. "Close the door."

Swiftly striding away from the area towards the prison cells, Bedi continues the report into her cell.

Kieron is already in the main below deck security area. The floor covered in blood. He lifts the blanket covering the bodies of Selma and a guard. Bedi arrives; only momentarily taking in the mess, she goes to the guard at the back near the cells.

"Open. Let me see."

Without question the guard reveals they are empty apart from the last.

"What happened?" she demands, ripping the binding from Banjo's face.

"Let me out!"

Bedi slaps Banjo so hard, her head nearly comes off. Banjo looks up, not needing to be reminded of the question

"Your men are both dead," she snarls.

Bedi slams the door closed.

"Lock."

"They were alive leaving here, but both bleeding. They've been taken to the medical centre," the guard says.

Kieron and Bedi rush off, Kieron on his cell.

"Izzy. Two dead security crew in the cells, double murder. Status of Hunter and Croc unknown, they are with medics. Possibly bleeding."

Kieron ends the call before he is questioned. HQ has all he knows.

39 – IN THE DARK

"I'm supposed to know everything!" Izzy screams at the blank screens. Blue flashing EMT lights flicker into their unit through the darkened windows. She fires up the cameras to see Dwight being brought in, on a hospital chair pushed by a nurse and with a medic. Her frustration increases as she goes to the door.

"Dwight!"

"There," Dwight says, as with a few taps the large screen fires up and Amy continues her call to the huge screen at the end of the hi-tech desks.

Doctors can be seen running to a helicopter and equipment is loaded.

"Need to fly, team," Dwight urges.

"Just waiting for blood," the medic replies.

"I want you airborne, I'll get that sent on a second bird," Dwight says, from behind Amy. He is standing, holding onto her at his left and gripping the solid screen on the desk to his right.

"We don't have a second bird, sir. The blood is coming."

A trolley is pushed fast towards the craft, under the rotating blades. It topples, at least one blood bag breaks as they crash to the floor.

"Slow down," Amy calms.

They watch as the blood is recovered, the loose empty bag collected, the door slammed, and the bird cleared.

The medic and his camera look down at the roof they are leaving behind.

"We've never left like that, sir," he shouts in a gasp.

"Well done, soldier," Dwight says.

The call ends and Izzy is left looking at Dwight, standing. Amy turns and looks at him, then nods to Jake who has already noticed.

Dwight realises he is standing on his artificial limbs.

"That normally takes a little more effort," Amy says.

Dwight is left nodding at himself, then looking at the flabbergasted Izzy.

"I told you; no taller than me. And, you've got no pants on, and we've got guests."

"Don't worry about me, I'm used to seeing him with no pants on," Amy says.

Dwight is left only able to introduce everyone.

"This is Izzy, ignore the height thing. That's Jake, and this is my new pocket rocket, Amy."

Confused, Izzy points at Amy.

"Rocket?"

40 – BLOOD TRAFFIC

"How are you?" Kieron asks Croc.

The lad has been cleaned up a little, his shirt has been cut away from his torso and he has a clean bandage putting pressure on the wound.

"I've been cut before. How's Hunter?"

"They're working on him."

Bedi walks in and stands the other side of the bed.

"You rest," she tells the boy, genuinely concerned.

It is an order, but she bends over and kisses him on the forehead.

"Don't get excited. You will bleed more."

Kieron shows Croc his cell, the still video message of Dwight standing up, next to a smiling Amy. After Croc has taken in that he is standing on two artificial limbs, Croc reaches forward, and presses play.

"Get yourself well. That's an order from me, and from Rocket," Dwight says.

Amy nods.

"Get well. I look forward to meeting you all," she says.

"He's standing. Who was the woman?"

"That's his girlfriend, Rocket," Bedi says.

Croc looks from her, to Kieron, confused.

"Apparently," Kieron says. "She's no avatar I've ever seen."

"But, I'm…"

"Life's strange. You were yesterday's Rocket, if you ever were at all."

"I'm confused" Croc says weakly.

"Worry only on getting better," Bedi says, and they both leave him.

Kieron and Bedi walk from the treatment room into the medical reception area which is quiet. Apart from two security guards posted outside the entrance, it is as if nothing had happened. Once again, Kieron and the senior nurse meet over the computer on her desk, and she remembers the time after the fight and the confused COVID test results

"You're beginning to worry me," she says to him.

He acknowledges her, but he is waiting for an answer to his cell ringing out.

"Dwight," he starts into his phone, and listens to an update on the helicopter. "I might need blood for Croc."

The conversation is factual.

"This is a double crew murder, plus the thefts. You better speak with head office and have Izzy rewrite that bullet clause for all weapons," Kieron finishes.

"You do worry me," the senior nurse says. He looks at her badge. Her name is Bjørg, and she is as cold as her native Iceland, but no match for Bedriška.

"I need to move a small communications hub down here for young Winston Crocket. He's safe here behind guard."

"You are going to have to ask the Captain," she says.

"I know. Hello Captain Walker," Kieron says, slowly turning to her. He saw the unmistakable woman's reflection in the nurse's shiny name plate on the desk.

"What killed two of my security team?" the captain asks.

"Greed," Kieron states.

"This is not a time for riddles or jokes. What killed Selma, and her guard?"

"Greed," Kieron states again. "If you need a medical answer, that's one for senior nurse Bjørg."

"Explain yourself," the captain demands.

"I'm Commander Kieron Philips, with Cruise Crime Investigators." He too has automatically used the shorter punchier name, CCI, whether unconsciously or out of respect for Croc. He holds his glance to Veronica Walker for a second too long and he knows it. He turns to Bedi; she can explain herself using whichever tale and title she wishes.

"Bedriška Kossoff, ex KGB, now investigator."

"The crime doesn't make sense, ma'am. The killer had diamonds from two other ships. When he failed here, he had more than enough to escape with."

"But we were locked down," Veronica Walker suggests.

"He'd find a way to go. He must have been under orders to get all diamonds," Bedi adds.

"Greed, as I said."

The doctor joins from the theatre, dropping his blood-soaked gown on the way.

"I'm losing my way here, and I need blood," he says.

"Two thoracic surgeons and blood, will be dropped on this ship within minutes, doc. You just have to hang on," Kieron encourages.

"There'll be no more killing on my ship," the captain states, full of unresolved suspicion. She nods demanding Kieron continue as the unmistakable sound of a helicopter draws near and hovers.

"We have a killer to catch," Kieron starts.

"He left on lifeboat with supplies to other ship," Bedi explains.

The doctor goes back, calling Bjørg to help. He has more pressing matters.

"We have a team on that ship watching the boat unload," Kieron says.

"I'll make sure Captain Spinazzola is aware and his team arrest the thief," captain Walker says.

"No. We need him to lead us to his boss or his partner who has to be an IT specialist with tendrils deep inside your systems," Kieron adds.

"Too late," Bedi says bluntly. "He has lifeboat and going towards islands." She is looking at a text from Dwight, and it turns to an incoming call. "Dwight. We should get on chopper?"

"Only one of you. One stays with the team," Dwight insists.

"I go," Bedi says, closing the call to Dwight and looking at the captain. "Now, next killing not on your ship."

Kieron puts his arm around her waist and holds her, giving her a look of concern. They break and she is gone.

41 – TWO DOWN, ONE UP

Pulling the headset off the surgeon's head as his feet touch down on the ship's upper sun deck, Bedi fits it on her head. She puts her arms in the loop for a quick lift and eventual release, then waits impatiently for the blood and the other medic to be untethered.

"Go pilot, go pilot," she shouts as soon as she can. "Put me on lifeboat going to the island. Go!"

In the strong downdraft from the rotors, the medic and doctor run away. Like a spider dangling on a thread the chopper raises Bedi up and then dips forward and powers away in the direction of the lifeboat, which is heading for Freeport, hours away.

On the MS Amatheia Billy has a gun to a ship's engineer. He forces the able seaman to swing a new lifeboat out over the sea on its cradle arm. Hanging over the water, the two men have no connection with the ship apart from its cables. Billy takes the remote and lowers it on maximum speed. The craft is dropping faster than normally happens but not fast enough for Billy. He looks at the mechanical release handle and takes the safety pin out.

"No, too high," the engineer panics. "No!"

Billy pulls the release. The boat drops. Crash! It hits the water and both crush to the floor, shocked and winded. Billy is up first and climbs to the driver's position.

At sea, the thief drives the first lifeboat flat out sitting with his head above the open top. Bedi hangs on the wire as the chopper swoops in. He fires at her, now swinging and twisting like a spider on a thread in the wind as the chopper slows.

As her arm comes around, and her sight is on the boat, she fires back. Bullets are exchanged, neither with much chance of hitting the distant moving target.

"Get me closer," Bedi shouts into her comms-set.

"Negative. You will be shot."

"Get me in before I shoot you!"

The chopper swoops lower and shots exchange back and forth. The boat is hit, once, twice and a third. The thief drops to the inside, a more protected driving position, and pulls the craft from one side then the other, still aiming for the islands. The chopper swoops after it. He pops up and fires.

"We're going up, I am not risking the bird," the pilot says.

"Drop me," she shouts, firing again.

A bullet rips through her side and flesh and blood fan out in the wind. She falls free of the harness, hits the top of the small boat, bounces on the orange roof leaving red blood, and then bounces down the side.

The chopper dips low and powers away as the chord is pulled in. It circles around looking for her with every intention of getting her out of the sea. The boat driver sits back in his seat and powers to the island.

"Come in agent. Come in. We're coming round for you, over," the pilot says, he and his crew looking down at the sea.

Billy powers past the search area to pursue the thief. The two boats, both fitted with twin 170hp diesel engines begin a 6-knot chase just minutes apart. If Billy can catch him, the twin rudders will mean a cat and mouse weave and pounce until there is a winner.

Seeing Billy coming in from the side to cut him off, the thief pulls his boat hard about and heads in the other direction, towards Freeport, which is back past his ship.

Billy tries to second guess the move and pulls a wider circle, hoping to keep the killer near the Aerwyna. The move puts a greater distance between the two orange boats, normally a preserve for life and now out to kill each other. He needs a second player to box him in; he needs Kieron.

42 – I'LL FIND IT

Like a whirlwind as powerful as the rotor blades they left behind, the surgeon dashes down the steel crew steps with his medic who carries a backpack full of blood. Bypassing all guest areas, they arrive at the medical centre ten decks below their drop zone, sucking for air. Disrobing from their jumpsuits, they are both totally focussed on Hunter's state and listening to every word of the medical history fired at them.

"OK. His veins are shutting down, let's get a new cannula in," the surgeon demands, pulling on clean scrubs and gloves.

His medic pulls out the blood bags and hangs them, them draws the nurse's attention to check them.

"O-positive, O-positive, O-positive. I have four more in the cold bag."

The nurse who had been assisting begins to tap along Hunter's arm in search of a new vein. None of them have any swelling, let alone enough to insert a needle. Kieron moves in, lifts his arm, and tightens a plastic tourniquet around the upper arm.

"I'll get it."

He grabs the top of the arm and squeezes down, pushing all the captured blood down holding it below his strong hands. The veins have no option other than to bulge. The nurse easily gets a long cannula in and tapes it. Kieron lets go and removes the tie.

"Nurse, I need irrigation on this neck," the surgeon demands.

The ship's doctor is fascinated at the in-the-field-like operation, but Kieron needs him to save Croc.

"Doctor, can you move next door and work on young Croc?" Kieron asks the ship's medical chief. It is as much a demand as a request. "Killing and mending, guess that's what they taught us all."

"I was never taught the killing."

"Never met a doctor who couldn't handle a gun."

"I never served."

"You are now. It's part of staying alive. Now, I need these two fixed up."

"He's A-positive," the medic says handing him one blood bag and showing that he has more.

Captain Veronica Walker enters.

"Your Russian KGB agent was hit by a bullet and dropped into the sea; the helicopter is running a grid looking for her. Do they bring her here or take her to Freeport or Miami?" she asks.

"Miami, we have our hands full here," the surgeon says, without taking his eyes off the blood leaking from the new father, Hunter Witowski. "And if I can keep this guy alive and make him fit for flight, this one's gonna need a flight to Miami. Not a winch, he'd be dead before he got to the helicopter. There's a Cessna Citation Bravo in Fort Lauderdale permanently installed with intensive care equipment. I'm gonna need to be with him every step of the way."

"Can he not go on the other ship, overnight into Miami?" Kieron asks.

The surgeon's look is a firm negative answer.

43 – THE CHASE

The sea might be flat, but at six-knots the lifeboat is finding a rhythm as it bounces on the water that resists it. Hanging onto one of the small mooring buoys at the side of the killer's boat, and on the blind side of Billy's view, is Bedriška. She is gritting her teeth, fighting for air, and using every muscle to stay on, let alone trying to rise out of the sea. With every bounce of the boat, she is slammed back onto the water. Her blood mixes with the white horses made on each painful impact, and the bubbles turn red. With the groan of a tennis player, she lifts her leg up and weaves it into the rope that loops the buoys around the edge of the boat. She twists over so her face is down in the sea raging under her, and she pushes up. Then grabs up in search of a grip, any grip.

Using his complex watch, the killer locks the route destination on Freeport. He checks the chopper, which has left him and is making an obvious search and rescue sweep. He can see Billy the other side. He takes the crew's bottle of water and steps down to take a moment, sniggering at the ship he will pass again soon and toasting it. He is hit hard, and plunges face first into the steel floor. Bedi is on top of him screeching like a banshee.

Her forearm digs hard into his throat under his chin, and she pulls, harder and harder, her nostrils bulging wide as she sucks in for oxygen and power.

"Die, motherfucker."

He struggles, not to release himself from the grip but to wriggle forward. He pulls them under a bench, where they are squeezed in and his demise looks certain, but he reverse-headbutts her upwards, and again. Her nose splits, the back of her head plants into the steel and wood of the bench and she loses grip on his throat and control. He rolls over and with an outstretched arm wheels her into the floor. He then brings his raised elbow down into her messed-up face. Blood runs from her side, her nose, and her head. She looks finished.

But as he stands, her leg kicks hard into his crutch making it his turn to suck air. She has little left to offer, no power, no acceleration and she is a sitting target. He has discomfort but is less impaired. He stamps down into her face, then again. She is finished. He bends and lifts her limp body onto his shoulder.

"Big mistake, miss KGB. Never underestimate," he says, with an angry Mexican accent.

44 – 2 DIMENSIONAL

Macey sits alone in the middle of the theatre stalls on the MS Amatheia. She is lamely sketching the flashing curtain in front of her that lights the whole theatre. The young Hotel Manager accompanied by a security officer, both in their white short sleeved uniform shirts, drift in. The Hotel Manager moves along the row towards her.

"May I?"

"Please sit," Macey says, offering one of her huge smiles. "Macey."

"I know, I've seen some of your work. Spectacular," he says, with just a hint of a flirt.

"Thank you."

"I'm James, the hotel manager. This isn't your normal subject matter."

"Does it show?"

"Perhaps I shouldn't judge until the final work."

"That's very respectful of the art," she laughs. "But this is not engaging me, and I fear will never be finished. If it is, it won't be in any recognisable form."

"What's not engaging?"

"Flat light. Two dimensional."

"Yes, the lighting team have to learn a whole new way of working. The subjects are back lit by the show on the curtain. The technical team have to front light, and we hope for three dimensions."

Macey is nodding, but not necessarily in agreement.

"The last hotel I worked at, on land. They brought in the same changes. I think they're here to stay."

"And the audience present a fourth dimension?" she asks.

The officer laughs.

"Always. Hey, someone's just stolen a lifeboat and jumped ship. It wasn't the two guys who came with you?"

Macey looks to him slowly.

"As if I can escape management. They're backstage. No, we are walking the ship for clues, but I'm happy to sit this out and chat with you."

The hotel manager gives the slightest of nods and his attending security partner makes for the stage. Macey lifts her camera phone.

"He couldn't do a little dance and give it some dimension?"

"I doubt it."

Covertly, she fingers the pad. 'Security looking for two of you.'

Ricky is walking from the dressing room access steps at the back of the stage. From his perspective, the back of the light curtain is in front of him, and the focus of its light is out to the audience. Hidden in the dark he watches Sandip and four other stagehands move the old wooden sets sideways, the ones he was shown yesterday on his tour. The light spill becomes harsh sunshine as a large stage door is opened and he can hide no longer. He walks forward, watching the sets lifted out onto the promenade deck

"Where are they going?"

"They will be taken off in Miami, sir," Sandip says.

"So, are you out of a job?"

"No, sir. I hope not sir," Sandip replies, lifting the next section, Ricky takes the other end.

"You switch the curtain on and off?"

"No, sir. He does that," Sandip says, pointing at a colleague, Kusay, as he passes back into the stage."

"I work the lighting desk; I start and stop the show," Kusay says lingering in the doorway to reply.

"That easy?" Ricky asks, as they put the section down against the bulkhead.

"I hope so, sir. I have been taught the show, and I take the cues from the stage manager."

"Sounds easy. Where is it loaded?"

"In my lighting box, at the back."

"On a computer?"

Kusay nods.

"How does it get onto your computer?"

"It arrives in my downloads."

"From where?"

"I don't know. There is an email address for questions."

As they walk back into the dark the security officer is waiting.

"I have some questions, so I'll need that address," Ricky says. He watches Kusay and Sandip lift the next section.

"I give question to production manager, he gets answers, so he knows everything," Kusay says walking out into the sunlight.

"Come on lift the other end," Ricky says to the security officer taking the last and biggest piece.

"I am working, sir. I will return to my office. Where is your friend?

"Outside, for a cigarette. Come on, lift."

"Kusay and Sandip are here now," the security officer says, and he leaves.

"He will not do manual labour, sir. He is an officer," Sandip says, smiling. The three lift the last section out.

"Stupid one," Ricky laughs to himself.

45 – THINK TANK

The Miami hub is as dark as ever. The light comes from a large screen where Billy looms large, bouncing with his camera as his boat races on.

"Dwight, I'm on him. I can take him, but there's no evasive action. It worries me."

"Could be a trap," Dwight suggests.

"That's what I figure. If he was in the theatre, and had explosives, I'd expect it to blow as I jump on."

"Theatre?" Amy asks Dwight.

"Of war," he tells her, then he is full on to Billy. "It's full of fuel so let's expect he's been busy. He's no clown. Just give it a nudge."

"I've got a plan."

"Billy!" Dwight warns, but too late. The picture went before he finished.

Amy and Jake look at Dwight shocked.

"Will he be alright?" Amy asks.

"It's how you get your customers," he tells them.

For most of their medical careers, Amy and Jake have dealt with the many who have lost limbs. However, they have never been close to the risk-taking and listened to a soldier before the incident.

"His calm is frightening," Jake says.

"Billy's good. We concentrate on our job." Dwight twists in small shuffles. "The killer's in the wind with the diamonds. His partner, the brains in IT, could be anywhere, but they don't have the diamonds. The killer could be going rogue, and, on the run, but the brains could feel trapped and let down. Macey has had suspicious crew sniffing around, but maybe they're simply confused."

"Don't you want the crew on-side. Enlighten them," Amy suggests.

"We don't know who's who. Or, where the killer's partner is hidden?"

Izzy steps in.

"The ambulance is the air. It'll land by the ship in about 20 minutes. I've told Kieron." Izzy pauses, she is noticeably uncomfortable. "We don't normally operate with an audience."

"Is that in your new rule book?"

Izzy looks reprimanded and does not pursue the point, but Dwight can see she feels wronged.

"This is my medical team," Dwight defends.

"Hey, look, as fun as this is, I have a family at home and a dozen crime channels on TV," Jake says.

"I've no one at home, and I'm free until seven if you don't mind," Amy offers.

"She looks after me," Dwight says, to finally close the book on Izzy's concern.

Amy smiles, enjoying his company and learning more about a man she hardly knows.

"The plane's for your man who went down?" she asks.

"Three down," Izzy cuts. "Two I expect on that plane, one is my brother."

Dwight turns to her sharply. "Sorry, Izzy. I completely forgot."

"So, do I get to go to the hospital?"

"Sure, if you need to. We should also tell Mary and Stan," Dwight adds.

"You mean, would I call our mom?"

"No, you don't have to, Izzy."

"I can do it," Izzy says, firmly.

"Are you sure?"

Izzy fires him a look to ask why she might not.

"I've been speaking to Croc on the phone, he's fine. The doctor on board wants the clinic free for further problems."

"Two on the plane," Amy starts. "You said three down."

"One is lost at sea," Dwight says, thinking. "I've got just over an hour to get to his wife Elaine, take her and the baby to the hospital, then get you back."

"Me?" Amy asks, thinking.

"I can go with you to Elaine's," Izzy insists.

"Then who runs point here?" he asks her. "Elaine's a baby-sitting job."

Too late, he realises he may have insulted Amy.

"I could do with your help," he says to Amy. "Just until seven."

Amy smiles at him. He has no idea where she is going at seven, or who she is seeing, but he needs her now. He turns and opens a voice channel.

"Billy come in."

46 – TURNAROUND

Billy's boat sweeps in sideways and rams the Mexican killer's boat side on, and they both bounce. He can see Bedi is tied to the wheel, upside down, her legs trying to reach for purchase to help hold her up. Blood runs down her face and into her hair. She keeps spitting out, so as not to drown in her own blood. He knows she is alive and conscious. He takes his belt and ties his steering wheel to hold his boat pushed into the side of hers.

"I've found Bedi," he shouts into comms. "Get that chopper hovering on stand-by."

He drops the comms and goes to back to the side door at mid boat. Using his strength, he positions the two boats welded together by rudder force, he needs to get the door openings lined up.

"Hang on, Bedi!"

As keen as he is to get on, and as hard as his body is working, his eyes are searching and his mind evaluating.

"Bedi, where is he?"

She is not capable of speech. He sees no signal from her, but as the doors line up, he can assess the back of the boat where the garbage blocks are burning. The killer had expected Billy to catch up and the fire is set to blow the full fuel tank. The killer is not on the boat, the boat is the new killer. Billy jumps. He looks to the flame, then to the front where Bedi is dying slowly. She will die for sure when it blows as she is bound and incapable of survival. He rushes to her, determined they survive any blast and better still get to the other boat first.

Bedi is a mess. Each arm is cable-tied to the wheel, and there is a very tight tie around her neck, keeping her head down. She has used every ounce of energy to suspend herself and keep her bodyweight off her throat. The two boats crash into each other again and the sea forces them up and bangs them down. Holding her up, Billy flicks his knife open and carefully reaches for her neck. But they are hit by flaring fire burning a build-up of waste fumes. He drops his knife and her and she gags. Darting to hold her up again, he grasps her tight as they are hit by a second flare. His knife slides away across the deck. It is out of reach. Their boat comes off a rise and hits the sea hard as the boat next to them catches a wave side on. They duck as it lumbers up over them and rolls away. Every muscle in Billy's face is ripped tight as he looks back to assess the fire, then down to his knife.

"Hold-on, tight, now!"

He drops and grabs the knife, rises, and carefully forces the razor-sharp blade between her neck and the plastic tie. The boat bounces, and he pulls, her head is free. Both arms are released, and he folds her gently to the deck, placing Bedriška on her side to stop her choking on her own blood. He has two lives to save. He stops the power and the boat calms, now the other boat can circle them, having righted itself and the wheel is tied to a tight side rudder steer.

"If he jumped on there as I jumped off, he ain't going anywhere," Billy says to himself.

Bedi tries to speak.

"Enough, rest a moment, I'll be back."

Although the flames are no longer being fanned by headwind, the fire is looking death in the eye. He breaks out the fire extinguisher, charging into it and spraying, while pulling life jackets from under a bench and tossing them back at Bedi. The fire extinguisher is not meant for such a fire and runs out without the job complete.

Checking Bedi as he steps over her, he climbs up, powers the boat even though he knows the fire will be re-oxygenated. He drives at the other circling boat from inside the wide circle in is making around him. He leaves the wheel a moment and sits Bedi up.

"We're gonna have to jump onto the other boat."

Bedi nods, and tries to talk, but he won't allow it. He forces her arms into life jacket straps then jumps up.

He is back driving at the sister boat, which he hits and nudges, so they are together. He takes another life jacket and arranges the straps to hold the boats together.

"Bedi! I'm coming for you."

Right hand on the wheel, he uses less and less force and tests the bond. He leaves it and squats for her.

"Arms round my neck."

Bedi tries to grip him, but she has little left. He drags her to the door with the fire is raging around them.

"Come on. One push."

But he can't pull the boats together and hold her. The fire starts to flare and crackle again.

"Go," she says to him.

Billy heaves her around his back, but Bedi knows she can't hold on. She knows the boat will blow; she knows he must get safe. The boats bounce away, then together and Billy jumps, Bedi drops into the sea. The boats crash together over her. He momentarily looks back for her, then at the flames, and he runs for the driving position and cuts the power. The rogue boat races ahead. It blows covering him in debris.

Billy runs to the back of his boat and sees Bedi in the water hanging onto the lifejackets. He dives in and swims to her. His instant thought being it will be so much quicker to swim than trying to bring the craft about.

"Don't you die on me," he spurts, getting to her.

She forces a smile.

"Killer jumped off near ship, he's gone back to the Aerwyna," she manages and then she passes out. He needs to swim back to his boat, with her, and warn them.

47 – GOOD LUCK

The pontoon at the side on the ship has unusually been fixed longways out to sea so the ICU plane can draw up to it and the wings just be safe. It is an operation that would only be attempted in the flattest sea. Kieron gives one last look inside and fires an order.

"You hang on now bro'."

The engine increases power and Kieron runs inside where he is met by an officer holding a phone.

"Dwight," he answers, and listens a moment.

"Plane has taken off, warn Croc."

Kieron rushes back to the pontoon and looks up to the plane which is just going behind the ship so it can't be seen. He looks all around the pontoon but can see nothing.

"I want armed guards watching this pontoon being brought back in and staying aimed at the sea until that door closes," he demands, then he turns and looks all around him.

"You're already back on, aren't you?" he says to himself.

In the air, the medics are still working on Hunter and trying to stabilise him. Blood bags hang above him, a plasma bag and another clear bag. Croc is being redressed but is on his mobile.

"What?" he exclaims, still listening. "You think the killer's hitching a ride on this plane? It ain't a box-car,"

Despite his humour, he is concerned, and he moves away from the work being done on him and looks out of the window.

"What?" the aircrew asks him.

"We might have a passenger. On the floats."

"Good luck to him, we've enough worries inside."

"No, he's the guy that did this, he's a killer and will kill us all to take the plane," Croc explains. "Pass me that flare gun, loaded."

"Are you crazy?"

"No, open up and hold my legs."

"No."

"Or we all die," Croc says, wrapping his wrist around the leather strap beside the door and holding himself waiting to be handed the gun. The door opens.

Aircrew hold the door back. Croc bends over the edge, held by the legs, and looks below.

"Pull me back, pull me back!"

His second fight is to get back inside.

"No one there right," aircrew snigger to him.

"Not below, he is being towed behind on a rope."

They look at him shocked as they try and look before closing the door. Croc is on his cell.

"Dwight. He's not here. He must have gone back to the ship," he shouts.

"Wrong ship, it's not the one going home." Dwight shouts back via Croc's speaker.

"There's something he wants on that ship. Something else that was in that safe. Something worth more than the diamonds, which makes sense of why he stayed," Hunter says.

Croc and the aircrew turn to the patient in shock. He is awake. Hunter smiles and passes out again.

48 – BABYSITTING

Sitting in the back of a Miami taxicab, pulling into Coral Gable, an upmarket domestic area of Miami, Amy is blown away by the houses, as much as the escalation of the conversation she has been allowed to hear.

"Do you need to go back?" she asks.

"No, I need to see Elaine, and get her to Hunter," Dwight says. "I'll get you back by seven."

"I can make a call and cancel."

"An understanding boyfriend," Dwight fishes.

"I'm not a one-man girl, never have been."

Dwight is confused but decides not to become a fool by asking further. He is capable of being that without opening his mouth.

"Your buddy is not the usual soldier. Homes in here must start at two or three million."

"Money means nothing to him at the moment," he says softly, pulling into their drive and preparing himself for the moment.

"Are you OK?"

"I've had to do this too many times. Far too many."

Elaine opens the door with surprise. She met Hunter on a cruise ship and was never his wife while he was serving. The presence of Dwight, with a female colleague, takes a few seconds for her to equate the necessary fear. She collapses.

Inside, Amy is nursing the baby in the bedroom, as Elaine flusters around.

"Slow down," Dwight consoles. "He ain't gonna get there any faster; he's in the air."

"I want to meet him at the plane."

"Let's not slow him down, just slow you down."

Elaine had been kidnapped long ago in the heist of a cruise ship. She wished that had never happened. She wished he had never met Kieron. She wished the agency had never started. She stops.

"Let's go. What I've got will have to do."

Amy is not about to hurry, and Dwight had never walked up the stairs before on his temporary limbs, and down will be slower. He hovers at the top in fear, as the two girls wait at the bottom.

"Dwight, you're walking," Elaine says.

"Not quite."

"Sit down. Come down on your ass," Amy orders.

"Yes, fast," Elaine agrees, impatiently.

Orders like these and the situation have moved Dwight's progress on faster than weeks of gym. However, later, he will be tired, and sore. He uses the rails to sit.

Amy drives Elaine's car back into Miami with Elaine asking questions that neither her or Dwight can answer. Dwight sits quietly enjoying the baby asleep in her seat next to him. His cell-phone goes again, and he is quick to take the call; he does not want it on speaker.

"The plane landed; all is good. He'll be at the hospital waiting for us," Dwight says, knowing the last bit was dressed up a little by him.

The reception area is calm, cold, and business-like, often thought to be without feeling, engaging only to root for information which will allow them to be efficient. Inside is the opposite. In the theatre there is a controlled urgency driven by the need to save Hunter, and he is critical. He is now in an induced coma as they work.

In the observation room above, Elaine stands pressed up against the glass. She is being allowed to say a few words via an intercom into the theatre, coached by Amy, who the medical staff have immediately seen as an assistance.

"Hunter. I love you. Macey-Isabella's here. She loves you, get better for us."

The doctor acknowledges the input, and Amy knows that means the pair of them should go, even though neither can see behind his mask and gown.

Dwight lays the baby in a room they have been allocated and he spreads out the things that were cobbled together. It appears a lot of stuff, but he has not had a baby. Elaine returns with Amy.

"I wanna be alone now. I want to wait for him."

Amy looks at her watch and immediately feels guilty as Dwight has noticed.

"Look, I'll take Amy, and come back," Dwight suggests.

"Take my car, Dwight. Take Macey-Isabella, and some feeding bottles and let me concentrate on Hunter."

"I'll be back real soon," he says.

"I just want him back. Mai sleeps for the night, she's good. But feed her if she wakes."

"She sleeps?" Dwight asks.

"Why? Did Hunter say she kept him up all night?"

Dwight nods, she acknowledges, and they prepare to leave.

"I'll take you to the clinic for your truck," Dwight suggests to Amy as they leave.

"I don't wanna be late, you can come with me."

"And meet the boyfriend, boyfriends?"

"Yeah. All of them."

49 - BASKET CASE

Dwight is thinking while he is entranced by Mai sleeping deeply, rocked by the gentle rhythm of the journey.

"What do you think of when you think of diamonds?" he asks.

"Bling. Excess. Bullshit."

"I was asking Mai but as she's asleep, thanks. Although, they weren't the answers I was looking for. What do most folks think of the word?"

"Oh! What would a younger girl say? Well, maybe engagement ring, or gemstone. Older women like me, maybe forgery, stupidity."

"OK. Try and help me out here, you're not getting this game. More on the wealth, sales, theft, greed line."

"Money. Richness. Investment, maybe. Safe deposit. Rich old people. Rappers. Footballers with ear-rings."

"Stop there, Amy. I like the safe deposit."

"You're welcome," she grins, as he is once again holding his cell to his ear.

"You were a lot more relaxed before today," she says.

It is Dwight's turn to grin.

"The pandemic meant no cruising, so no work. I was all yours," he teases.

"Well, let's try and get back to that."

"Izzy," Dwight starts into his cell. "If he's gone back to the ship, he's after something he has yet to get. Think on things we missed, like a key. A safe deposit key. Or, what else could have been in that safe?"

The car stops at a large modern sports centre. Dwight looks up, none the wiser.

"Can I rush in, you come in with the rug-rat? It's got ramps, grab bars. Well equipped, and easy entrance."

Dwight is floored by her terminology and haste.

"How will I know where you are?"

"You'll see me," she says, fascinated by the complexity unfolding before her as she throws the over engineered baby-stroller open. "Wow, bet this is a few months rental on my apartment. Here, use this as a walker, and go slow. You are going to be beat tonight."

Dwight walks into the normal noise of a gym with an active game and crowd cheering. But the building's access features, for so many different disabilities, is not lost on him. He follows the noise and walks around past the fabricated stadium-like seating to the court where he sees a fast-moving, wheelchair basketball match. Amy is the coach. She is on the side-line, gesticulating, and shouting, then giving precise notes in the time-out.

"Well, I never. Would you look at this, Mai?" Dwight says to the sleeping baby.

He takes a seat in the corner on the lower bench, stroller beside him with the child turned away from the match's flying ball. He is still working, his cell tight to his ear.

"Izzy, set up a meeting first thing tomorrow morning, with the cruise line Chief Operations Officer, Casey B. de Michelle. I think she's in the Palm Beach office. Tell her I'll drive to her."

The court erupts as an incredible three-pointer is netted.

"You taken the evening off?"

"I'm still working, and I'll be back at the hospital before Hunter wakes up. Croc can come with me in the morning if they discharge him and he's up to it."

Dwight ends the call. He is enjoying every twist and turn of the game to the point of neglecting any updates on his cell, until a call demands his attention. He sees the caller is Mary, and that he also has one message. He decides to read the update before he might be questioned on matters that he has no knowledge of. 'Croc has taken a turn for the worse. In surgery. I'm worried. Izzy.'

"Mary!" he answers, immediately recognising her barrage. He puts her on speaker to hear her as the crowd noise is so high.

"Don't you Mary me! Why's Macey ring me and call me mom? What's wrong? Then the girl can't speak. Something happened to my boy?"

"He'll be fine. He's being fixed up at 'the general'. So is Hunter, who has been stabbed. Elaine has a family room. I'll send you a cab."

"I'll get my own cab. My boy in hospital and you went to a game? You left Elaine looking after that baby while you went to a game?"

"The baby is with me."

"In that noise?"

"It was impossible to get you and Stan to the hospital before I had to leave…"

"To be a baby-sitter when my son's hurt?"

"I didn't mean that."

"Well, you get my god-daughter back here out of that noise, she must be frightened senseless."

Dwight looks at Mai in the stroller and she is fast asleep and smiling.

"Mai's smiling."

"That's wind, get her back here. Stan can look after her," Mary orders.

"I think as parents you should be with Croc, not baby-sitting."

"Stan ain't Croc's father."

50 – THAT MEXICAN

The ship's sea door is open again, but no pontoon is out. Billy has pulled the lifeboat alongside and is smiling as he always does. He looks a little wrecked, but jokes about it.

"Annoying little mo-fo, that Mexican."

Inside, the ship security officers stand each side of the opening to protect against the killer. The team of medics climb on board the boat, with a stretcher for the wounded Russian agent. Bedi walks out.

"I need a drink."

Kieron steps forward and hugs her, then produces a half bottle of vodka. She grabs his head, and kisses him hard on the lips, then spins the top off and glugs a good amount down. Shocked, she stops to address him.

"You added water!"

Kieron offers to take back the faulty product, but she keeps it.

Billy joins them.

"She's hard. Hard as concrete nails."

"Yeah," Kieron agrees. He shakes Billy's hand and hugs him. "Thanks."

The medics insist they should take her away, but she is not moving.

"They got better alcohol in the clinic. Get that bullet removed and then a bandage," Kieron says.

"I want proper drink sent down."

"Go. I'll get it sent. Billy, you should go too and get checked out"

"I don't need to, I'm fine," Billy says, even though he looks wrecked.

"Get washed and changed, we've gotta have dinner with the captain," Kieron tells him as Bedi leaves.

"Be a dear; ask one of the staff to get my case from my yacht," Billy says sarcastically, in a mock English accent.

"Use Hunter's room, his clothes are your size."

"The man's a gentleman."

Kieron turns to a junior officer sent to work with him.

"Officer, show him to A617 and let him in. I'll be up to change within minutes, then you can take us both to join Captain Walker."

Although the officer has been sent to shadow Commander Kieron Philips, he is torn. He has two agents to watch. Three if you count Bedriška. As he thinks, they ignore him. Kieron walks to the lifeboat where security have boarded. He watches them search every nook and cranny of the craft. Billy walks to the elevator and presses for a lift but looks back as the doors begin to close.

"He ain't that easy to find."

Kieron knows. He also knows it's likely he's already on the ship.

"Check over the edges and in the water then get this door closed," he orders. Kieron has no standing on the ship, so the security officers are confused. However, they have lost their leader and they have been told to keep the killer off. The boat pulls away, losing contact with the ship. With hi-beam torches tracing the sides, it spins around slowly so it can be watched. It settles under its winch and the new crew attach it to be lifted. Kieron sees it rise with water falling from it, lit red from the setting sun.

"Let's get the ship door closed and locked," he says, leaving. In the elevator, he checks his watch and his cell-phone for messages. There is the one from Izzy about her brother.

Outside, the raised boat swings into its place on the ship by its dedicated cradle arm. Kieron walks along the promenade deck by the rail and looks from the sea to the lifeboats hanging above him. He doesn't see the Mexican holding on the blind side like a limpet, but the Mexican sees him, and is moving around the rim. He walks towards the front and speaks with the officer who has been posted to watch the ship's main anchoring chain. It is nearly dark now and in readiness, the heavy chain is lit with a search light.

"Nothing?"

"No, sir. He has not come onto the ship."

"Oh, trust me. He's back on. Somewhere."

51 - DINNER

Billy looks very smart in Hunter's dinner suit. He walks with Kieron into the main dining area. The Maître'D then leads them to the captain's table, which is large and oval in the raised centre area of the glittering gold and silver main dining room, but it is only set for four. Dressed immaculately, the captain and her officer companion, the hotel manager stand.

"Captain. Sir," Billy says, respecting rank.

"Captain Walker. This is Billy, one of the men we had on the MS Amatheia."

"I'm James Grüner, Hotel Manager," the other senior officer says.

They nod in acknowledgement and sit. The wine-waiter pours white wine, as the head waiter hands the menus out and greets them.

"I could get used to this," Billy says.

"Please don't. Not on my ship," the captain Veronica Walker says. "Strangely, my company still insists they never booked your agency."

Kieron is attracted to her calm control.

"The head of our Miami office is going in to see your COO tomorrow. Let's suggest they get that ironed out, but to rest that matter for now, we have been paid a first payment by bank transfer," he says.

"From our main company account, which is even more worrying," the captain agrees. "Something is going on, which we might have well booked investigators or brought the police in for."

The captain controls her distraction better than James as Bedi swans up to the table in her body-hugging, glittering dress, that reveals the line of the bandage but as usual, no underwear lines. She can't remember the last time she left the uniform to wear an evening dress.

"Ah. Our KGB officer. I thought you were in the medical centre," Captain Walker says, as she attracts the staff's attention to set a fifth place.

"Normally just rehab," she says.

The waiter offers her wine, but she refuses the glass.

"Big glass, like red wine. Please fill with Vodka, some ice," she says, before the self-introductions.

"Captain Walker."

"James Grüner, Hotel Manager," He smiles, his blue eyes wide open.

"Bedriška Kossoff, hired killer," she grins. She loves pushing boundaries with people who feel they are important and although she respects rank and ship etiquette Bedi also took on board that the captain did not offer her first name. Kieron knows Bedi's style.

"Haven't I seen you somewhere before?" Billy asks Bedi, amused.

"If you see me, you remember," she jokes.

"To the matter in hand; we have a killer trying to get back on my ship?" Captain Walker asks.

"I've posted guards to walk the decks all night, and a man on each anchor," James says.

"He come back whether you like it or not," she says.

"I will try and stop that happening," James suggests.

"My guess is that he's on," Kieron says.

"Maybe even eating dinner and watching us," Billy smiles, toasting the room.

"He's after something and it's not a few diamond rings," Kieron reveals.

"But he's a diamond thief?" James continues to probe. He appears to ask most of the questions so the captain can take in the answers and think.

"He's too well trained to worry about a few more rings," Billy says.

"Maybe he's in love."

"You mean he's come back for a partner?" Kieron asks.

"Exactly. The IT expert who is opening doors and safes, someone deep in our systems as you suggest," James says.

"No. Even if they were here, and I doubt it, they'd be better off without him. They can walk off next time you dock," Kieron offers. "He has a different task."

"Whoever booked you appears to have had a different purpose in mind to the one you imagined," the captain suggests.

"I think you're spot on, Captain," Kieron says.

"They wanted us to find the diamonds and take them back to Miami," Billy says.

"But they don't need these low-end diamonds. What they needed wasn't in what we or he found. Or he would have gone, and it would be over. The diamonds are a cover. We were a cover, and it's gone wrong for him," Kieron suggests. "So, we would like your help, ma'am."

"You need my help? I'm down my head of security and an officer. Plus, I've lost a lifeboat since you've been on this ship," the captain says.

"We need each other," Bedi toasts with her large glass of vodka, which they watch her drink down. She holds the glass up at arm's length for a refill and the partners can see her silver dress is red with blood.

Billy is quick to go to the serving stand and requisition a white tablecloth. Within seconds, the two men excuse themselves, and walk the relaxed Bedi away, dangling the cloth to avoid a scene.

The captain nods for James to follow them. James agrees without any further encouragement.

52 – TIME FLIES

The wheelchair version of basketball normally has four quarters lasting 10 minutes each, as opposed to 12 minutes. The midweek league, with its travel and complications is kept to 7 minutes a quarter. At nine thirty the stadium erupts. Dwight leaps to his legs without thinking. The stroller rocks and he has to save himself from stumbling. He is celebrating Amy's victory, but it is still lost on the sleeping baby, Mai.

At the right moment, he walks onto the court with the stroller as his prop. He waits for the much in demand Amy.

"Ritter!" He hears. It is a shout from a soldier speeding to him with a hand high. "Sorry you had to join us, man."

"Nelson," he says, hi-fiving his old buddy. He smiles from ear to ear knowing he is one of a new comradeship. He remembers sending Nelson off on a medivac. Amy turns and hugs him.

"I haven't enjoyed myself that much for I don't know how long," he says, euphorically. "I like basketball, why'd you never ask me?"

"You weren't eligible?"

His cell goes, Mai wakes, the crowd cheer the team's victory run. He now needs to multitask in a different way.

"Weren't what?" he asks Amy.

"All my guys have mastered their prosthesis before they can try-out. I've gotta small dance troop too. They are amazing and should be doing displays. You can help in many ways," she tempts.

He takes his cell call.

"Dwight," Izzy says to him.

Amy watches as he listens and his face drops. She waits to be informed.

"I gotta go," he tells her. He is a mixture of shocked, sad, and serious. "He's not gonna make it."

"Is that Hunter, or Croc?" she asks him hesitantly.

"I didn't ask," Dwight says, surprised. "Izzy was an emotional wreck. I just assumed Hunter. I'm sure she said 'he.' Yeah. Bedi was at dinner on the ship, she's fine. It must be one of them."

"I'm coming," Amy says. We're stronger together."

53 – CHARTING

The captain has not joined the reformed group for an after-dinner drink. James, the hotel manager sits with Billy in the dimly lit, well-polished dark-wood and brass Chart Room. Kieron is not there, but his drink is. Only they know the confusion the day continues to bring. The few others in the bar are merely enjoying a quiet evening. Kieron drifts back.

"Izzy's not picking up. We should focus on our job. The Mexican wants something; what?"

"Just had one-line from Dwight," Billy says.

Kieron looks at his cell phone again.

"Think safe deposit boxes," Billy aims at James, curiously.

"Yeah, we have them. Safe deposit boxes are available throughout the fleet. You can order as you book, or ask at the purser's desk," James explains.

"I guess they're not connected to the IT system?"

"No. They're old-fashioned keys."

Kieron smiles thoughtfully. "Let's assume, the real prize is in a safe deposit."

"They're small."

"How small?"

"Smaller than the room safe. You wouldn't get a laptop in there. They're really used for special pieces of jewellery, maybe money."

"Why don't people use the cabin safes?" Billy asks.

"They do, but if they use the cabin one for cameras, cell-phones, keys, money, and passports, then maybe special jewellery and money will utilise a safe deposit box," James informs them. "No different from on land. Actually, some guests just like the idea of using them. It makes them feel special."

"Is there a master key?" Billy asks.

"No. We have spares locked away."

"Would he be after the contents of every box, like a heist," Billy asks.

"We have no guests."

"No," Kieron says. "It's one special box. The key should have been in one of the diamond safes. On the other two ships, he cleaned the jewellery shop's commercial safe out and there was no key. Here, he was interrupted. Then someone else cleaned the safe out."

Billy likes the idea.

"Feasible," James says.

Kieron is typing that into his cell.

"Let's open all the boxes," Billy grins. He brings a simplicity to most things.

"We can't do that," James hesitates. The captain will not allow it, and the purser looks after those keys as if they're the most valuable thing on the ship.

"Well, James. The Mexican will," Billy says.

"He can't do that," James says, thinking.

"If he wants to, he will. Then he'll set a huge fire to force an abandoned ship," Billy says. "He doesn't care."

"That's ridiculous. He can't go that far."

The two men look at James as if he is stupidly naive.

"We need security guards with the boxes," Kieron says.

"I don't have any more. They're already pulling double shifts to guard the decks."

"He might have already done it. You might have a safe room just full of dead people," Billy suggests, pushing for more immediate action.

James leads them off.

54 - WHAT'S SAFE?

The safe deposit box room is a narrow space behind the purser's office, which is at the rear of the hotel office, behind reception. The long and narrow area runs back between the small cabin size offices on either side of the middle section. It is full of workstations, desks, computers, a huge, large-paper-size copying machine, commercial paper trimmer, and piled up reams of paper. Everything appears normal and it is not, as feared, littered with dead bodies by the time they arrive.

The safe and boxes are at the more private far rear, where it is narrowest, and even more obviously squeezed between cabins in the bulkhead, squared by reception and the aft staircase at either end. Three big men is a crowd. The room contains many financial solutions: some larger safes, and then a small wall of boxes at the end.

"What are these?" Kieron asks, pointing to the bigger safes.

"This one's for foreign currency. This one is the purser's and the larger one is the casino's," James explains.

"How much does the casino safe carry?" Billy asks, keenly. Casinos form part of his Wild West enthusiasm.

"It can be a lot."

"No," Kieron says. "He's not after those. Without guests, those safes are not prime pickings. There's something going on, maybe illegal, that is worth far more. It sits in one safe deposit box, but he has no idea which one, until he finds the key."

"They," James corrects him. "The Mexican, and the person who sent him, who is well into our IT system. We have lots of IT engineers onboard."

"No, just the Mexican," Kieron says, still thinking. "They don't know which box, nor do they know which ship."

"How do you know?"

"Just possibilities, but serious conjecture."

"IT might be at head office," James suggests.

"More troubling, the Mexican has no idea it's this ship until he finds out who cleaned the safe out here."

The three walk out into the open work area and meet four junior officers that have been called to guard duty. James addresses them with Billy eavesdropping, as Kieron attends to his cell-phone again. When Billy and James turn back to Kieron, he is frozen like a statue and white as if the blood has drained from him.

"What's up, boss?" Billy asks.

"Hunter died."

The pause is chilling.

"I'm wearing a dead man's clothes," Billy slowly realises in a breathless whisper.

55 – NEW ERA

Midnight pierces the start of a new day. For this group it will be a new era. The agency has lost one of its owners, Elaine has lost her husband, and baby Mai has lost a father.

Until today, Amy was a nurse at the clinic and only knew Dwight as another amputee. Never did she see soldiers lost in the field, nor the effect it had on their families. Whilst all the amputees she worked with had lost something; maybe an identity, sometimes a family as Dwight had done, her clinic was a place of positivity. The staff made sure of that, but here she is powerless. The day that has just slipped away, taking Hunter Witowski with it, has rocked her life. With no idea how being positive is possible, she stands in a room, hugging a weeping woman she doesn't know. She never knew Hunter, though she will never forget this night, nor will Elaine, but baby Mai is asleep and will remember none of it. Time is a strange currency. Life is just a breath in the earth's 4.65-billion-year history. Elaine's hurt will be shorter still; but it won't feel that way for any of the group.

Dwight walks into Croc's room where he appears to be asleep. Mary and Stan sit at his bedside. Stan holds his flat cap in his lap with one hand, and his other hand holds Croc's ankle through the bedclothes. Stan looks more than lost; he is drained. Mary stands and faces Dwight.

"I'm gonna go and tell Macey, I doubt she knows. She might not be respectful, and gives me hell, but she should know," Mary says softly but full of anger.

"There's gonna be a lot of people we should tell, Mary. But does anyone know who they are? None of us knew anything about Hunter Witowski. My guess is Elaine doesn't. He lived an anonymous life and had his future and family stolen from him. And why?"

"Yeah. Why?" Mary says, and she bursts out.

"I've asked myself many times, never found the right answer," Dwight says.

Stan rises slowly, a broken man. Dwight knows he needs to hug him.

"You OK, Stan?"

"Just had the family I was never allowed to have, ripped away from me again," he says. He shuffles out.

Croc rolls over. He is not asleep.

"Twenty years old and I find out I have a real mom and dad. Hard enough to take in. Then, I find Stan's not my dad. And he finds out I'm not his son."

Dwight sees the subplot that has escaped in the night's other tragedy.

"In one night, I lose two men who felt like a real dad to me. Done stuff for me, like a real dad does," Croc says.

Dwight grips the steel bedframe and sits.

"What the fuck! You're walking?" Croc asks, as he sits up in amazement and some pain.

"Stan is still every bit a dad to you, son," Dwight says. "So's Kieron, and me."

"When did this happen? The world's changed."

"Yeah," Dwight drools. "How are you?" he says firmly changing the focus of the conversation.

"I'm alive."

"Good. Fit to go to the cruise company with me tomorrow?"

"Tomorrow?"

"The world doesn't stop turning, just because you can't feel it spinning."

Croc lifts the bedsheets and checks his bandage. Dwight looks.

"Sure."

"Get a good night's sleep. Kieron and Billy are still on that ship with a killer, and we've all had enough loss."

"Why is the killer back on the ship?"

"We reckon he hasn't got what he's after. Diamond rings are just a cover. It's probably in one of the ship's safe deposit boxes and he was looking for the key."

Croc nods, the work helping him. "If he's gone back to search again for a safe deposit key, we should plant keys where he'll find one. Trap him and kill him."

"Oh, I think they'll be a queue to do that."

56 – TOMATO WHAT?

Screaming for food, Mai is most definitely awake now everyone is back at the house. Mary is making cups of tea, and Stan is passing them out.

"Amy, can you take her, she must be able to sense my distress," Elaine says, passing the baby over. Amy has no choice but to take her. Elaine rushes out and the others feel she needs time on her own.

C.S.C.I. Series - Book 6

Dwight edges Mary away from the tap at the sink. He fills a milk bottle which already has the powder in. He takes it to Amy.

"Here," he says, handing her the milk. The baby is silent as she drinks, oblivious of events. "I should take you home. Sorry, you need to get some sleep."

Amy is as natural nursing Macey-Isabella as she is the soldiers at clinic.

"Too late for sleep now," she says. "I have people who need me from early this morning. And a dance rehearsal at lunch time. Maybe I can take some time off to help you in the afternoon."

"Think of yourself for a change," he says.

"Macey-Isabella is gorgeous," she says, ignoring him and looking at a happy child.

"Macey-Isabella-Mary," Mary corrects her.

"Oh. You must be the Mary."

"The Mary?"

"Yes, I've heard about you."

Mary looks at Dwight very suspiciously.

"Tomatoes," Amy says.

"What about my tomatoes?"

"I love tomatoes."

"You're welcome, when we open again," Mary says.

"I have a host of great recipes for you. Not fried. You'll love them."

"I'll love them? So, how you cook green tomatoes?"

"Jam, chutney."

"Tomato jam?"

"Perfect addition for breakfast."

"Oh."

"But the best…" Amy pauses, and Mary waits. "Is fried green tomato ice-cream."

"Still fried."

"It can be dry fried; wok fried," Amy suggests.

"Not only have I gotta be woke, speak woke, I've gotta cook woke!"

"No. A Chinese wok."

Dwight and Stan both watch from either side of the room, waiting for Mary to explode.

"Amy, we cook for a lot of people. It's not a home thing we do."

"I often cook for fifty or sixty servicemen, and staff. We also do cookery classes."

"Oh. Ice-cream."

"It can be boiled tomatoes, and the real prize winner is green tomato and ginger ice-cream," Amy enthuses.

"Must try it," Mary nods and she walks out to find Elaine.

Elaine is curled up on the bed. Mary lies behind her and cuddles her.

"My life's over, Mary. It's finished."

Dwight knocks on the door.

"Elaine, Mary. Amy's taking me to the clinic. I'm gonna pick up my truck, then pass by Dodge and meet the MS Amatheia which should have docked. Elaine, a drive out might be good for you."

"I need to stay with the baby," Elaine says.

"She'll sleep, Stan's got her," Dwight tries.

Mary gives Dwight a look. "Stan's good."

"Maybe you need to tell him that, Mary."

"You go. I'm staying," Elaine says.

57 – NOT WHAT IT SEEMS

Hospitals wake everyone at six in the morning and the lights go on. But Croc is already sitting on his bed, dressed and thoughtful.

"You need to lay down and rest," the nurse says. "Your doctor is gonna want to see that wound, and I'll need to re-dress it. You can get undressed again."

Croc unbuttons his shirt. The nurse moves off but manages a smile, even though she has a full workload. Patients must be readied for surgery, others washed, tablets handed out, and tests done before the surgeons do their rounds. Croc waits for whoever comes first.

Dwight appears, walking on his new legs, though no one would suggest easily or correctly yet. Amy is just behind him.

"How are you, buddy?"

Croc slowly turns to him and nods a greeting to Amy.

"The nurse said I've gotta be checked and redressed."

Amy lifts the chart from the end of his bed and studies it.

"I didn't sleep much," he says.

"No one did," Amy says.

"I'm going to take Amy to the clinic, pick up your sister and Ricky, then I'll be back around eight," Dwight says,

"It's not a game anymore, is it?" Croc asks.

"Hunter knew the score. He wasn't playing 'shoot 'em up' on a console. He knew people died," Dwight tells him.

"And lost limbs," Croc says. "You're walking!"

"Been a few months of work, but I'm alive. I owe it to Hunter to walk."

"Wrong time for him to die. How's Elaine?"

"There's never a right time," Dwight says. "She's a strong lady."

"You knew it was me in that game?" Croc asks.

"All along. Would you have expected anything less of me?"

"And Rocket?"

"That's me, is it?" Amy says, not knowing the history.

"Kieron and Billy planted some keys around the ship, we'll get him today," Dwight says, to change the subject.

"I didn't see that. I need my cell," Croc says, indicating the cupboard.

Amy walks around and retrieves it for him.

"Rest," she says.

"Two hours," Dwight says, leaving. Amy follows.

In the corridor, Amy links arms with him and walks with him. She knows the rhythm; she has done it a million times.

"Who is this 'Rocket'," she asks him.

"He made an avatar called Rocket. Too easy; it's just Crocket without a C. He pretended a woman was behind it, so I strung him along. I knew it was a false identity, then guessed it was him."

Dwight is in one of his thoughtful modes.

"Why would he do that?" she asks.

"It was lockdown, he was bored, and he was playing," he says, thinking, as they get to the steps at the front of the hospital.

"Do you want to try these?" she asks, indicating the steps.

"No. D'you know why?"

"No idea."

"Because I don't have to, and you don't take risks you don't need to. No Wild Bill, no Calamity Jane."

"Pardon?"

"Both were dropped in as a teaser. A bored amateur. A risk is something you take when you have to."

Dwight shuffles to the ramp, which is hard enough.

"So, no more risks?" she asks.

"I didn't say that. I explained the steps weren't necessary."

"I'm getting the feeling I need to stay and watch you all day."

"Amy, there are soldiers who need you. I'll take Ricky and Macey with me as well as Croc."

"To the cruise company?"

"Yes."

"Is it dangerous?"

"No, I've just got an itch."

"Itch? That itch is worrying me," Amy says, as they approach the taxi rank.

58 – BUFFET BREAKFAST

Kieron is used to death, but seldom has he lost a night's sleep over it. Soldiers rarely dwell on death. As their mission continues, death continues. This seems different, but it isn't. There is risk to life and the mission is incomplete. He is daydreaming at a table for two against the window near the coffee and tea dispensers. Billy approaches and joins him. As a mirror reflection of Kieron, he also sits angled inwards watching others. If the buffet restaurant were full of guests, they would no doubt be looking out to sea. The difference is that they would be on vacation.

"How do crew get to use a guest safe deposit box?" Billy asks.

"I guess it's down to the purser."

"So, if he says no, the ship's not useable to carry whatever this high value asset is". Billy ponders.

"It's a good puzzle for Croc's computer; which crew get safe deposit boxes on this ship, that don't on the Amatheia or Ianassa? Although we don't know for sure that it's all about a safe deposit box. What HVA is small enough to go into a box?"

"That's what had me going all night," he pauses. "You know I love the Wild West, the gold rush, the great stories?"

"You're a natural gunslinger, Billy."

"But I'm an adult," he says, coldly.

Billy is not normally one for such a dark comment and his tone is concerning. Kieron searches the younger man's face for an indication as to what is in his head as he leaves the enquiring silent gap.

"I missed the gold rush."

"I'm sure the myth is bigger than the reality was," Kieron says softly, encouraging a further step into the black hole that appears to be eating Billy up.

"It might have been depraved, degenerate, debauched, but it didn't go out to destroy mankind."

"Where's this going, Billy?"

"Will God ever forgive us for what we do in His name?"

"That's deep."

"I doubt He'll forgive any of us. Not one. Except those who claim they did nothing." Billy obviously needs a moment. The man who never seems to be affected by anything, and who never knew Hunter, is uncharacteristically soul searching. "And you know what they did?"

Kieron gently shakes his head.

"Nothing. They did nothing. The people who think they did nothing, they actually did nothing. They avoided seeing children being made to bear arms and kill villages of women and children."

Kieron has seen war, he has seen children with guns, and he knows the second after they have aimed the weapon at you, you can be dead. It is how he met his adopted daughter, who invited him onto his very first cruise ship when she became a dancer. It is where he met Hunter Witowski, and his wife Elaine who was held captive in Madeira while the ship he was on was subject to a Heist. A million memories flash through his head.

"No Kieron. I don't mean what we saw. Africa has about a quarter-of-a-million child killers. I went out to protect diamond mine traders thinking it might be the Wild West, but it was just wild. I couldn't work there."

"We said diamonds were just a cover."

"He still took them," Billy argues.

"Greed."

"Sure, but they're just chips and small cuts. I doubt any of them ever saw a mine or Africa."

"Forgeries? He was employed to remove forgeries?" Kieron asks.

"No. Lab diamonds are real. Absolutely no difference between mined and grown diamonds," Billy says.

"There must be."

"No, that's official now. They haven't had to call grown diamonds synthetic since about 2019."

"So why do they still mine diamonds?" Kieron asks.

"As you said, the myth is bigger than the reality and the myth's gotta be nurtured for the product to have value, because what is it? Coal! I bet they've gotta chunk of coal; a big chunk of coal."

"But small enough to fit in a box?"

"Worth more than gold, more than drugs, and more than cut diamonds," Billy says.

"Conflict Diamonds?"

Billy laughs rhetorically. "That's the term they prefer. Removing the word blood is cunning marketing. Helps people not to feel guilty wearing them. I reckon over 150,000 people, including children, died in the Sierra Leone civil war funded by fancy coal. Lab diamonds don't sound romantic or valuable."

"So do they have still have a value, other than the myth?"

"The myth doesn't end there. It's like all politics and big business, they demean the small freelancer digging and panning to buy food for their family. They call them artisanal miners and say their diamonds are not as good."

"Are they?"

"Oh yeah. Your queen's got the largest cut of the Cullinan in her crown jewels. That piece of coal was the biggest diamond ever found. A priest found one recently. It got called the Peace Diamond. The government thought it was worth 50 million, but it only sold for six-and-a-half."

"This ship's never been near Africa," Kieron says.

The two men let the conversation settle. Kieron collects the empty coffee mugs and takes the few steps to the dispenser for a refill. As he fills them, he watches a guy fill a small jug with water, then tip it into a bottle. The decanting is meticulous and complies with the rule stopping bottles being filled at water stations. The rule is not there to sell bottled water, it is there to stop cross-pollution. He returns to the table and starts to type into his phone.

"Let's say the water is the High Value Asset," Kieron re-starts.

"The diamond."

"It's in a dispenser, moved to a jug, then put into a bottle, then carried off a ship. It keeps moving, to get from start to finish. Basic smuggling." Kieron looks up, thinking further. "Ship to ship. Port to port. Start to finish. If Croc and Dwight plot the ship meeting ship to get a ship from Africa to meet this one, and link safe deposit box use, they might find the smuggler. But then, we are only equal to the where the Mexican's IT expert is. Our thief is stealing from the real smuggler."

"That's what I reckon," Billy says, glad he has got it off his chest.

"But he didn't take any of the keys we planted overnight. Why wait for the day to get busy? Unless there's somewhere he hasn't looked," Kieron muses. "He took Arif, he searched Banjo's room and had the diamonds we took from her."

"He must have figured the sex with Arif was not Banjo but another partner," Billy says.

"He's right," Kieron confirms.

"We need to plant a key on them," Billy suggests.

"That's human bait," Kieron thinks out loud.

"They're a target with or without us. You don't think Arif will have resisted torture?"

"It was a man, Ramesh. You might not have had that depth of information in your report," Kieron explains. "What we should do, is take him in to protect him."

"Exactly. Meet the new 'Gunslinger Ramesh'," Billy says, standing.

59 – CASEY B. DE MICHELLE

The truck pulls slowly into the spacious grounds of Meecho Entertainment. Set in a manicured park of grass and palm trees in Palm Beach, the pink, art-deco curved building could be straight out of the Jetsons. The spacious car park is almost empty.

Ricky is driving; the other three, Macey, Dwight and Croc have slept the entire journey up the Florida turnpike, which he took just over an hour from Miami. The truck's deep exhaust relaxes as it idles as he considers the wheelchair bays near to the building. He is indecisive as it would take both slots.

"Find a truck slot," Dwight says wearily, trying to wake himself. "I've got my chair."

"I was hoping to see you walk," Macey says, stretching.

"It's not that impressive," Croc says, feeling a little pain and stiffness as he moves.

"That was the deepest I've slept in a long time. Walking takes it out of you. Ow!" Dwight moans, as he tries to move. "I must have worked muscle groups I forgot I had."

Inside, there appears to be a skeleton level of staffing. Casey B. De Michelle walks into reception to greet them personally. The Chief Operating Officer of the cruise line leads them to her office. She is a very firm and confident lady, who is choosing her moments.

"These are sad times," she starts. "But confusing, and I don't like not knowing everything that's going on."

"Me neither, but that is how every job starts for us," Dwight says.

The office is big enough for a large, curved desk as well as a mini meeting table that would easily seat twelve. Coffee has been laid there.

"I hope you don't mind helping yourself."

Croc instantly pours for them all as Dwight introduces his team.

"You have a young team, Mr Ritter," she says. "I admire that."

"The agent we just lost was very experienced, and a new father."

"I'm sorry," she pauses. "Call me Casey."

"Likewise, Dwight. I haven't been referred to as Ritter since Afghanistan."

The attraction of looking out of her large, curved window on the top floor is too tempting for Macey, but Ricky is tight and listening. He knows things may have moved on a lot in the last few hours.

"I'm sorry for your loss," she says. "But as you know, this has all been a shock to me because I never booked you. No one here did."

"Sure. We agree to park that bus in the light of what's been happening, but you've seen our bank statement and received our emails. We were booked and paid for," Dwight says.

"No argument that the money has been removed from our bank account, and the booking was from my computer."

"Do you mind if I use your station, and go in deep myself?" Croc asks.

"I think I do," she hesitates. "There is sensitive material in there."

"Like your memo last night to your board about this meeting. Or your email to your daughter's maths teacher after the complaint that she'd been disruptive."

The astonished woman stiffens in her formal suit which is more than the weather suggests might be worn.

"After the current problem, my sister Izzy would like to spend a while with you discussing our other service, digital security," Macey suggests.

"I can get in from this," Croc says, waving his large tablet, which is a powerful computer. "Took me less that ten minutes to get into your computer from my hospital bed last night. I can do it from here while we sit and talk, but I can see more from inside. I will find how they got in."

Dwight watches as the youngsters take over a business that has a lot he doesn't know about, and he knows how Casey feels.

"Ok," she agrees reluctantly. "Do you need my password?"

"No, your daughter's pony told me that."

She sits joining Dwight at the table, and Ricky follows her lead. At each space is a company letter-size pad and a company pen for the guest. As the others take coffee, Macey doodles in ink, trying to find an image.

"I know you," Casey says to Macey.

"I don't think we've met."

"No. Mai.I.See. I just bought one of your pieces."

"The company did," Croc says. "I have the purchase price here Mace, so you can check with your agent."

"What are you trying to find?" Casey asks, a little annoyed at the intrusion.

"Anything that might be relevant. A lead. A line of code dropped in as a back door, or a route out," Croc explains.

"Given how easy it is for you to manipulate our system; how do I know you didn't break in, book your own services and then authorise your own payment?"

"Then kill one of our own two founding agents?" Ricky asks.

"The other thing I want is our team to open and inspect every one of your purser's safe deposit boxes," Dwight says.

"Impossible. That's a breach of privacy."

"This is either a terrorist attack, or at best smuggling blood diamonds. D'you want the ship blown up, or locked down under investigation when you pull into Miami?" Dwight suggests.

60 - BAIT

Kitchen support staff begin staggered breaks after the breakfast rush. It is just gone ten o'clock when the first enter the restroom, which has a small stage for karaoke, a DJ, or maybe a small band. There is a bar, which is closed, and a pool table, and the room is decorated with posters made to advertise events the crew invent.

Billy walks out with his arm around another worker, both dressed in the same white uniform. Under his white flat kitchen hat, his hair has been blackened and his skin is slightly darker.

"What you give me for this?" he says, flaunting the diamond ring that now belongs to Bedi. She is also dressed as kitchen staff but is about four people behind and by herself. They both notice the Mexican siting on a table at the side swinging his legs. He is not pretending to be one of the kitchen staff.

"OK. Play pool; ten dollars," the new Billy says, in an unknown accent. He leans over the table allowing the key on his neck-chain to swing freely. He makes a thing of it being a nuisance and stands upright to tuck the annoying chain in. "No one will play me?" Billy shakes his head pretending to be annoyed, but he can see the bait has worked. He storms out. Another member of the staff follows him out.

"Show me ring. I have fifty dollars."

The Mexican slides off the table and follows them. Bedi tracks him staying just out of his sight. In less than a minute there are loud screams and the noise of a skirmish outside. The staff run out to see what has happened.

The Kitchen staff rush to the two men on the floor outside the green room. Both have been knocked down. The first gasps for air as he is lifted, he is not used to any kind of physical confrontation and is in shock. The second is Billy. He checks his neck for a missing pendant and feels a little blood from the line of bruising where the skin is broken. With the help of the others who do not know him, he stands. The Mexican is long gone.

Bedriška is on her cell. "He has key." She ends the call and goes to Billy. Taking over as the one to hold him up, she excuses them. "I take him to medical centre."

Without a look back, the two agents have left the group who did not know who they were. Billy passes the ring back to Bedi and she slips it on her right hand. He is now losing the over-dressing of whites. Bedi begins to do the same as they get to the steel crew staircase. They pause, looking up to see how far the killer is in front, but he is not to be seen. Bedi leans out for a better view of all the stairs above. It is clear she wants to run up, but Billy stops her. He smells a rat.

61 – THE TRAP

The narrow room of floor-safes and previously organised locked drawers is in chaos. The purser is failing to open drawers as quickly as Kieron checks the contents and pushes them closed, to be re-locked. They need a third person, but there is no room for them to work even if they had one.

"Faster, he's on the way," Kieron demands. He is dressed in officer's whites with his cell-phone in the officer-shirt breast pocket live to Bedi.

"It's not possible to open them faster," the purser insists. He is annoyed, not just because his authority has been wiped away, but also because he can't take the pressure that is being forced upon him. The purser pauses to change to the second bunch of keys on a chain to his belt.

"Give me those," Kieron says, taking the new keys with his right, and unbuckling his belt with his left. He yanks the belt from him. "Start re-locking."

Kieron pushes him behind to the easier task, as he opens each drawer.

"Touch me again and I'll stop."

"One more word from you and he won't need to kill you, I'll do it myself," Kieron threatens.

"That's it," the purser says, stopping work.

Kieron whips him back around, snatches the first bunch of keys and throws him out. He grabs his own cell-phone without removing it from his shirt pocket or looking down at the overweight and sweating purser hitting the ground.

"I need help, one of you," he demands.

"Negative," he hears whispered from Bedriška. "We've lost the mark."

"One of you, risk passing him," Kieron orders.

Against the clock, Kieron locks each of the checked boxes, then side steps tossing the first bunch of the keys at the purser. With the second set of keys, he opens the remaining boxes. He has a good routine going for changing one key to the next on the ring as his hands move along, box to box. He is much faster by himself.

"Don't ever volunteer for bomb squad," he says to the fierce looking, but physically incapable officer on the floor. He slides drawer after drawer open until he gets to the last one, then he is back to the first of the sequence to check the contents, close and lock.

Bedriška appears.

"Walk him out."

Bedi has started before the last word from Kieron has finished. The heavy man's weight and resistance does not even register with her as she forces him into the side door.

"Open it first."

"This is my area," he argues.

Bedi twists him into the first office, kicks him behind the knee and as he drops, she puts him to sleep by pushing her thumb into his neck.

As Bedi re-enters the safe area she must catch one, then two, huge un-cut egg-sized rocks.

"Evidence," Kieron says, quickly checking the last boxes. He moves past her giving her the keys, holding the first one ready. "Start with this one and lock the drawers. I'll stall him."

"If not, I'll kill him."

Kieron smooths the line of his uniform whites, breathes in, smiles then rounds the wall to the public face of reception.

"We also need to ask the purser who rents box A90."

The disguised CCI agent joins one of the ship's two female crew behind the reception desk. One has just started to deal with the Mexican. Kieron hopes Arif never picked him out from any of the pictures the killer was able to show him, and that he does not know him. However, he is ready if the thief does. He has no intention of falling at the killer's hands.

"Sir," she says, "I have never done this."

She is perfectly calm and operating as instructed by Kieron when he set the sting.

"Good morning, sir," Kieron says to him. "Mel is one of our aspiring new crew." He looks to her. "The guest keeps his key. We must make an entry of his visit in the log, using his digital identity." Kieron looks up and invites his identification. "Sir?"

The Mexican holds his cell-phone up but does not hand it over. The female officer scans the phone. The computer screen below the counter level shows his details. Kieron ignores them and acts as if he is waiting, he needs a few more seconds. Kieron hits the screen as if it is the cause of a technical glitch.

"Try again," he instructs her.

She scans the cell once again. Kieron's helpful face looks across the atrium and smiles at Billy, then back at the screen, then up to the Mexican.

"Ah. At last. Mr Cazo?"

The Mexican killer nods.

Pacing himself, Kieron now instructs Mel, the trainee.

"With guests, we ask to meet them at the side door, then we escort them to the safe deposit area. They use their own key to open their own box. We don't touch the guest's key," Kieron explains. "Mr Cazo. Perhaps you could meet Mel at the side door, here on the right. I might just watch her, then I can tick off another of the many tasks she needs to learn."

Mel goes into the back room, the killer walks around to the side without the need to engage. Kieron knows Bedi is inside, and he knows the killer previously saw her hanging from a helicopter shooting at him. He hopes she is finished or there will be the sound of a huge battle. He pauses but the silence is not broken, so she must have gone, he has no need to rush. A report is more important. He uses his cell as he calls the other receptionist and Billy to him.

"Dwight. Two large rocks taken into evidence. The rat's in the trap. He already has a safe deposit box of his own. We have two huge uncut diamonds in evidence from box Alpha-Nine-Zero. We'll see how he reacts when he finds it empty."

"My guess is, he'll report up."

"Mine too."

Kieron uses his cell to take an image of the information on the screen and send the man's details back to Miami.

'Alfonso Cazo. Senior Testing Inspector. Department: Communications Hardware. Company: Ocean Testing Central. Guest Staff. Dates: 02:12:2021 to 05:19:2021. Cabin: B421. Account: Charge to ship's account. The picture is clear.

"That's Hunter's killer." Kieron ends the communication and addresses the receptionist. "Print that and issue a key to that room for this agent. Billy, I want any link he has, to anywhere."

62 - PUPPET

Dwight's team approach his truck in the Meecho car park. Shadows from the palm trees have started to shorten now the sun is higher in the late morning sky.

"Why didn't you tell her we know her ship's carrying conflict diamonds?" Ricky asks.

"We were giving her more than she gave us, and all I wanted was the new contract and payment."

"I could have done that," Croc shouts back to them. He has gone ahead.

"Her captain will update her, then she will want to talk with us again. At that point we might need a lot more from her," the big man says.

Croc has the tailgate open and operates the ramp on Dwight's customised truck. The big man drives his chair straight on to it. Although he has a well-worked method to get into his cab using his incredible upper body strength, life is changing fast.

"Someone, pass my legs."

As they leave Indiantown Road and join the fast toll at exit 116, they can see the more familiar Interstate 95, which is no more than a quarter of a mile away. West Palm Beach is behind them, and the two roads run parallel. They meet again in Miami, but the i95 can be busy and slower.

Ricky is driving again. Dwight sits as passenger making a report. Croc and Macey are sitting in the back, both thoughtful. They have an hour of puzzle-solving before they reach base.

"You're quiet, Croc," Dwight says, expecting some input.

"There's a lot to take in; a ship is a mini-city. A fleet is like managing a country, its people, businesses, food, staff, money. Hell, there could be a lot of connections."

"Does that make Miss Casey B' president or dictator?" Macey asks.

"Or a puppet?" Ricky adds.

"What do you mean?"

"Leaders are nurtured by those who are really in power. They're positioned, elected, ready to do what they're told."

"So, who is she a puppet for?"

Macey's pencil hovers to shape the powers pulling the threads above a puppet princess.

"Money and power are normally a good place to start, and when we find it, it won't be what we expected," Dwight suggests.

"The ship is just a vehicle," Ricky offers.

"For moving people or making money?" Croc asks, "or is that the chicken and the egg?"

"That's the point; its only existence is to make money."

"But, if management get so removed from the threads below that are developing their profit, they are open to abuse," Croc suggests, looking at the list of outlets and services on board. "The ship takes a percentage of everything that it moves."

"Unless they don't know they're moving it, then the inherent problem is that the system they set up is so strong it avoids the rule structure; Catch 22," Ricky offers. "The question: does our princess dictator know it's broken; is she trying to beat it back into shape or is she totally unaware?"

"Golden rule, kids, for your new training manual. Track the greed. Greed for money, or for power. This is a commercial set up, so let's follow the money first," Dwight says, reminding them that he knows of their own ambition. "Somewhere in the structure is a revolution based on greed."

"Dwight, that's not what Izzy has planned for our agency," Macey defends.

"No bro," Croc adds, "The company's new. Like you, it's finding its legs, and we're just keen to see you walk, and us to have a future."

"So, is there a revolution on board?" Dwight asks, which could have two meanings.

"No, the companies are all too small for that, but they can eat each other," he explains, still sifting through the information. "I feel like a pan-handler looking for a grain of dust in all this rock. The list of freelance business and services is huge."

"I'm sure it's the only reason our team has the killer alive. He might fly us nearer to the sun than your research, Croc."

"If I hear he died, I know we got this solved," Macey suggests, drawing all kinds of demons peering down through a hole, each holding a string.

"A lot of these services have common denominators," Croc suggests.

"Like what?" Dwight asks.

"Like the same service-agents or bookers. I reckon one of these has seen what another is doing and got greedy."

"Big jump to killing," Ricky says, re-joining the unravelling.

"Agents don't kill. They just book people who do. Mr Cazo is a hired killer. We need the agent," Dwight says.

"It won't surprise you his name's not Cazo. I've found seventeen identifications for him so far, none link to any cruise companies. He's wanted for everything from drug smuggling to murder, and in at least ten countries," Croc reveals. "I need more time."

63 – KILLER

"Is everything alright, sir?" Kieron asks, approaching Mel, who is standing adjacent, though neither watching nor interfering. He gently eases her away. Mel walks a few steps then is gathered by Bedriška and guided straight out of the side door to safety.

Kieron holds the standard cruise-smile as if he had been doing the job for years, even though he is watching Cazo, who is faltering. The thief's attention moves from the lack of content in two open boxes to trying to close one. The one that is not his.

"I thought you only had one box, Mr Cazo?"

"I lost my key in the cabin. Then I find two. I try both, but my things are not in either. These are not my keys."

"Let me try and solve this problem," Kieron offers, going to a computer screen. He has no idea how the system works, but also has no intention of looking at anything. He knows which key Billy was wearing.

"This one is yours," Kieron says, offering it back. He keeps the second key. "This one appears a spare. If you say there is nothing in that drawer, I will have security check its history and get it back into circulation."

The killer is nodding gently but thinking harder. His eyes search the empty work area.

"I know. It's like a graveyard here without guests," Kieron says.

"But this is not mine. The box is empty."

"Oh dear."

"I can't remember," the killer says, waving his hand in zigzags across the front of the boxes like an orchestra conductor. "Open every box. I know what is mine. Open."

"I can't open the boxes, sir. The contents are private."

"You can, you will."

"Was this box opened for you by your company? Is that where the confusion lies?"

"Yes. But I collect rock. Like quartz or amethyst. I know my box."

"Which is it like, sir? They are very different."

"My company find stone. They leave it for me. I will know when I see."

"I understand. Let me just contact your company, and they can tell me the box number. Because the key you have matches our paperwork."

"I don't have time for this," the killer says, beginning to get impatient.

Kieron, however, is very calm, if not enjoying every moment before the kill he keeps telling himself he mustn't execute.

"It is not as if either of us can go anywhere. Let's not be hasty, and I'll get them all open with the purser, and we will find your clear, blue, red stone. Whatever." Kieron backs off slightly. "I have your company on file, I will call them. Would you like a drink while you wait?"

"Not my company, the agent who book us for job. They know me," he says.

It is becoming obvious he is searching for a play. He is making himself ready to pounce. All he needs are the keys and time, then an escape. All Kieron really wants to do is kill him. Bedi is not in either of the two men's sight, and she is even more unpredictable.

"Look. You get the purser, I get a bottle of tequila, and we party," the killer says, now moving forward. His terms were an order. His hands are raised to the height of his stomach, and open as if suggesting there is no other option.

Kieron steps back.

The killer walks forward.

Kieron shrugs and backs away one more step.

"But sir, surely you understand."

"You, open the fucking boxes. Comprendez?"

As fast as the snapping tongue of a lizard, Bedi captures and pulls the killer's right hand towards her, under the blade of the commercial 43-inch paper guillotine. She jams his wrist right up by the hinge. As she nuts him; her forehead to his nose, she drops her whole weight on the lever made of a shiny silver steel.

It slams down, turns red, and his hand drops to the floor.

Bedi doesn't stop as he recoils in pain, screaming. Her left-hand wheels him down on the copying machine, flat on his back, as her right hand lifts the cutter, then flips his stub up. As he spins away, she grabs his other hand and pulls hard.

"Who do you work for?"

Face down he looks at her in horror and hatred.

"No one, he insists with a venomous spit."

She slams the lever down.

"Correct. You never work again."

He loses his other hand, but she doesn't stop, she takes his ornate flick knife from inside his belt. This has happened so fast, Kieron had no chance of stopping her, though this is one time he wouldn't. He would rather applaud.

"Stop blood. Squeeze your artery with your finger," she mocks. "Oh, you can't; no fingers."

She picks up his hand and throws it at him. He recoils, still screaming, still mad he charges her. She side-steps him and with a trip sends him to the floor. She steps on him.

"Who do you work for?"

"I never tell."

Bedi flicks the knife open.

"So, you no need your tongue."

64 – NO HANDS

Billy searches the standard cabin, but without success. Cazo travels light, just as the cruise investigators do, or any other agent, thief, or hitman would. There are no pictures of family around the cabin, no sense of belonging or home. There are a few clothes folded in a bag ready to go, nothing in the drawers or cupboard. He lives out of a bag. There is no attempt to make the space homely, no attempt at anything.

He turns abruptly to a knock at the door.

"Billy. It is Bedriška."

Billy knows her voice, but he still holds his hand over the spy hole in the door. If someone was going to shoot him through it, they would do it when the light goes. He looks through the hole and she is expecting him and pulls a face.

"Nothing," he says, opening the door.

"Did you expect to find anything?"

"No."

"We find huge uncut diamonds."

"I knew it," Billy says. "Where is he?"

"Medical centre."

"Alive?"

"He lost his hands."

"Where?" Billy asks.

Bedi tosses the severed body parts on the bed.

"Oh."

"You might need fingerprint to open something."

"No. Save them for Croc with his phone."

"Good idea," she says, tipping Cazo's clothes out and using his bag to keep the hands in. "I have confusion."

"Confusion?"

"Why we get booked after third ship is robbed? Why not first?"

Billy turns to her; he can tell she has something of interest to work through.

"Because they didn't know the first two ships were cleaned out," he offers.

"No. You fall into trap."

"I did?"

"You assume that cruise company book us, but they say no. I believe them."

"You think the thief's IT partner booked us?"

"Yes. Their man failed. And they did not have second shooter."

"Hmm, the Kennedy theory."

"Would you plan big mission with only one chance of hit?"

"Probably not," Billy says.

"Maybe they did, and they fail. Maybe we booked to be second chance," Bedi reasons.

"We didn't fail," Billy muses, taking a moment for more thought. "The diamonds could have been on any ship; maybe there are more."

"No. Croc found pursers on other ships do not allow crew to use safe deposit boxes," she says.

"I saw that report while I was in the atrium. You think that the thief's IT person found that out?"

"No. Cazo found out when on first ship, he can't hire a box. When on second ship, he can't hire a box. On those ships he open gem safe and take diamond rings, but he does not expect to find safe deposit key."

"On this ship he can use a safe deposit box, so, he and IT boss know this is right ship. He expect to find key in safe."

"But he opens the safe and he gets disturbed."

"No. He opens safe and finds diamond rings but no key. That is problem. Time is running out, so they use plan B," she says.

"Plan B?"

"We are plan B. They need help finding key, or mission lost."

"Why is it lost?" Billy asks.

"When ship go into Miami, real smuggler gets diamonds. Opportunity gone for thief. Now Amatheia go back to Miami, time running out. Aerwyna maybe next."

"Thief must be more than just killer and IT," Billy says. "There's always a boss."

"Maybe someone else on ship. But not killer. Not puppet. Yes, maybe puppet master."

"And they don't have to leave ship?"

"But diamonds must leave."

"So, why not plan C?" Billy asks. "Go in there and force all the boxes to be opened?"

"Harder to survive, harder to get free, or off ship. With us, diamonds must go to head office. Thief must know he can get diamonds back from us, in journey, or head office."

"He's a nasty killer."

"Bigger problem," Bedi states. "Who thief stealing from?"

"Smugglers who trade in conflict diamonds; they will be an even nastier bunch of killers."

65 – CASINO CITY

Dwight's double cab holds four people together in a tight space, where there is no option other than to interact and bounce ideas. The engine is off as they sit parked on the dockside, watching the MS Amatheia being loaded. The goods are well organised to go in sequence, from the dock, over a short connecting ramp in through the watertight door.

"Someone books all that food, all that kit, onto the ship," Dwight says.

He looks to the other end of the ship. The wooden stage scenery is being craned from the promenade deck onto a large semi flatbed truck in a safely taped off area.

"Someone collects a shopping list from every department on the ship, and they order it. Those orders are then given to who?"

"I can trace that line of command," Croc offers.

A bus pulls in. A group disembarks and begins to stretch.

"They look stiff," Ricky says.

"Gotta be dancers," Croc offers.

"Why?" Macey fires at her brother.

"Sorry, sis. They're probably pastry chefs."

"Don't profile people."

"It's the industry we are all in," Dwight reminds her, watching them.

"And you give people profiles each time you reveal their souls in a painting," Croc continues. "To be stiff and still bend like that, they must be dancers is what I meant."

"Sure, you did."

"Long bus drive," Ricky says. Being the journalist, he is on the detail.

Dwight captures the name on the bus with his cell-phone camera and checks the picture, zooming in to read it all.

"Night Sky Entertainments, Deadwood, Lawrence County, South Dakota," he says.

Croc keys the detail into his tablet.

"Don't they have an airport in South Dakota?" Macey asks.

"Wow, two thousand miles," Croc says. "That's a thirty-hour drive from here."

"More in that bus," Ricky offers.

"Cheaper than flying for that many people," Dwight adds.

"They're not all dancers," Macey says. "That guy is huge."

"Singers, magicians, comics," Dwight suggests. "Entertainers from Casino City."

"Where's that?" she asks.

"Deadwood."

"Dead's not a great name to associate with an entertainment company," Macey suggests. "Neither is wooden."

"Kevin Costner owns a casino there; he's a pretty good entertainer," Dwight offers.

"He sold it," Croc adds, still reading.

"Billy went there once. Was a pilgrimage. He loves stories of the gold rush, the Wild West, the old films. He hated the tourist trap it had become, did the museums, and left," Dwight says. "Let's run this from some other angles. Why did the woman who booked me want to keep our team at two agents?"

"Invoice control. She didn't want the real Casey to be alerted," Croc offers.

"When you checked in at the ship, your report said the IT team got a call to warn them of your inspection."

Croc nods. "Yeah. As Bedi and Kieron checked in."

"Then I had a call from the CEO of that same IT company, Miss JJ Easterbook. How did she know we'd got booked?"

"You think she's the person who employed us?" Ricky asks.

"No; that was a video call. We have her image, and this controller would not risk facial recognition. The real person we want, the real line of command is hiding amongst the agents. Someone who knew about the smuggling of blood diamonds," Dwight says. "Someone booked us and booked the killer."

"How did they want you to deliver the diamonds back to them?" Macey asks.

"Is that the rings or the huge rocks?" Dwight asks, dialling on his cell. "Bedi and Billy are asking the same question. Asking who is pulling the strings."

"Miss de Michele. It's Dwight; I need to walk around the Amatheia." He pauses as she tells him it is impossible. "I'm not sure you have an option. My team found huge uncut diamonds being smuggled. You want this ship delayed a day or two? We're gonna park the truck, in one of your company spaces, then four of us, who just left your office, need access while you chat with my boss and your captain on the Aerwyna. We'll be off this ship before it sails."

66 - AERWYNA

Billy and Bedriška flank Kieron who has been summoned to meet the captain on the bridge. Bedi carries the killer's small bag. Captain Walker is once again teamed with her hotel manager, James Grüner and both are deathly serious. With the security guards who brought the CCI team, they outnumber the officers in charge of the ship, as the ship is still anchored off the Bahamas.

"A man is maimed, his limbs are missing," the captain delves, knowing she has less than half the story.

"He must know what happened," Kieron suggests.

"He's no doubt still in shock! What happened?"

"Lost both hands, you say?" Billy asks.

"You removed the purser from that office," James accuses.

"For his own safety," Kieron insists. "Murders are piling up on this ship."

"Who knows what happened in there, but your purser still has hands," Billy says, annoyed with James.

"There must be yet another rogue on board," Kieron offers, as the matter is inconclusive.

James is less capable of containing his anger than the captain. "No. You know more than you're sharing."

"We think your ship is being used to smuggle illegal diamonds, sir," Kieron directs at the captain.

"You know they're illegal?" Captain Walker asks.

"They're illegal," Billy adds.

"You have shown us no proof," James insists. "If you took anything from any of the safe deposit boxes, you need to declare it. It has to go back in the box and be investigated correctly."

"Diamonds or no diamonds. Illegal of not, I want everything entered in the log. The doctor has requested the man's hands are found and sent to the medical centre."

Bedi shakes her head; a not-knowing look.

"Where did he leave them, sir?" Billy asks.

The stand-off produces no conclusion and no evidence other than the thief is not talking and the captain is frustrated at not knowing.

The three agents leave the bridge knowing they have no need to volunteer any help.

"She doesn't have a clue what to do. She's never been in a situation like it," Billy says, as they walk away down the corridor.

"It's not a military ship, Billy. She's never been through what we have. We can't expect support. She's normal," Kieron says, defending her. "Croc should have worked the route out within hours, the ships, the safe deposit boxes, and which name passed diamonds to which name."

"But we not asked to find smugglers," Bedi adds, bluntly.

"It will never lead to the dealers and the mining companies. And even if it does, they'll deny everything, and nothing will stick."

"Maybe, smuggler and killer same person," Bedi suggests.

"No. They wouldn't need to steal their own diamonds and risk so much," Kieron offers.

"Maybe yes. Ship not meant to come here. Ship not meant to go into Miami. So, maybe diamonds in wrong place," Bedi adds.

"Surely they can wait until it goes back to normal. If they are the smugglers, if they are diamond traders, it is no more than a slowdown in product line," Kieron says, answering Bedi.

"Greed. They're all greedy," Billy adds.

"What if the cruise line change route of this ship when sailing restarts?" Bedi offers.

As they arrive in the buffet, Kieron leads them to a table. They have no food but are feeding on a new line of thought. Kieron is looking at his phone.

"Croc has some route plans and connections up already," Kieron says.

"From West Africa, diamonds would need to go the other way to be cut in India. They cut most stones. China are challenging India for the trade, but again, the other way," Billy suggests.

"Are they just bulk cutters? These are special diamonds," Kieron asks.

"There's Dubai, maybe Tel Aviv."

"Then you can go either way from Africa," Bedi says, knowing the cruise routes better than the other two.

"Coming this way, we have New York. Or there's Amsterdam," Billy lists from memory.

"How long did you work in diamonds?" Bedi asks.

"I worked various sites in Africa. Six-month contract. It's not hard to pick up how the industry works. Mine, design, cut, sell."

Kieron is still reading his cell as the others pick through the ideas. "The web says, the Cullinan Diamond was sent to Amsterdam to cleave and polish. I like that word; cleave."

"It's all c's with diamonds; cut, carat, colour, clarity," Billy says, offering terms used in the industry.

"This ship was on routes from the United Kingdom to the Canary Islands, off Africa," Bedi says. "It could meet ships coming up the African coast. It get diamonds and take them to Europe, or the Baltic, so Amsterdam is possible."

"The call to anchor here brought it across the Atlantic and off target," Billy states.

"OK. Smuggler not killer," Bedi has worked out.

"Why?" Kieron asks her.

"If they steal their own diamond, they must know which ship. Which box," Bedi states.

"Yes. It must be somebody else," Kieron offers.

"Someone who know diamond is being smuggled. Someone who knows routes. Someone who knows these gems not where they should be. They pounce," Bedi concludes.

"Stupid enough to risk stealing from some nasty killers," Billy reminds them.

"Maybe smuggler does not know yet," Bedi offers.

"Or do they? They might think we have their diamonds?" Kieron says.

"We do," Bedi says.

"Maybe that's why we were contracted. They are meant to see us steal their diamonds."

"Why do we care?" Billy asks. "We've been paid, we've found Hunter's killer, and we recovered diamonds most of which have no legitimate owner. Let's go home."

"Not yet," Kieron labours.

"Why not?"

"Because, someone is pulling the strings somewhere. Whoever may have ordered Hunter's killing may be setting us up. That's the real murderer, and I want them. So, who is it that knew the diamonds were sitting in the wrong place, waiting to be taken?" Kieron asks. He is determined the job is far from finished.

67 - WRONG SHIP

They may have travelled for thirty hours on a bus, but they are on the ship to work; the dancers are blocking routines on the stage they will be using.

At the back of the theatre, separated by nearly one thousand empty seats, Macey watches them. Dwight, standing on his sore legs, concentrates on the sound and light technicians in the control box set in the rear wall. At the choreographer's call, the dancers stop. A moment later, the show playing on the LED curtain is stopped.

"Looks like you've been working with them for months," Dwight says to the engineers. It is a compliment, cast out to fish for information.

"Same, same, every show," the head sound mixer says. He looks at his watch. "They finish now."

Dwight looks down to the stage and he can see that the stage is being set for the seven musicians. The larger man from the bus is talking to the orchestra leader who takes the offered music sheets and passes them out to the other musicians. Macey has walked to the front and is aiming at the dancers.

"Very slick," Macey says, clapping.

"Same shit, different stage," an apathetic girl dancer says.

"Whatever, it's impressive and you could be in a worse place."

"Right there, we've worked worse places."

"Where?"

"We have to do our time in the casinos before getting a ship."

"Macey," she offers, holding her hand out.

"Sorry, I'm not touching. But hi. Linda."

"Sure. But, great, you get to see the world, eh?"

Dwight sits in a seat to rest. Using the strong seat backs to lower himself down. He is near enough to hear.

"If I don't go stir crazy; we just saw the size of our shared cabins."

"Didn't you share rooms in the casino?"

"Never lived in the casino; we were in an RV park. Static vans; too old for guests but they were roomy."

"Static vans? Where's that?"

"The Hide. Near Deadwood. We're all from Night Sky Ents. Everyone's from Night Sky."

"Not everyone."

"Pretty much. They train the beauty techs, shop staff, everyone."

"Lifeboat drill," The choreographer shouts, clapping her hands to command her team. The stage is no longer theirs.

"Catch you later." And the girl is gone.

"Nice work," Dwight says, as Macey sits in front of him, offset by one chair.

"Is that me or him?"

They both watch the tenor singing just enough for the musicians to get the dots right. He walks forward and shouts to the light box. "I'll be moving from here, to here."

Ricky and Croc walk in and sit behind Dwight. They lean to him and talk softly.

"The purser is adamant that crew should not use the guest safe deposit boxes and told me to go to ask at crew reception. If there is room they can store money, but it is more normal for them to transfer the crew's excess money to wherever is home," Ricky says.

"This can't be a smuggling ship. Routes don't match up either," Croc adds. "I have a ship-to-ship trail, and names and boxes, and so far, all the names who hire safe deposit boxes are shop staff."

"Shop staff?" Dwight asks.

"Here's the thing," Macey says slowly, making them all wait. She turns to the three behind her. "Just like the art thefts, we're working for a crook?"

"I thought you liked working for the art crook; he's your mentor now," Ricky says.

"It's art. You've gotta work for one crook or another."

"And are diamonds any less corrupt than art?" Ricky questions.

"Quite a question," Dwight says, thinking.

"No. The real question is which crook are we working for?" Macey grins, as Dwight tries to catch her point. "See, you thought we were working for the thief, and some clever IT dick like Croc got us involved. What if the smugglers know they were being robbed and they loaded us in the barrel?"

68 – WHERE NOW?

The three CCI agents stand on the promenade deck and look across the sea to the nearest island. It is another sunny day with perfect visibility.

"We're certainly not within twelve miles of any US coast, so the FBI are not interested yet," Kieron says.

"Other than Hunter's murder. That's a crime against a US citizen," Billy says.

"We might be more that twenty-four miles from any mainland including the Bahamas, but this ship is registered in Nassau and flies their flag."

"More convenient laws," Billy smirks.

"Unless you are gay; then not so good on this ship or in Bahamas," Bedi sneers.

"The killer's on a tender to that island. That was the captain's call, not ours. I wasn't present at that crime, I'm not a witness," Kieron says. "I can't offer any help to the FBI should they ask me."

"Me neither," Bedriška offers.

Billy reads from his cell. "The Royal Bahamas Police Force is seeking the public's assistance regarding a deadly shooting. The Force has established an Incident Room to facilitate this investigation & is asking members of the public to contact them. They ain't quite the FBI, US Marshal or Homeland security across there. The FBI will be all over us."

"I know nothing," Bedi says.

"I get why we've been brought in. As always, we sit between jurisdictions, and we get results," Kieron says.

"Thief is killer," Bedi says, throwing his hand into the sea and watching the fish gather to nibble. "Evidence gone."

"I wish you wouldn't do that just before lunch," Billy says.

She offers him the other hand. "It is special dish, international cuisine, and we not need finger prints."

Billy turns his nose up. "I just turned vegan."

She throws it in with the first. "Thief or smuggler. Who do we work for?"

"Interesting conundrum," Kieron hesitates.

"But it's not. It never is. Let's just find out who ordered the killing of Hunter and go home," Billy says.

"Kieron turns around to look at the other two on his right. He leans against the rail, relaxed. "Sure. But what do we do with these?" He produces the two large rocks from his pocket.

"Someone will come and get them," Bedi grins. "Someone will know we've got them."

Kieron smiles. The danger she infers has not eluded him.

"Give them to the captain; let her stick them in her bloody log," Billy suggests.

"But is that the devious plan? Are we not playing into their hands?" Kieron asks.

"No. The captain could have opened any of the boxes at any time so it can't be her," Bedi says, pushing the empty bag in a rubbish bin.

"Then who?" Kieron turns, scanning the entire length of the ship. "Is there another player?"

"Doesn't have to be anyone on ship," Billy says. "They booked us as second shooter."

"Whatever. They can't know we found anything."

69 – YOU SHOULD BE DANCING

Although Izzy is torn between showing she can cope running the CCI hub in Miami and moaning about being left alone, both pale to hunger. The others are boastful about having eaten lunch on a cruise ship and are replete. They are bringing her to the point of losing it, then they each hand her a transparent plastic evidence bag stuffed with food. It is more than enough for a few people.

"I though Mary would be here," Dwight says. He is still forcing himself to stay on his new legs.

"No, she's with Elaine."

A solemn moment of silence shows the respect they all have, though they are helpless to change anything.

"Croc's here, so do you want to take this feast to Elaine's?"

Izzy nods but must relay updates before she leaves.

"The FBI has a copy of all the files. I asked them to stay away from Elaine, convincing them that she knows nothing. But they will want to see you all."

"That's fine, but if they could start here, I need to go and see Amy."

"You only left her a few hours ago," Macey says, surprised at his eagerness.

"The FBI went to her about an hour ago."

"You didn't suggest she knew nothing?" Dwight questions with edge.

"She can take the inconvenience. Then they're going up to Meecho. They want to see you all, but for now it's just a two-man team," Izzy says.

"I got things to do."

"Go. I got the hub," Croc says.

Dwight leaves and the triplets are together for the first time since this started.

"I think his legs hurt," Ricky offers.

"He does have a chair," Macey offers.

"And an Amy," Izzy says, leaving with the food.

Further south in Miami, Amy is rehearsing a dance troupe. Dwight enters the hall at the back of the clinic and stands by the door, watching. He has been attending fittings and rehabilitation sessions for some time, but he has never seen this group. Lifting his cell phone, he films the spins and turns of each of the seven performers in formation, as an interacting comedy routine. Two have one limb replaced by a carbon-fibre spring-like blade as prosthesis. One with no legs at all and using a chair. Dwight realises how lucky he was to keep enough to use the units he is testing.

With her back to Dwight, Amy is laughing raucously, as are the others. However, she turns as they react to Dwight being there. Her demeanour changes when she sees him. Memories of Elaine flood back and the others notice her reaction. She knows they deserve an explanation.

"This is Dwight; he lost a friend yesterday."

The soldiers offer condolences in genuine but short exchanges.

"I'll see you again tomorrow," Amy offers.

"I'm sorry. I didn't mean to end the session," Dwight says.

"How is she?"

Amy asks the question but they both know Elaine is going through hell.

"I've got to go up country overnight, to follow a lead."

"Its' a big country! Where?"

"Thousands, well, two thousand miles."

"I was going to offer to drive you, but that's not a drive."

"No. I'm flying. It's only five hours in a plane," he says.

"Are you taking your chair?"

"I hadn't thought. Normally I do."

"You should. You've been on those legs much more than is good for the beginning."

"I do ache in places I never knew existed. My glutes are killing me. Poor choice of words," he says, rebuking himself.

"D'you have time for Joaquim to work those out with a massage? It's a must."

"Erm. No. I need to go.

"Let me come. When are you going?"

"Now. It's an agency in South Dakota that book the entertainers on the ships."

"I've got a few clowns they can have," Amy says, smiling for the first time since she saw him.

"You've got something they might be interested in," he says, thoughtfully.

"That they 'should' be interested in!"

"I don't think they do anything that ain't driven by profit," Dwight says.

70 – OFF GRID

A cruise ship is a floating luxury hotel. When the sun is out, as it is this late afternoon, no excuse is required to sit with a beer or a cocktail. Bedriška has her usual vodka with ice in a long glass, Billy has a beer, and Kieron has a glass of Rose. Just as guests might be doing if they inhabited the ship, the agents look at their cell phones.

However, they are not on any social media. They are all reading the same reports.

"Croc's getting a dressing down from the FBI," Billy laughs.

"He was the only one present when Hunter was killed," Kieron says, but without any force in his delivery. "It'll be a good lesson for him, but I guess he won't be available for a while."

"They're gonna ask about the missing hands soon," Billy says.

"None of their business," Bedi states, abruptly. "And Croc doesn't know."

"Will he keep his cool?"

"Where's Dwight?" she demands.

"I would have thought he vanished so he could stay operational without interference, but I can't raise him," Kieron says.

Bedi looks up, concerned.

"If Dwight's not answering, he doesn't want to," Billy says, annoying both of them.

"Has he got any reason to avoid the FBI?"

"Not that I know."

"Look at Croc's report," Bedi says. "He find entertainment agency design shows. They supply show designed to LED curtain. They must have code writers."

"It all makes logical sense," Kieron says.

"Dwight would add Deadwood and IT expert together quicker than we did," Billy suggests.

"What would he do next?" Bedi asks him.

"The old Dwight would have had us get right up their nose."

"The new Dwight just got legs," Kieron says.

"And man in his unit just die," Bedi says.

"I bet he's on a plane," Billy says.

71 – FRESHLY SQUEEZED

After a never-ending private road verged by attractive picket fencing, the SUV taxicab pulls up at a large white ranch glowing in the low evening sunshine.

Amy is out first and helps Dwight as the driver opens the tailgate to access the wheelchair.

"How the other half live, eh?" Amy says, as the driver helps lowers the electric chair down.

"It's fine there. I'll get it if I need it," Dwight says.

"You want me to wait?"

"I don't expect to be thrown out that quickly."

"Good luck," the cabbie says, as he slams his doors. The cab circles around and out, leaving Dwight and Amy looking up at the property. It is a huge four-storey wooden ranch, curved like a horseshoe. Each floor is set slightly back from the one below, like the rear terraces of some cruise ships. There are four sets of windows on each wing. In the left wing, there is an arch that cuts through the centre to stables and buildings behind.

They stand inside the moon shape by a small fountain. On a ship, it is where a pool would be. A woman rides up on a horse and stops next to them.

"Mr Ritter, welcome. And Miss Polson."

"Well. Look at this amazing looking creature," Dwight says.

His actions ask if he can stroke it, and the rider allows, as she swings down off the horse.

"Miss Ginsburg. So nice of you to see us. I was on a fund raiser…"

"I hope that's not why you're here."

A stable hand takes her horse and leads it through the arch.

"No, no, no. I was told about you guys, and wanted to see what you did before returning to Miami."

"Or rather you wanted me to see what you do," Fiona Ginsburg says, as she climbs four steps to the pillared porch. "Do come in."

She never looks back, and strides through a wide-open double door into the large hall.

Amy lingers with Dwight who is slower. She is ready to assist as he fights to step up, using his hands to help lift his already punished muscles. Stairs are still a very new challenge to him, one that he will not be seen to give in to.

They turn right into a reception room where all the windows are so open, they appear to have been removed. A soft breeze acts as a soothing natural air conditioning.

A tall thin, young woman enters with glasses and two jugs on a tray.

"Melanie has drinks. Would you mind if I leave you with her while I shed my riding jodhpurs and boots? I'll be a few seconds."

Fiona leaves; it was not a question.

"Would you care for iced water, or lemonade? I can recommend this. I just squeezed the lemons, and it has a refreshing bite. It's not too sweet."

Both take the lemonade, Dwight angling to use her while she is alone.

"You have excellent balance."

"I'm a dancer," Melanie says.

"Fantastic. D'you get to work on the ships?"

"I hope so."

Dwight leaves his drink and walks over to look at the pictures on the back wall. There are both free standing frames on furniture and shelves as well as pictures mounted on the wall. He video captures them all, trying not to be obvious but the image is more important than being caught.

"You must hear the others boast of being at sea?" he asks.

"Not dancers. Once they get to sea, they never come back here. I spoke to Miss Ginsburg's son-in-law once when he was home. He loves it. He's crew."

"Which one is he? Dwight searches the pictures, many of ship's crew, some at galas and fund raisers. There are also pictures with stars. Dwight works fast to cover them all. Melanie studies them too, as she has never really looked at them.

"I don't know any of these people with Miss Fiona."

"Miss Fiona?"

"It's a dance term. Respectful," she smiles, but still looking at the pictures.

"Like Sensei?"

"I guess."

Amy can see what Dwight is doing and she uses her cell and records the pictures in the hall as she watches for Fiona's return.

"Wonderful place you have, Miss Ginsburg," Amy expresses as a warning to Dwight and trying to slow her down.

72 – THE GALLERY

Dwight hears Amy clearly and scrambles across the large room.

"Don't worry, Melanie," Dwight says to her softly. "I wouldn't know any of them."

He manoeuvres around a chair to the low table and reaches for the tray where he rescues his glass. He wouldn't normally be short of breath, but he is tired. Looking up, he can see the security camera and he knows he has been watched.

Fiona arrives. She is now wearing a loose cotton dress and soft shoes.

"That's better. Now, why are you really here?"

She fixes him with a questioning look. Dwight is thinking, but not fast enough.

Amy, who has followed Fiona, rounds her, and jumps straight in, saving him having to decide what to say next.

"We have the most amazing, entertaining dance act you will have ever seen."

"Bold statement. I've seen a lot of acts. A lot of dancers."

"Few who've lost limbs, I doubt."

"None. I produce entertainment shows."

Dwight feels the prejudice of the remark but stays silent. Amy is less capable.

"These individuals have overcome horrendous loss and become the best they can be."

"The first question; is it entertaining?"

"And what's the second question, Miss Ginsburg?" Dwight asks, eventually speaking.

"Price," she says, eyes wide open, her amazed expression unforgiving in its bluntness. "I work for commercial companies."

"Do you mean price, or value?" Dwight asks.

Fiona again fixes him with her stare, this time demanding he quantify his offer. But he is not here to sell a dance act, he wants to find a killer and he feels he could be looking at her. He is desperate to use his cell phone again but can't take the chance.

"We are talking of an art form," he says.

"Art?"

"Art has a value," he suggests.

"Art has a price. Its value is perceived, often never achieved," she responds.

"Sometimes exceeded," Amy interjects.

"That is when something is really wanted," Fiona suggests.

"You have a house full of art," Dwight says.

"I sell entertainers, not art. I know what will sell, and where and how to sell it."

"I can see why you're a successful agent," Dwight smiles, allowing her point to win. The discussion is getting him nowhere.

"We'll show you what we have, you tell us the price."

She now shows her awfully expensive teeth in a huge smile as she pulls her hair free and shakes it out. Fiona enjoys winning.

"Their new state-of-the-art limbs don't just imitate their body's natural movement but become a source of amazement. Here," Amy says, offering Fiona her cell phone to watch.

"Can you bounce that onto the screen through here?"

Fiona leads them into an a small room where she no doubt sells acts to invited guests, bookers, and club owners. "It's an open guest network. I don't get too many walk-ins trying to steal the Wi-Fi."

Amy is with her, but Dwight lingers behind capturing more pictures of Fiona with crew.

"So, why do you need such an elaborate security system?" Dwight asks, seeing another camera in the corner of this new room.

"As you said, art has a value."

"Some risk. One way in or out; a long-gated road."

"You work in security?"

"No. I was a soldier."

Fiona turns away from the screen and addresses Dwight.

"Then you understand a high value asset might be worth the risk of a long road out, but not with cameras," she says.

"I do. That's why we want to encourage you to take the risk of this act. You must take some risks?"

Amy takes just seconds to connect her cell to the large screen. It shows a wheel spinning meaning something is trying to work.

Behind the two women, just seen by the camera, Dwight types a text message and sends.

73 – CLOUDING OVER

It's just gone seven thirty in the evening, and as it is getting dark the sky clouds over. The islands sit in the hurricane belt so can suffer between June and the end of November. From December through until May the weather can be almost guaranteed, which is why it is the playground of the rich and famous.

"Is this the lull before a storm?" Kieron asks, looking up as the small plane in the sky above reduces engine power ready to drop down into Great Harbour Cay.

"I feel air pressure change," Bedi says.

"Same feeling of dread as an attack might be forming somewhere out there," Billy mocks, walking to the rail, then looking back.

All their cell phones bleep. They read a message from Dwight. 'Rogue in member of normal crew, married daughter of agent.'

"That's short and sharp," Bedi says. "He cannot talk, no?"

"Where the hell is he?" Kieron says, looking at his watch. "He wouldn't be in Deadwood yet, it's too soon."

"If you're paying, and he took his girlfriend, then he hired a jet," Billy says, thinking. "And he's onto something."

Cell to ear Kieron waits.

"Croc, did Dwight get a jet to Deadwood?"

"I don't know. I've been drilled with questions, all afternoon!"

"Look at the account."

There is a silence.

"Yes. No return booked, no hotel booked," Croc says. "What's that noise?"

Deck hands are rushing to pile up the plastic sun beds and chairs on the deck. After thumping them into piles eight high, they lash them back safely.

"There's a storm coming. Stay awake, circulate everything," Kieron says, to report back to Miami. He looks across the deck, and as well as the deck hands who are not in a formal uniform, there are uniformed security officers approaching them. "I think we are about to get arrested, and I'm not sure we should be out of circulation."

Kieron ends the call. He nods to Billy and Bedi who have already noticed the pincer movement towards them and have spread out to weaken it. He shakes his head just twice, slowly, and they know they are not to be taken.

"Take them out," he mouths. He then walks down the side of the bar and vanishes into the ship.

Billy gently floors three security guards, one after the other. The bar staff notice the altercation. One takes the house phone at the end of the bar to raise an alarm. Bedi is faster and it is ripped from the wall and her look alone tells them they can never be scared enough. She walks over to one of the three guards on the floor, lifts him, then holds the man that stands at least a foot shorter than her, over the rail and high above the sea. Another officer approaches her from behind.

"Come close, I drop him."

The officer stops.

"Who sent you?" she demands.

"Our office says to arrest you," the man squeals. She drops him anyway.

"Man overboard."

She and Billy tie the other men.

"They have no idea who sent them. It's just an order as always. Just following orders," Billy says.

Kieron turns left into a small unused bridge room where the card tables and chairs are stacked. There is also a covered, upright, rehearsal piano. He lifts the cover and opens the top. Grabbing a cloth from a table he wraps the diamonds and pushes them down, resting them against the strings and on the keys. The cover is replaced, and he then deliberately runs into the two approaching security guards. They are both spun over onto their backs, and cable ties taken from them and used to disable them. Seconds later, Kieron is back on the deck. There are no bar staff, no workers, just security officers cabled to rails. Billy and Bedrıśka have gone. He walks over to a security tied officer and takes his radio.

"Billy come back."

"Roger."

"Bedi come in."

"Roger."

"Whoever else is listening. Your whole operation is about to come tumbling down."

74 – THINK ABOUT IT

A video of Amy's performers ends, and she turns to Fiona Ginsburg, full of pride and keen for approval. She has invested a lot into those she works with at the clinic. She has seen them come in broken and leave inspired and wanting to help others. Fiona is stoic.

"Did you see Patrick Swayze dance with his wife at the world music awards in 1994? I'd have paid good money to have been sitting in the front row," Fiona starts.

Dwight is tired and he knows that Amy will be upset by the response. The politics have also seen them drift away from the investigation, even if it has made for a perfect cover story. He needs to work back to the real point of the visit.

"Did you have that kind of money back then?"

She stalls, not expecting that question. As a negotiator and one who expects to win, she offers a powerful silence. Dwight doesn't need to play the silent card; he knows he can annoy her.

"Time's a currency worth more than money, and as talented as Swayze was. As in love with his wife he was, time was not a currency he was paid in."

"Where is this going?"

"Pardon me, as someone who lost both legs, and a wife, when it comes to these magnificent guys, it's personal."

"I don't see a reason to disagree. It's sad you lost your love; sad Lisa Swayze remarried, but that is life."

"I didn't know she'd remarried," Amy says, hit with innocent surprise.

"Yes." Fiona lets slip a slight wry smile. "A diamond jeweller, I think." For the first time she has hinted at the red cards she may be holding. She recovers, "I have to be real about what you're offering, and I'm struggling. Although, there will be a market somewhere."

"No, they struggle," Amy offers. "They struggle and succeed."

"How about Hollywood, working on movies?" Fiona suggests.

"They can do that. There are agencies who love using them in war films. To get blown up looking like their limbs are coming off again, and they're used to that. But what a way to relive your loss. We want to show they have another talent," Amy explains.

"But will they make holiday makers feel great? Will the act be uplifting?" Fiona asks.

Dwight sees the opening that has been coming.

"We are talking about guys who are used to taking a risk. Who are highly trained security operatives, offering to work on a ship."

He lets the agent hear her own interpretation of what he just said. He watches her eyes like a poker player sitting at a table in the tourist city of sin, not so many miles away. He watches her consider her cards and decide to stay in the game until the river.

"Maybe it's me. Maybe my choreography is shit. I'm not a dancer. I just help them. I'm not a cook, but I teach them to cook," Amy says, now getting emotional.

Dwight eases over to his pocket rocket and puts his huge reassuring hands on her shoulders. He is now holding a couple of aces.

"Surely, people see the need for equality and understanding now," Amy pleads.

"We've got off on the wrong foot. Not me, I don't have any feet. But, before we leave, humour us. There must be a use for these guys. Let's brainstorm this," Dwight asks.

"Come and see the set-up we have here," Fiona says.

75 – INSIDE I'M DANCING

Outside, Dwight takes his chair. Seated, he powers on the flawless flat concrete, following the two women to the huge barns at the rear of the property.

"These buildings are perfect, they have ramps," Amy says, not having given up with her new need to sell the act.

"Equipment is moved in and out, so they all connect by access roads," Fiona explains, but not to knock her down.

Dwight catches up, drives past her, and goes inside. The large building could not be less farm-like. There is a stage with wings either side and flies above where there is basic rigging. A trapeze is being installed by two guys who look more like cattle-ranchers than construction workers. In their belts are the normal holders for the basic wrench, screwdriver, and a power tester, but also a gun. They watch the three below, ignored by Fiona.

A hanging LED curtain forms the backdrop to the stage. The walls and ceilings are fitted with some lighting. Away from the stage, at the front of the audience area, a huge original digital projector hangs down, looking very dated in an otherwise modern facility.

"Guess the projector's a bit old school now?" Dwight asks, wanting to push her on the demands of digital technology.

"But if I remove it, I'll need it. And it does produce a ghost-like effect in front of the LED curtain. I'm working with some ideas," she explains.

"You have good technical help?"

"Sure. The best. We're always using code writers, but they change jobs quicker than any profession I know; ambitious and always looking for something more. And they're not a-dime-a-dozen like dancers."

"Tough when you've got ongoing projects; I guess you need to keep one or two main ones on side."

"Yes."

"And like any profession, they take some incentivising to stay."

"Where are they based?"

"Can you dance?" Fiona asks Dwight, to redirect him.

"Maybe I'm having a middle-aged crisis, but inside I'm dancing."

"We send dance troupes to ships. I've over sixty new kids learning routines. I'm designing a circus type show and a new magic show using the curtain. We also train kids who have studied sound and lighting. Cruise ships are huge employers and it's year-round."

"Do you visit the ships?" Amy asks, feeling lost.

"That's a different full-time job. We serve three fleets, a total of thirty-seven ships. The teams work six-month contracts, which means my assistant is away every week of the year settling a new team on another stage."

"Wow."

"You have seven guys?" Fiona asks.

"There are a few others," Amy says.

"I have a show based on Frankie Valli and the Four Seasons. Who doesn't?"

"It's great music," Amy agrees.

"How many in the act?"

"Five. Frankie plus four."

"Wrong. Four. Which is two shared cabins. That is the total bed spaced reserved for that stage act. There are not three cabins. Seven is way too big, and these are not special rooms."

"They don't need special," Dwight adds.

"If you don't mind, I would let lawyers decide on that," Fiona says.

"You have to know maritime law as well?" Dwight asks.

"I supply entertainment staff, masseurs, beauticians, croupiers, fitness instructors, shop assistants, and train many sound and lighting technicians. I have to know everything that is happening on a ship, before the ship leaves port."

"How about Veterans' Day. A special act to honour those who have served in the United States Armed Forces," Amy suggests.

"That is a great idea. But with a dozen performers, we would be making a show for just two or three ships? I would need at least ten versions of the four guys. And after that investment, I need to keep them working. They would want more than one wage a year for all the training it would require. Then, they will be moving from ship to ship, plane to port, port to plane. Can you give me ten versions of an act?" Fiona asks. "And make it funny and upbeat, last forty-five minutes and performed twice in a night? Plus, a completely different second show, better than the first? Each act does two shows in a four day stay on ship."

"I know someone who can do that, easily," Dwight says.

Amy turns to him, worried he is about to nominate her for a job that is way beyond her ability. Fiona stands waiting for the proclamation. He turns to her.

"You can, Fiona. You can, and this will make you famous. This is not just a business but an honour. Ships are mobility friendly, right?"

"I've never seen anywhere that could match them on that, so, understand, on a ship, you would be nothing unusual," Fiona says.

"No, they will be very special," Amy says.

"You'll make them more than special."

"I like your candour. But a warning, we've had a few magicians win major TV talent shows. Shows that involve stories about the war, and their families. They work well on television, as do the performing dog acts. They didn't work on ships."

Her cell phone bleeps a message, and she hesitates. It would be rude to answer. Dwight's cell also bleeps a message. Excused, she smiles, and they both read. Fiona's face turns serious.

Dwight has no idea what hers says. He can only guess. His says.

'Security tried to arrest 3x team on ship. Security down. Team in wind, being hunted. No idea who pulls strings. Check in with Croc.'

Dwight looks up at her, profoundly serious.

"Plus, in the day-time programme they could play a basketball match against a guest team."

76 – NO CONTROL

While Izzy, Mary and Stan stay with Elaine and the baby, the others try to focus on the future threat to the agents still in the field. The Miami headquarters may have a younger feel with Dwight absent from point, and the diner closed, but it is reserved. The cloud of sorrow that hangs heavy over the agency, following Hunter's death, is far greater than after Georgie's murder. Then the office was closed in lockdown. Both losses were tragic, but few people ever met Georgie; she never actually worked for CCI, nor did she visit the office. She was close to Bedriška, who is harder since that loss. Georgie was also very much loved by Kieron, and now the triplets - Macey, Croc and Izzy - all sense he has less interest in the agency.

Croc is totally focussed, cropping faces from pictures and numbering them. The full-face pictures are then dumped into a face recognition programme. It would be boring work if he thought about it, but the sole aim is to finish the vast number of images sent to him from Dwight and Amy in South Dakota. Working fast does not mean a lack of attention to detail, but he has not recognised anyone from his brief posting on the MS Aerwyna.

Macey is watching another screen, which only shows results of faces once recognised. Machine aside, she has not recognised anyone from her time on the MS Amatheia. Once stage one offers a name, that is sent to yet another software programme, which is Croc's own invention. It looks for connections whether family, leisure, or work. It operates by looking for any form of link between entities. The first software of its type was developed to catch serial killers, and versions are used by every crime agency all over the world.

Ricky is at the far end of the long desk, away from the large screen. Not in that chain of work, he has a pen and paper-pad like many good journalists still do. His investigative but creative mind still enjoys writing notes in circles, adlib across a page. He may assemble them many different ways to think of a connection, and, if writing copy, it would be man-made, not a machine fed story. He uses the computer station to try and find worm holes to information-treasure.

"There's nothing about Fiona Ginsburg having a daughter. That must be deliberate. It must be to keep her out of the spotlight," he offers.

"Yet entertaining is so in the spotlight," Croc replies, automatically.

"I've even used her first husband's name. He had an accident too."

"She killed both of them?" Croc asks.

"Try her stage name," Macey says.

Ricky dives back into the computer.

"I'm not seeing that either. It would normally show a mother daughter link as trivia."

"Except, let's be fair. Is the mother famous?" Macey asks.

Croc slides to another station and taps away like a woodpecker digging for ants. "Huh," he grunts.

"What?" Ricky asks.

"Many of these pictures are photoshopped. That's on top of any work she's had done on her face. So, up the age. Think much older."

Ricky looks at images of Fiona Ginsburg's face as Croc enlarges them.

"Look here, and again. This woman appears with her, again and again," Croc shows them. "They ain't sisters, which is what the photos are meant to imply. That's the daughter. I'd put money on it."

"Yeah. Look at the way she is holding her as opposed to the other posed shots. She even looks like she's trying to be as young," Macey says, enjoying it.

"That one slid under my net. Who is she?" Ricky asks.

Croc punches up one, then another, cross referencing answers.

"Martha Jane Mitty," he says slowly, as if someone has told him a bad joke that he dislikes.

"Who calls their daughter Martha?" Macey asks.

"Someone from Deadwood. How unoriginal," Croc says, annoyed.

"Explain?"

"Sis. Martha Jane Cannary, was the real name of Calamity Jane."

"The daughter's never done TV or film. Not under that name. Not even trivia," Ricky reveals, hitting a dead end.

"Don't need to if your rich ma has an empire," Macey says.

"You think Martha put her name on the door of the stock room on the MS Amatheia?" Ricky asks. "That she's a dancer or the choreographer."

"If so, why next door to Wild Bill?" Croc asks.

"Sick family, sick joke. Sick rich kid bored doing the same job, week in, and week out," Macey says.

"Or," Croc offers. "It's the boyfriend. History claims they were lovers.

"Dwight's report was that the son-in-law is someone in a ship's crew," Macey offers.

"Were he and Martha, lovers?" Ricky asks.

"You mean like carving names on a tree," Macey mocks. "Posh people's gang tats; name on cruise cabin door."

"OK. Who she marry? Who's Wild Bill?" Croc asks.

"We need that wedding photo," Ricky says. "We need the date of the marriage. Can you ask Dwight?"

77 – DEATH TRAP

James Grüner approaches the captain in her office, which sits between the bridge and her personal suite. His sense of panic reflects never having had to deal with murders and ongoing attacks, not at sea, nor in any of his previous land-based positions.

"Ma'am. Three security staff were attacked and tied to the rail on the pool deck."

"What?" she says, standing and collecting her cat to her.

"It has to be those agents. Are we sure they're real? Do we know if they're a risk to us, to life, to the ship?"

The captain picks up her cell phone.

"I'll report this and ask for more security staff. They'll demand more detail. I need a proper situation report to me on the bridge. I'll be locking it down."

James leaves, knowing he cannot ask his head of security to do the requested work; she is dead. He must do it himself. He rushes down the empty corridors, fearful of every stairway opening. He is not attacked, he can see no one. Emptiness and silence have become his enemies.

The captain leaves her office and enters the bridge where the night lighting is modest. It is dark outside; the only lights visible are of other ships in the distance. The sea might be peaceful, but it is too dark to see. Only three officers are in attendance. Two are in the cockpit facing forward, not that the ship is being driven anywhere. The officer of the watch is on the other side of the bridge, a full ship-beam away.

"Lock the bridge," the captain orders. She has far more urgency in her voice than is usual.

No one moves. No one takes any notice of her command. She freezes when it becomes obvious that she has been ignored, and the silence is oppressive. Her reaction, far too slow, and driven by fear, is to raise her cell ready to call an alarm. Tentatively, she takes a step forward, but her cell is snatched from behind her. The cat screams and leaps free. She turns in fear and backs off, into her two officers in the pilot seat. They are bound and gagged tight, sitting upright. Both are deathly scared. The captain turns defiantly, but she is in panic, fearful of her fate, long before she looks up to see her assailant.

78 – HIDING

"Why are you whispering, boss?" Croc asks, throwing the image of Kieron between two beer barrels up onto the large monitor in the Miami hub. "Have you been shot?"

"No. Not today. Not yet."

"Then that looks a heavy night out," Macey says, reading a story into the picture. "Save that image."

"Who ordered our arrest?"

"It's not the Palm Springs head office. I've been monitoring the backdoor the thief's partner left on the CEO's computer, but I reckon his code writer is good, and cunning. Probably left phoney backdoors everywhere to make the real one a tough discovery."

"You need to find it fast. Dwight thinks there is someone in the crew. Who is it? Who am I fighting?"

"Don't worry. I'm on it. My guess; it's either with Dwight in Deadwood, or locally with you."

"Croc. Know this. When soldiers, or sailors are given an order, they don't question where it's from. They don't guess. They do it. No guesses please: find out who is giving the orders for our demise on this floating death trap?"

"I'm on it, boss. I'm on everything. I have my own back door. The order to arrest you went to all security staff, but it would take me more time to trace the origin. Plus, I have face recognition going, connections being sought, staff and safe deposit links being made. This hub is hot and trotting."

"It needs to canter. Faster."

"I'm at full speed. I also have a list of alarms it has raised so far, ready for me to manually check," Croc says.

"A list?"

"That's normal. I just work through them. As normal. You don't see a fraction of the work I do."

"Send me the list. Share the list with Dwight, Ricky and Macey. I'm feeling very exposed here."

"Relax, have a drink," Macey mocks.

"Are you sure they're after you?"

"I'm sure they couldn't give a shit about me, Ricky. But they think I've got the diamonds they want."

"Do you?" Croc asks.

"I hid them."

"Where?"

"Not saying, in case there's a leak in communication."

"But if you're killed, no one will know where they are," Macey interrupts, stating the obvious.

"Ask Stan."

"How would Stan know?"

"He's good at hiding stuff," Kieron says.

"Damn right. Hid the fact he's our dad for long enough," Macey says.

"He ain't," Croc tells her.

"What?"

"Mary's our mum, but Stan ain't our dad."

Mary goes quiet. Whatever is going on in her head does not show externally.

"That's enough. I don't want anyone after him," Kieron says.

"They won't go after him he's at …"

"Stop there, Macey. Just know, if the thief's tentacles reach out, they heard our conversation. Now they'll come for you, to find out where Stan is. Lock yourself in. Work fast."

They are shocked at the threat Kieron left them with before he vanished abruptly from the big screen.

79 – LIGHTS OUT

"Shall we leave you to lock up, Miss Ginsburg?"

The two men that had been working in the rigging of the Deadwood rehearsal barn have finished work and are waiting by the door. It is dark outside.

"No. We're leaving. Then you can switch off and lock up," Fiona says.

She is now standing in the middle with Dwight and Amy. Dwight is reading reports whenever he can, and he fixates on the request directed at him. 'Dwight, get a wedding picture. Daughter and member of crew.' He looks up and around one last time. It would be an auditorium, but there is only one-half-row of just ten seats.

"Do you ever use this for public performances?" Amy asks.

"Goodness no, we're in the middle of nowhere," Fiona says, leading them off.

As the three approach the door, the engineer turns one bank of lights off behind them. Then another. Darkness chases them as they walk, like a threat in a horror movie. Fiona misses nothing, she turns and looks behind her.

"I like that effect."

The stage goes dark. The light they are in goes dark and just the area between them and the door they approach is lit.

"This space is used for warming up, and the artistes prepare while something else is being worked on stage. There are more seats somewhere."

"Stacked at the back miss," the workman says.

"I have open weekends. Bookers from each of the ships are invited to watch new acts, new shows, and decide what they feel will fit their ship."

"We need to perform for them," Amy is quick to say.

"In the evening I throw a huge party, and they stay in the main house overnight," Fiona smiles, turning back at the door. "I do know what I'm doing. I invest a lot of time and money into it."

Dwight brings his chair to a stop just outside under the exterior doorway lamp.

"Forgive me for asking a question," Dwight starts.

"Shoot."

"No mention of family, no family pictures in your state room. Although you have a daughter, and she married a crew member?"

Fiona is unsettled by Dwight's question, and the two ranch engineers notice. They switch off the final internal lights and lock the door.

"You need us to hang around, Miss Ginsburg?" the first ranch engineer asks.

She shakes her head.

"We've time," the second worker says, ignoring her. The two follow the group of three as they move off. Fiona notices that Amy finds their over-protective concern strange.

"I lost my husband a few years ago; an unfortunate accident," Fiona shares. "They look after me."

Fiona moves off. Amy follows.

"I'm sorry."

"Long forgotten, and she is his daughter, from his previous marriage. I just keep her employed, busy, and as far away as I can."

"Your choreographer?" Dwight asks.

"I do the choreography. She's the company dance captain."

Dwight has dialled Miami and the line is open. He hopes they can hear him, and he wants to report more, but he knows he is being followed and watched carefully.

"Your stepdaughter," Dwight repeats.

"Thought we saw you walking earlier, buddy," the first ranch engineer asks, over his shoulder.

"I'm tired, big league; lower back and glute muscles are screaming."

"Don't forget your piriformis," Amy says.

"Yeah. They're all singing the blues. I'm a bilateral above knee amputee and these legs are temporary."

"What's that mean?"

"The real legs that we're making for him will fit perfectly, have perfect alignment and a much better function," Amy says, swinging around. "I'm not sure how he's managing so well on those."

"Maybe he's obstinate. Doesn't give up easily."

"You can say that again."

80 – LOCKED IN

Dressed in the officer white trousers and shirt that she stole earlier from the ship's laundry, Bedi searches cupboards and spaces on the Bridge of the Aerwyna.

"Where you keep the drink?" Bedriška asks.

"There's no drink in here, my officers don't drink on duty." Captain Walker replies, as Billy ties her up.

"The ship goes nowhere. We could party here," Bedi says, annoyed.

"Have it ordered."

"The bridge is locked Captain, and it's not opening up," Billy says.

"You won't get away with this. You're in the middle of the ocean. No one has ever stolen a cruise ship. No one. What do you want?"

Bedi leans into the Captain's face.

"Shut up."

"Officers in number, will be here any minute and they will overpower you."

"I have no worry. Some of you Americans you have bucket list. Not me. I have fuck-it list," Bedi says.

Billy is using his cell phone.

"OK Croc, we have secured the bridge. Inside we have First Officer Freeman, and Second Officer Jacobs and Third Officer O'Keefe."

"I have no red flags there, but the CV of James Gruner has alarms all over it. He has only been in hotel management during the lockdown period. He started as an assistant on the Amatheia, and he was moved across to the Aerwyna just four weeks ago. I'm working it through."

"James?" Billy says.

"Yes," he hears back.

"James was the real name of Wild Bill Hickok. His name was James Butler Hickok. Check it."

"I've got it. You're right. I'll get back to you with more detail on James Grüner."

Billy looks at the Captain and grins. The Captain adds nothing.

"Croc. Don't worry about Mr Grüner. We know where he is, we're waiting for him. Find his wife, she could be behind this," Billy says.

"Tiva," the captain smiles.

"Tiva?" Bedi asks her.

"Everyone calls her Tiva. She's a handful. I've only met her once. She thinks she could captain the ship."

"Tiva. It's Cherokee. It means dance," Billy explains, his cell in hand, typing.

An alarm goes on the control panel.

"What's that?"

"Someone is opening a watertight door."

Bedi goes to the edge of the bridge that overhangs, with windows back and front so you can look along the hull of the ship, front to back.

"The other side," the captain says. "Maybe it's time for your diamonds to leave."

Billy goes to the other side and joins Bedi now looking back at an approaching boat.

"No, Captain Walker. Your ship is being boarded by pirates," Bedi says.

"C3 go 5," they hear on the radio.

Billy changes to channel five and hears the command. "Double."

He changes to channel 10.

"Fifteen."

Billy follows.

"By 5."

"Billy settles on channel 3."

81 – PIRATES

Kieron moves out from behind the bar and goes to the rail of the pool deck. He has an earpiece in, connected to the stolen ship's radio. It might be night, but light comes from everywhere and he is exposed. In the sea below, he can see the boat easing towards the ship. Its idling engine gives bursts of thrust to reshape it in the now choppy water.

"I see one, two, three men with automatic pistols," he narrates softly, into the ship's radio. "Go nine."

Kieron switches to channel nine, leans out to send pictures of the boat with his cell phone. The only noise is the slight drone coming from the air-conditioning and generators running on reduced power.

"We're watching. Boat driver looks like Havana Rock, the guy we met in the plane," Croc says, from the hub via the cell. "He must have come to take us fishing."

"Good spot. I wondered if we were going to see him again. There's a woman with them, boarded last. Four total, boat waiting," Kieron says, quietly.

"Zooming in on her face." He hears Croc say in his earpiece.

"Three guess?" Macey challenges him via the open line on his cell phone from Miami. "I'm offering three because she's probably not called Calamity Jane, Martha Jane, Martha Witty or any other version. Why does everybody change their name?"

"Sorry was that Macey, or Mai.I.see?" Croc asks.

"When you're breaking the law, don't use your own name," Kieron says. "Just like Voltaire, my favourite satirist. Real name was François-Marie."

"Careful, boss. Whoever opened that watertight door for them, could be on board looking for you. Even if the IT is not local, these guys will have been given orders to detain you," Croc says.

"Those who can make you believe absurdities can make you commit atrocities," Kieron whispers, scuttling to a crew door.

"And that could be James, the Hotel Manager. Their guns look like semi-automatic CZ75s," Croc tells him.

"Kieron, come in."

"Go, Billy," Kieron whispers, into the stolen radio.

"Watching, God-like. Do I need to roll away the stone? I'd like to come down and get me one of those."

"Negative. Standby."

"No guessing," Billy orders.

Unarmed, Kieron moves inside the ship through the white painted steel crew door. He knows Billy meant he wasn't to take risks trying to count bullets. Whatever gun they are carrying is likely to be fitted with an extended magazine and a spare.

Looking below him, he quickly alights the steel stairs making no noise. He knows one sound could be his last.

82 – BRIDGE

Bedriška is watching from the overhang of the bridge. She goes to the door and looks out through the spy hole.

"No one, they do not make alarm. I can go and cover Kieron."

"There were only four. Kieron can cope."

"We do not lose another agent."

"Do you have a soft spot for him?"

"And Hunter. I hate he is dead."

"I'm surprised you didn't kill the Mexican."

"He won't live."

Captain Walker's cat jumps onto her lap, which causes Billy to notice that she is watching a cockpit screen. It shows the raiders walking down i95.

"Now d'you believe us?"

"Yes," the Captain says, softly.

Bedi goes to the panel and switches the picture until she finds them again. She then zooms from their guns, to the ammunition they hold in their belts and across to the gun the woman holds.

"That's midships stairwell," the Captain offers. "Go to her face."

Bedi widens the shot and goes up.

"That's the dance captain. They call her Tiva; it means dance."

"In Cherokee," Billy finishes.

"I think so, on her father's side."

"Kieron: dog channel," Billy says, into his radio communicator, while on channel 3. He changes to channel 4. "Spider." Then he moves to channel eight. "Three hostiles with CZ's at midships on i95. Extended clips, two spares in the belt. Plus, female known as Tiva with a drum fed EVO."

"Roger that."

Both men know a drum means she doesn't need to reload like the clip fed guns. Her Scorpion EVO3 will have either a 50 or 100 bullet capacity.

"Guess that she's going for the safe deposit boxes," Billy offers.

"Call reception, clear that area," the captain panics. "Dial 614."

Billy dials, then he puts the phone to the captain's head. He does not want to have to explain or argue.

"It's Veronica. Clear that area now. Avoid stairwell and lifts, we've been boarded by pirates."

Bedi operates the joystick on the security camera controls and has found the atrium at reception level. There is no one on deck six. She changes to the dance floor below; atrium deck five. The three gunmen are moving around the lift and stairs bulkhead. One approaches the curved Cinderella stairs on the port side, the other the starboard side. Tiva goes to the middle and looks up, nodding to order them forward.

Billy is on a video call to Miami, and as he pans around the bridge, his cell shows them Captain Walker and her cat.

Croc screams: "What the heck is that?"

"I'm not sure, Croc. It's a disturbing little shit," Billy says.

"It's a Dwelf," Veronica informs them.

"Exactly. A thing that's escaped from some weird horror movie."

"It is a hairless cat, a cross breed of an Elf with a Munchkin."

"That's a wind-up. Cats don't have curved ears," Croc says.

"Or those stupid short legs," Billy agrees. "It's gonna bite one of us and draw blood soon. Look at how it stares at me."

"Are you surprised, the way you're insulting her? And her name's Butt."

"Butt?"

"Short for Butt Naked. It's a playful, affectionate, doglike cat," Veronica says.

"It's not right," Billy says, panicking as the cat goes to him.

Bedi slips out of the bridge. The door locks behind her.

83 – MIAMI

The tension has increased in the Miami hub, and Croc is flicking between ship cameras which he has access to. The whole ship looks quiet, until he comes across a gunman and the armed woman waiting at the side office door of reception.

"That cat was like an alien," Croc says.

Macey has it on her screen and is studying it.

Croc throws the four main atrium cameras as quarters in multi-screen format, onto the big screen. There is a gunman each side of reception, pointing their weapons over ready to shoot.

"If it ran out now, those two would run for miles," Macey says.

"That's her. Tiva the diva. Stepdaughter of Fiona Ginsburg," Croc informs, filling in detail vocally and typing a text report as they research her.

"Marries Assistant Hotel Manager on board the MS Amatheia," Ricky says, sharing a picture from a ship crew newspaper.

They watch one gunman slip over the reception desk and slowly sidestep inside the back office.

"Watch," Croc says, knowing what will happen next.

On the other camera, the second gunman buckles at the knees. Kieron catches him and quietly lowers the unconscious man to the floor. He pushes the gun a safe distance away, cable ties his wrists and feet in seconds, then drags him to the side and into the woman's toilet. He takes the unconscious man's ammunition, then moves back into the atrium and collects the weapon.

"Calamity," Macey says, looking at a picture of the CZ75 gun on her screen. "Those guns get called Calamities. This is like one of those bad dreams."

"She married James Grüner, assistant hotel manager on another ship at the beginning of lockdown. Just the other dancers and some crew there. But his CV looks phoney, and I can't substantiate any of his previously claimed positions at land hotels," Croc says.

"Grey area, the curriculum vittae. Resumes are not official legal documents, so it's not technically illegal to lie on a resume," Ricky offers. "It's done all the time."

"But his has been digitally dropped into the shipping system, and his promotion looks to have been machine triggered."

"Meaning?" Macey asks.
"He promoted himself?" Ricky adds.
"An IT expert did," Croc explains.

84 – GOODNIGHT

Two ranch engineers follow Fiona, Amy, and Dwight. In the arch that cuts through the main building, they enter a side door. It takes them into the few ground floor rooms separated away from the rest of huge main ranch house.

"This is the media area. Film editing is on one side. That's my favourite. The boring information technology is on the other side. Nothing is going on at this time of night," Fiona explains.

She opens the door to a dark room, lit by several edit screens. One has the timeline and digital cutting tools showing, the others have pictures of a stage show. The desk is long and there are many sound faders on one side, and a simple computer keyboard on the other. On the back wall of the room are two guitars and a musical keyboard.

"Miss Fiona, shall we take your guests into town and drop them at a hotel. I'd like to be making that move now," the first ranch engineer offers.

"Why not? I'll talk to you about the act, Amy. But it needs to be just that, an act, and I need to think on it. I promise we'll do it."

Fiona and the ranch engineers turn their bodies indicating that Dwight and Amy should lead out.

"I'd like to see the digital technology office," Dwight says, hesitating.

"It's just a computer, buddy," the other ranch engineer laughs.

"I don't think anything Miss Fiona Ginsburg does, is 'just' anything. I've been mightily inspired by everything I've seen, and if that's just a computer on a desk, I'll eat my hat," Dwight says.

"Feast on it, buddy. A computer's a computer."

"No, let him see." Fiona pushes the door open, surprised to find the head of IT working quietly in the dark. The pictures he has live on his three screens, are of safety deposit boxes being ripped out of the wall and passed back. Tiva is seen sorting through the boxes and throwing them to the floor. "Tiva! What's going on!" she shouts at the screen.

In a spin he might never control and may never end, Dwight wheels Amy out. He throws her towards the safety of the editing room. He directs his lack of balance into the second ranch guard, powering him backwards and down. They both hit the floor of the IT room. Dwight is a big unit, with the huge upper body strength of a man with no legs. He snatches down and takes the man's gun, at the same time rolling the ranch hand around to be a human shield in time to stop the bullets from the first rancher.

Amy appears and reaches for Fiona and pulls her back.

Dwight swings his legs up into the rancher's gun. Bullets rip through his pants until with just one shot from Dwight, the rancher takes a fatal blow between the eyes.

The coding engineer draws his weapon, but as he twists and stands, his hand explodes, and his gun goes flying.

Amy is back in to help untangle Dwight. Fiona is one step behind. As the IT expert tries to recover his gun, Fiona hits him hard and snatches it away. As she holds the gun to his head, she screams, confused at what is going on.

"Tiva?"

Tiva can't hear her.

85 – ONE DOWN

Kieron quietly rolls over the counter and onto the floor behind reception. He checks the acquired gun again because it is not his and he does not know how well it has been kept. He ponders, first switching it to single, then double shot. This model is easy to keep accurate even on full burst, but ammunition runs out fast. He checks the spare clip, attached upside down, under the nuzzle at the front where it is used as a forward grip. He may need to switch clips quickly if it gets hot in there, extended clips only hold 20 rounds.

Worm-like, he pulls himself along the polished floor using his elbows and positions himself ready to be in the opening to the backroom, where there are two men with similar guns, and Tiva with the larger but lightweight polymer EVO 3 Scorpion: all deadly. Assuming she is not trained she will just pull the trigger and spray. His life could end in just a few seconds'.

Using his core strength, Kieron pulls himself into the gap and unleashes short bursts at the ankles of the man guarding the door. Both burst open with blood, flesh and bone going everywhere. He drops, no longer holding his gun. Kieron twists to the other man who has dropped the box and raised his gun. Kieron shoots first at the attacker's hands. The bullets make him drop his weapon and they carry through cutting into his body. The invader is dead. Kieron pulls back before Tiva unloads the Scorpion. He hears her run away and the door close. He rolls over and points up in case she has run around and is going to shoot down at him in reception. That would have been his first instinct; remove the danger. She, however, is not trained that way.

Kieron hears a movement behind him and knows the soldier with no ankles is moving. He rolls back in firing and the man goes silent.

"Billy come in."

"Go for Billy."

"Two dead, one cabled. Tiva in the wind, with weapon."

"Copy that. Crew and security all back under control. Bedi on her way," Billy says.

Kieron reaches out and takes a second weapon. He stands up, checking back and forward, then collects the spare clips from both men.

86 – AT SEA

Havana Rock is in the upper driver's seat of the attacker's boat standing by in the ocean just off the hull of the ship. He is genuinely concerned, having heard the gunshots. Apart from the lapping of the choppy sea and the idle of his large twin outboard engines, the ocean is silent.

He doesn't see, nor can he hear, Bedriška in the water behind his boat where the two black, Monster 600 engines drop into the sea. He does see the Bahama's Police Force boat approaching fast with blue lights cutting through the murky evening. He kicks the engines in.

Bedriška gulps as the propellors turn the water, cutting anything in their way. She fights for her breath, and a safe part of the boat to grab onto. It powers away, and she fights hard to hold on, to pull herself up, and to avoid death. The noise of the engines and the sea is deafening. By the time she is out of the water, her wound is open. Red blood shows through her white naval officer's uniform. She might be exhausted, but there is no way she is going to die there.

Havana pulls the boat around hard to go to the opposite side of the ship from the one the police launch is travelling to. He switches all lights off.

Bedriška leaps, dripping wet, and grabs him from behind and pulls and pulls as hard as she can, but Havana fights back. She is almost passing out, but strangles him, squeezing with all her might. Havana drops first, and she finds the strength to wrench his neck, so he won't wake to kill her if she stays unconscious.

The boat powers out in the dark with no driver.

The police launch bounces into the ship, and nine armed-police officers' board.

87 – CHAIN OF COMMAND

Captain Veronica Walker, now free and reunited with her cat, flicks between pictures of the armed police entering the atrium.

"Sorry about that, officers," Billy says, quickly untying the men in the driving seats. He is trying to watch the screen, untie the officers, and speak to Kieron on the radio. "We lost sight of female target."

"Roger that," comes back from Kieron.

"This is not our job, you have police on board now," Billy tells Veronica.

She changes her screen to the atrium, then another view. Billy notices something and leans over her, switching back to the previous picture.

On screen, Tiva rises above a chair, then ducks down with someone else.

"Behind chairs, in the bar below, port side," Billy informs Kieron on the radio. "It looks like she has a hostage."

Billy flicks the screen between pictures. He can see Kieron move to look for Tiva. He steps away from the exposed entrance to the staircase, curving down or climbing up, and moves to the other side of the round ornate area. With his gun up, he goes to the rail and checks down to deck five, the dance floor and the closed café. He glances up to deck seven. Towards the back of the ship, the double doors to the restaurant are closed.

"No angle," Kieron says, not being able to see into the bar below. "I'll go forward and take the stairs behind the lift," he whispers.

Behind him, the brightly lit windows of the closed shops expose him. He comes to the on-board jewellers which still look interesting, although the expensive stock has gone.

Glass shatters in a hurricane of bullets that destroy every shop window on his side of the ship. Kieron hits the deck then crawls away. After a beat, he rolls back to the edge ready to fire down.

"Can't see her," he reports, expecting information.

"Radio silence," Billy suggests.

Kieron gets up and runs towards the stairs, but he winces. Checking himself, he discovers blood oozing into the chest of his white uniform. He stumbles uncontrollably into the rail, even more exposed. He grips it, using it to move along because he needs to find safety, but he can't leave the rail. He can't make the stairs behind the elevators. He can only move around it until he reaches the opening and there is nothing to hold on to. Losing power in his legs he falls, tumbling down the Cinderella stairs, leaving both guns and all the ammunition scattered behind. He eventually rolls out onto the dance floor at the centre of the lower deck. Blood oozes from him.

"Call the doctor," Billy screams, rushing to the door out of the bridge.

"Can I remind you whose ship this is?"

"No. You can get the doctor there fast."

Veronica can see the police running into the atrium as she uses the ship's address system.

"This is the bridge. Medical emergency; assistance and gurney required in the atrium. Proceed with caution. Gunshot wounds." She goes to the door and shouts after Billy. "Local police are with him."

Billy looks back at her.

"They're not here for me, I'm one of the good guys."

At the end of the corridor, Billy takes the crew door and inside the business area of the ship he runs down the steel steps to i95. He checks both ways, concerned at his exposure. It is clear, so he walks along at speed until he finds the laundry. He needs to be disguised as one of the crew.

By the time Billy, in his white senior offers uniform, reaches the atrium, Commander Kieron Philips is unconscious. The doctor has him on a gurney with a drip attached and ready to travel.

"One moment before you take him off my ship," Billy says. He approaches Kieron and quickly slides his hands down his body searching him. "Ok. He's not carrying a gun."

Billy steps back, a senior police officer approaching him.

"Sir. Thank you for coming. There is still a female on board, armed with a machine gun." Billy turns to the medics. "Crew. Until the police have the ship safe, I want you locked in your cabins."

Billy sees James the hotel manager in the corner, and they lock eyes for a second. James leaves, Billy sidesteps everyone close to him, including the police officer, and he goes after the rogue officer, raising his cell phone as he goes.

"Croc. I'm chasing James. Tiva is in the wind, I need your eyes on these cameras."

"How about Kieron?"

"He's alive. Unconscious. Not carrying rocks."

88 – STAN'S HIDING PLACE

Mary and Stan walk into the hub, through the adjoining door from her diner. Elaine follows, carrying the baby Macey Isabel Mary Witowski. It is a shock for Croc, Macey, and Ricky to see her, just as it is for Mary and Elaine to realise it is the middle of an emergency.

"Elaine needed to get out," Mary says, embarrassed. "We thought Stan might cook a big meal for us all."

Macey takes the baby. Elaine can see the picture of the ship, split into four quarters on the large screen and she approaches it, horrified.

"Is that Kieron? Is he dead?"

"No. No, he's not. He'll be fine," Croc says, defensively.

"That's what you all told me about Hunter," she says, turning to him.

"It's not serious. He's not even being flown home."

"Where's he going then?"

"One of the lifeboats is going to tender him to Great Harbour Cay."

"You're forgetting, out of all of us, I'm the one who spent her working years cruising. The hospital is in Freeport, and you might as well come back to Miami. They don't have anything in GHC that isn't in the clinic on ship."

"It was the doctor's call, Elaine. That ship is in lockdown."

"Stan you gonna get cooking?" Mary asks, to try and change the subject.

"Croc. You get that man home. He saved my life once; he took a bullet then. I'm getting him back now," Elaine insists.

"Sure," Croc says.

"Dad?" Macey asks.

Stan stops. Not just because he has been called, but because Macey addressed him as dad despite now knowing he is not her real father. The room waits for a reaction. Stan smiles, his arms go out and he hugs her.

"Dad. You're always gonna be my dad," she whispers to him. He hangs onto her and is not going to let her go. "Kieron said he used 'Stan's hiding place'. What you two been up to?"

"Nothing!" he says, in an excited whisper.

"Where's your hiding place?" she asks him. Croc is listening, he gets up and puts his arm around the both of them.

"Kieron's hidden something, dad," Croc says.

"We used to hide our tips down the back of the old piano. On them bass notes. Bar owners always expected a share, but we had other ideas about that."

"You old fox."

The telephone rings and Ricky answers, being the only one left at the desk. Bedi's face comes up, she is in a bad way.

"Bedi!" Elaine says, going to the screen. "Where are you?"

The two are old friends having worked on the same ship for many years.

Bedi pulls herself up. "Elaine!" she smiles. "Boy did I need to see you." Bedi straightens up and looks around. "Looks like I'm in the middle of the ocean."

"Can you get back to the ship and collect Billy?" Croc asks.

"Maybe Kieron too. He's been shot," Elaine says.

Bedi is far from well, but she pulls herself onto the seat. The boat's lights come on and it banks hard as she powers it around. She is heading to the distant lights of the ship.

89 – A SHERIFF'S GUILT

The white ranch is ablaze with the blue and red flashing lights of police cars. For Deadwood this is a major event, and Fiona Ginsburg is a pillar of the local community.

Inside the living room, Dwight and Amy are drinking coffee with the sheriff. Mel and another dancer bring food in and lay it on the table.

"Sheriff Oakley, your men should have something to eat. Mel please."

Fiona waves her arm for Mel to take refreshments to the men outside. She then addresses Dwight. "And at this hour, perhaps you might stay, and we can talk more over breakfast. It appears we have a lot more to talk about than we thought."

"If you've got two spare rooms. Maybe, we both offer services to the cruise industry," Dwight says.

"I am going to need your agents to get to the bottom of this. I have no idea how much my stepdaughter infiltrated and ruined my business."

"The FBI have her now, Fiona," the sheriff offers.

"They'll be crawling all around here next," Dwight says.

"That engineer of yours is already squealing like a banshee. We'll have the complete story out of him before they arrive in their cheap suits."

"We have some good youngsters at Cruise Crime Investigators, who would really benefit from speaking to you, Miss Ginsburg. I guarantee we'll get to the bottom of all this."

The sheriff steps closer, and Fiona gives him a plate.

"Help yourself, Sheriff."

"So, Mr Ritter. Do you think they were smuggling the diamonds as well as stealing them?"

"I've no idea Sheriff. No idea. It has been a tragedy for us. We're gonna have to pick-up-the-pieces best we can. We've got a baby with no father and a wife without a husband."

"Will she be OK for money?" the sheriff asks.

"Do they have a home? Somewhere to live?" Fiona asks.

"I like the community spirit here. Don't worry; the house will be paid for. Witowski was one of our two main directors. Keyman policy should cover everything," Dwight says.

"Tiva didn't have that," Fiona says.

"Sad to say, I agree now. I should have taken things more serious," the sheriff muses.

"Sheriff?" Fiona asks.

"Her father was a good man. He came to me a few times before his accident. He was worried that she was into something on the ships, with some bad people."

"Suspicions of what?" Fiona asks, surprised at the revelations.

"He thought smuggling drugs. I told him to have a fatherly chat. Looking back; that was probably the wrong advice. She was using people to steel diamonds and who knows what else. That's an FBI thing now."

"She was always in self-destruct mode, and she couldn't have been given more. I don't think any advice would have saved her," Fiona says, walking away with the Sheriff.

"You think Tiva killed her father?" Amy asks Dwight.

"I know she killed young Macey Isabella Mary's father."

"Do you really have keyman insurance?"

"We'll find some money somewhere."

"The diamonds?"

"No. I think Kieron knows a nun in St Vincent who can ensure they get back to Africa and do some good. The proceeds might help African children not to join militia and become child-killers."

TO THE READER

Thank you for reading this story. If you are not familiar with my work (listed on IMDB.com etc), in the first book in the series, CRUISE SHIP HEIST, the pot of money that may help for Elaine was found and hidden; it just needs to be recovered. It was in that book Kieron met Hunter and saved his wife Elaine.

CAST LIST

CSCI
Commander Kieron Philips
Hunter Witowski (wife Elaine, baby
    Macey Isabella Mary)
Dwight Ritter
Bedriška Kossoff (ex-5th Directorate
    KGB – artistic affairs)
Billy

WILD MARY'S DINER
Mary
Stan
Macey 'Ma.I.see' Ricca
Izzy
Croc (Winston Crocket)
Ricky Hedgemont

Medical Prosthesis Centre
Jake – Prosthetist
Amy Polson (Pocket Rocket) -
Nurse

SHIP - Aerwyna
Captain Veronica Walker (cat is
called Butt)
Selma Gomez – Head of Security
James Grüner, Hotel Manager
Alfonso Cazo - killer

Chief Operations Officer, Casey B.
de Michelle.
Meecho Entertainment

Medical
Senior Nurse Bjørg
Nurse

Doctor

IT
Chad Roberts
William Stevens
Franklin Spender
Mike Summers
(& JJ Easterbrook, the Executive
Director of External Communications at
Easterbook/William)

Asian man 1 - Ramesh
Asian man 2 - Arif
Asian woman – Banjo

Deadwood
Fiona Ginsburg
Mel
Martha Jane Mitty (Tiva)
2 x Ranch Engineers
1 x Cab Taxi
1 x Coding IT engineer
Sheriff

SHIP – Amatheia

Captain Spinazzola
Damien - host
Susie – host
Sandip – man in the flies at the
theatre.

SHIP – Ianassa

CRUISE DORIS VISITS

Cruise Doris Visits is a cruise port guide channel on YouTube channel and Facebook chat rooms for ships. Just search Doris Visits. www.DorisVisits.com

THE TEAM

As always, the team is a must, and I cannot do without them. I have a vivid imagination, but the tools are another job. Thank you to Jean for her translation of my dyslexic mumblings, and David Withington for his eye on language and grammar.

Jean presents the YouTube Cruise Port guides.

David Withington - runs the online cruise resource 'How To Cruise'.

CSCI Cruise Ship Crime Investigators is a series of books

Whilst each is designed to stand alone, they are best read as a series. Heist, the characters meet with no idea of the future. Serial Killer they set up office in Miami. Laundry Wars the female agents join.

See you at sea …

Other books by the author

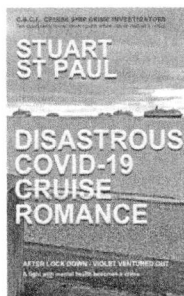

Printed in Great Britain
by Amazon